Peace In Paradise

Joan Lewis

website: www.poetjoanlewis.com

Copyright © 2014 by Joan Lewis.

ISBN: Softcover   978-1-4990-4648-9
        eBook   978-1-4990-4647-2

All rights reserved. No part of this book may be reproduced or transmitted in any form or by any means, electronic or mechanical, including photocopying, recording, or by any information storage and retrieval system, without permission in writing from the copyright owner.

This is a work of fiction. Names, characters, places and incidents either are the product of the author's imagination or are used fictitiously, and any resemblance to any actual persons, living or dead, events, or locales is entirely coincidental.

Any people depicted in stock imagery provided by Thinkstock are models, and such images are being used for illustrative purposes only.
Certain stock imagery © Thinkstock.

This book was printed in the United States of America.

Rev. date: 08/29/2014

To order additional copies of this book, contact:
Xlibris LLC
1-888-795-4274
www.Xlibris.com
Orders@Xlibris.com
650280

Peace In Paradise is dedicated to the author's husband. He is the love of her life and the kindest, bravest man she has ever known. He truly is her Hero. She feels gratitude knowing he has always loved, supported and encouraged her in all she has pursued.

Contact Author Through Website:
www.poetjoanlewis.com   or   www.authorjoanlewis.com

PART ONE

CHAPTER 1 -- MITCHELL

Mitchell Lauers was one of those kids who could not wait to be on his own and move far away from the picturesque small town of Cresaptown, Maryland. His mother, Matilda Lauers, did not want her second oldest son to leave; but Jeremy Lauers, Sr. felt it would make a man out of their eighteen year old boy. Mitchell knew he would miss his five brothers and little eight year-old sister, but he had to make his way in the world. Right after high school he left town and moved to Cleveland, Ohio to live with his older sister, Patsy, and her family. He had taken on a couple of jobs while in Cleveland. His uncle found him a job folding towels for Vick Tanning Health Club. At the end of his very first evening at the new job Mitchell took the city bus to return to Patsy's home. When the bus came to its final stop the driver told him he had to get off because the bus was at the end of its line. Mitchell walked many miles on Superior Avenue to get back to his sister's house. He quit the job the next day, and found another one.

After living with Patsy's family for nearly two months, Mitchell received a phone call from his mother. She asked him to return home. Matilda Lauers had become ill and she wanted her son by her side. He left Cleveland and returned to Cresaptown. Once he was back in Cresaptown his buddies and brothers had a whole lot of catching up to do with him; and he was happy in all parts to be back at home.

Matilda's other boys and her little daughter did all they could to help their mother through her illness. Though Matilda would never admit it, she was very partial to her son, Mitchell. She sensed a gentleness about the boy, and somehow his being by her side made her feel better.

It was towards the end of the week he decided he would take a break and go to the fair with his buddies. They had gone the night before, but the guys all wanted to go back since it was the last night the fair would be in town.

"Son, I'll be fine," Matilda told her son when he mentioned returning to the event.

"Can I get you anything before I go, mom?" he asked her.

"Yes son. Can you get me a glass of ice, please?" When he left her side, she decided she would just come right out and tell him not to go to the fair. When he returned with the ice that he'd crushed for his mother's consumption, she took it; then said, "Son, do you really have to go back to the fair tonight? You were just there last night."

"Mom, I won't stay long. Besides, I already promised the guys I would go with them," he rationalized with her.

Knowing how her son was when it came to keeping his word, she restrained herself from begging him to stay home. Besides, he had been sitting with her all day; maybe he needed the break. She gently nodded her head, giving him the okay to go. "Go on son," she reluctantly gave in. "Go on and have some fun."

"Thanks mom," he gave her a quick kiss on the cheek and left to go meet up with his buddies.

~ ~ ~

When the phone rang at eleven o'clock that night, Matilda Lauers had an awful feeling in the pit of her stomach. She knew before she even answered the phone something was wrong.

"Hello," she nervously said.

"Hello," the voice at the other end of the telephone replied. "Is this Mrs. Lauers?"

"Yes, yes it is."

The voice hesitated, then said, "Mrs. Lauers, I'm sorry to inform you, but your sons have been in an accident. There's been a five-car pileup and one of your sons is severely injured." When she was informed of the accident she almost passed out. Matilda had to get herself together. Her husband was working the late shift at the railroad station so it was up to her to make her way to that hospital, sick or not, to see about her boys. She put her clothes on and painfully walked across the alleyway to get Mr. Burns to take her to Cresaptown Memorial Hospital. When she arrived at the hospital, she found out it was Mitchell who was in the hospital with massive cuts to his face. She was told that at the moment of impact Mitchell placed his hand over the chest of his brother, Phillip, to keep him safe. That gesture left no support for him, so Mitchell went through the front window of the car. Matilda tried to keep from crying when she saw Mitchell's face cut, mangled and bleeding. She was in agony as she waited for the doctors to put stitches in his face.

With over thirty stitches in Mitchell's pale face, it was weeks before the young man was released from the hospital. The lawyers informed Mrs. Lauers if she waited a few years, she could get a healthy sum for her son's injuries and his pain and suffering. Mitchell's mother was quick to accept the settlement offer, giving her eighteen year-old injured son no say in the settlement matter. She received just enough to pay the hospital bill.

CHAPTER 2 -- RECOUPERATING

The pain had been unbearable. The aspirin barely put a dent in subsiding Mitchell's agony. The last time he was in such excruciating discomfort was two years ago when his appendix burst while he ran cross-country.

The scars on Mitchell's face took time to heal. A few months passed and still he was picking glass out of his forehead. Bottles upon bottles of aspirins he took to keep the headaches away. The only thing that kept him in a halfway decent spirit was his mother's comforting assurance that the scars were healing up very well. His skin was a fair tone, not brown like most of the other colored kids he grew up with; so he thought the scars would show even more. But when Mitchell looked into the mirror he noticed with his fair-skinned completion, he could barely notice the scars; even still he refused to go outside. Most days he would sit by the window and watch the people. That was all he wanted to do, because he did not want to be around anyone knowing they would gawk and stare at his face.

One day as he was staring out of the window, his mother came over to him. "Son, it's a beautiful day today. Why don't you go out and sit on the porch? Get yourself some fresh air," she said to him. She tried to cheer him up; but since the accident, he hadn't found too much to make him smile. Before the accident, many of his friends nicknamed him, Smiley. He missed those days. Often he would try to think of how things were before the last night of the fair. His headaches would flair up when he thought about it too hard. He was depressed, though he did not know it. He convinced himself he was alright; just not alright enough to be around other people.

~ ~ ~

One afternoon Mr. Harry, a family friend, came to visit. "Hey there Mitchell, boy. How you doin' these days?" he asked.

"I'm alright," he told the man. Mitchell hoped the friendly man would not try to engage him in conversation like he usually did whenever he'd come to visit. Mr. Harry, he noticed, came around more and more since he had been released from the hospital. Mitchell had once dated the man's daughter, Bernice, a year ago. When Mitchell gave the girl his class ring, she took it as a sign they were getting married. She even told her sister and mother that was why he gave it to her. Mitchell sat at the window thinking about that period in time. He laughed to himself; he remembered taking the ring back and Bernice and her sister ran into their house crying. It wasn't funny then, but thinking about it made him chuckle out loud.

"Hey boy, that's good boy. I'm tellin' you I ain't seen you have a good laugh in a while. Why this makes my day. Yeah, it's good to see you smiling again, sonny. You know my gal, Bernice, is havin' a party this weekend. You think you might want to come? She told me if I saw you, that I should be sure to tell you she wants you at her celebration." Then he turned and looked at Matilda, "It is okay, ain't it, Miss Matilda?"

"Mr. Harry, he's right there; and besides, you just asked him. I'm sure if he wants to go, he will."

Mr. Harry looked again at Mitchell, "What do you say, Mitchell, you think you would like to come to my daughter's seventeenth birthday party?"

It had been four months since the accident. Mitchell knew what Mr. Harry was trying to do. The man figured it would be good for him to go to the party. Mr. Harry knew his daughter was no longer romantically interest in Mitchell. She had long ago gotten over the fact that he dumped her. His daughter was a forgiving person and Mr. Harry knew there was no hidden motive behind the invitation. She was only inviting him because she was concerned.

When he showed up at the party all of his friends were happy to see him. He almost felt like things were back to normal. His biggest fear was one of his friends noticing the scars near his eyes and on his forehead. But no one did. He found that he'd almost forgotten about his accident while he was at the party amongst his friends. Bernice introduced Mitchell to her friend, named Brenda. Even though she was only fifteen years old the two of them hit it off well. As the teenagers were all having fun, and dancing with the lights down low, Bernice's mother came into the living room and flipped the light switch on. Teenagers pulled apart and squinted as they adjusted their eyes to the brightness of the light.

"What's going on in here," Mrs. Washburn asked. She walked around inspecting the teenagers as they reluctantly readjusted themselves from their petting and necking. The couples dancing closely to the love songs pulled apart unwillingly.

"Mom, what are you doing?"

"These lights; why were they turned off?" the mother asked her daughter as she went to the end table lamps and switched them on.

"But, this is my party, mom. How come we can't have some of the lights off?" After going back and forth with her mother about the party and the teenagers being too close to one another, frustrated and embarrassed, Bernice turned and ran upstairs in tears. At that point Mrs. Washburn chased everyone out of the house.

Mitchell knew how strange Mrs. Washburn could be. When he was dating Bernice, it was not uncommon for her to tell him to go home around seven o'clock in the evenings. And of course Mitchell can never forget the time Mrs. Washburn painted everything in the kitchen blue; chrome table and chairs, stove, refrigerator and all of the cabinets and walls. It was the strangest thing he had ever seen. Even though he felt bad for Bernice and wanted to console her, he knew it best to leave the property as her mother had requested.

When he and Brenda left, they laughed amongst themselves. They could hear Mr. Harry fussing with his wife about interrupting their daughter's birthday party. And when Mitchell glanced back he saw Mrs. Washburn hitting Mr. Harry on his brown bald head with a wooden spoon. Mitchell found Bernice's parents to be a strangely matched couple. He turned his attention back to Brenda, "Well, that was interesting."

Brenda laughed. "Yeah, it was. But it's okay because I couldn't stay long anyway. In fact, my dad is right over there, across the street, waiting for me," she pointed to the black car parked across the road.

Mitchell really wanted to see the teenager again. As he walked her across the street, he asked, "So can I see you again, Brenda?"

"Yes, I would love to see you again, Mitchell." As they stood on the back side of the car, she grabbed his hand. With an ink pen she took from her purse she scribbled her telephone number onto his palm. "This is my phone number. You can call me and maybe we can get to know each other a little better. I live quite a ways from here; almost ten miles." He walked her to the car door and opened it for her. The man sitting behind the wheel was stoic and looked straight ahead. He figured the gentleman to be her father, and he thought it was strange the man never acknowledged him. He decided to say nothing to him, but he did say goodbye to Brenda. As he walked back home he realized he had a most wonderful time. Not once did he have a headache. And none of his friends asked him about the accident, nor mentioned the scars near his eyes. And the best part of the evening, he met the beautiful Brenda who seemed to really like him enough to give him her telephone number. He was very interested in getting to know her.

CHAPTER 3 -- MARRIAGE

Mitchell found love with the beautiful Brenda Jamison. But her parents would not let her date the eighteen year-old, Mitchell, until her sixteenth birthday. When she turned sixteen her parents approved his visits with her. Because Brenda lived so far away, Mr. and Mrs. Jamison allowed him to spend the evenings at their home. A couple of months before Brenda turned seventeen, they had a big wedding and married in a beautiful church setting.

Knowing he must make a life for he and his young bride, Mitchell left his wife with his parents and went to Rochester, New York in seek of employment. He arrived on a Sunday, and with the help of John Hutton, found a job on Monday at the General Motors facility, Delco Products. Things were going well for him and he knew he had to get back to Cresaptown to bring his wife to Rochester. He did just that. That is when things did not turn out the way he would have liked them to. Once Brenda was relocated to the city of Rochester, things became a bit difficult for the couple.

Mitchell could sense his wife was not happy. He thought maybe it was the move to the city. If he had to, he was willing to move back to the small town of Cresaptown to keep them together. That was not what she wanted. She liked the city of Rochester. She had met friends while he was at work on his evening shifts; friends she should have never been involved with. And though Mitchell did all he could do to keep his wife, she did not want to be married to him any longer.

One evening, when Mitchell was at work, Brenda emptied their apartment. She took all of the furniture. The only thing left in the apartment was one light bulb and his clothing in the middle of the floor. This saddened Mitchell that his wife would leave him the way she did. All he ever wanted to do was to love and take care of her. She had once confided in him how rough her father had treated her when she was being raised. He wanted to protect Brenda and most important, to love her. But she did not want his love; all she wanted was to get away from the small town she was born and raised in.

When Mitchell contacted the lawyer regarding a divorce, he was told he could not start divorce procedures because his wife was only seventeen. He had to wait until she turned eighteen before he could move from the apartment they once shared. If he moved before she was eighteen, by law it would be considered as spousal abandonment. Once she turned eighteen he was free to move and start his divorce. Until then he must remain in the apartment, in case at the age of seventeen she decided to return.

~ ~ ~

It was Brenda's brother, Greg Jamison, who convinced Mitchell to make the move to Rochester. And though Mitchell and his wife were no longer together, Mitchell held no ill-will against Greg and his family, so the two men remained friends.

Greg was a pretty okay guy, with the exception of being mean to his wife. It was a bad habit he'd picked up from his father. Mitchell witnessed how sadistic Greg and Brenda's dad had been to their mother. And now here Greg was, a grown man and very belligerent to his wife, Helen. She was the mother of his two sons, but not even that made any difference in how he treated her.

One day Helen burst into Mitchell's downstairs apartment with tears streaming down her cheeks, and a swollen jaw.

Mitchell, concerned for her safety, asked, "Why do you put up with this nonsense, Helen?"

"I love him, Mitchell. And he must love me because he beats me when he gets jealous or if I make him mad. You just don't understand."

"Helen, please tell me you're joking. Tell me you really don't believe that. Greg does not love anyone except himself."

Helen did not like when people put her husband down for beating up on her. She was French and left her family to marry the colored man who could easily pass for white. In fact, her family disowned her because of her decision to marry out of her race. She did not care, because she loved him; and felt he truly loved her in return. The way she saw it, he was just going through bad times; and every now and then when he found himself in a rough state, he would take it out on her.

Helen knew how much family meant to Mitchell, even though his wife, Brenda, had left him. But she was not about to let him say awful things about her abusive husband without challenging it. To hurt him, she abruptly wiped the tears from her face, then shouted, "You have no reason to say that about Greg. He doesn't love just himself. He loves me and the boys too. If Brenda hadn't left you, you would understand what it's like to be married and to sometimes have problems." She looked him up and down; and then with a judgmental demeanor, she added, "Just because you couldn't hold onto your wife is no reason for you to be saying those things about my husband. He's a good man; good to me and to our boys." She hated she'd even bothered to come down to his apartment for a sympathetic ear. She had not expected him to say something bad about Greg and at that point, she did not care about hurting his feelings. In fact, she was hoping what she said had scorched him. Who was he to be making light of she and Greg's love for one another. After her poignant statement to Mitchell about not being able to hold onto his estranged wife, she turned abruptly and left the man's apartment.

Mitchell took the woman's words in stride. Sure, she was right to have her opinion about what happened between him and Brenda. Maybe she was even right in thinking the breakup was his fault. If she wanted to believe that, then she was entitled to do so. What she felt or thought presented no problem to him. He knew there was no way he could convince Helen what Greg was doing to her was wrong. Fact was, he felt they both were setting a bad example for their boys. Mitchell's father never fought his mother. Once in a while he saw his mother give his father a piece of her mind, or send the man to stay with his brother when he'd been acting a fool. But that was the most uncivilized behavior he'd witness between his parents; and that was nowhere near violent. How much harm could his mom do by telling his dad off and kicking him out for a night or two? He loved his mom and dad; and since he had witness the men in the Jamison family showing negative affection to the women in their lives, he loved his mom and dad even more.

~ ~ ~

Often Mitchell would hear Greg and Helen fighting and cursing one another. He tried to shield himself from getting involved with their disputes. After Helen's blowup with him, he resolved to stay out of their business. But sometimes it was easier said than done.

One afternoon he was trying to get some sleep before he headed out for his job. He'd worked that morning at his second job, Technique and Wood, and thought he could get a quick nap in before he went to his primary job at Delco Products. He was awakened out of a deep sleep by loud thuds and banging against the wall and floor of the upstairs apartment. Knowing the ruckus his brother and sister-in-laws often caused when they would have a disagreement, he jumped out of his bed and headed upstairs to their apartment. Beating on the door, he yelled, "Open up this door, Greg." The commotion continued inside of the apartment and Mitchell felt as though Greg was killing Helen. He was not going to stand by and do nothing. He would not turn his back on a woman being beaten by a man. He was determined he would get into the apartment to find out if Helen was alright. He placed his shoulder against the door then pulled back and slammed it into the door. When the entrance door burst open, Mitchell ran towards Greg and Helen's bedroom.

"Get off of her, you coward." He pulled the man off of Helen and swung back to punch him. He came within an inch of Greg's nose then brought his fist to a sudden halt. "You know what, you are not even worth me going to jail tonight." He shoved the man onto the corner of the rumpled bed; then noticed Helen crouching between the bed and the wall trying to cover her naked body with her arms. "Get up," he ordered Greg. The man did as he was told and Mitchell quickly yanked the bedspread off of the bed. He noticed a footprint in the middle of her small breast. He diverted his eyes and draped the spread over the small woman. "Come on Helen, go tend to yourself." Their little boys, Brent and Ted were standing in the doorway of their bedroom. They were crying about their parent's fight. "How can you take it upon your selfish selves to do this in front of these boys, Greg? Don't you know it ain't good for them to see this nonsense?"

The man sat there on the bed. He had no desire to tangle with Mitchell. In fact, he didn't even want the man in his apartment breaking up the fight between him and Helen. "She just make me so mad. She shouldn't have said what she said about my shirt," he defended his part in the fight.

"Your shirt? What could she have possibly said to you about your shirt that would have you stomping her in the chest? Don't you know you can give her cancer with the trauma you may have caused by bruising her like that? What's wrong with you man?"

Greg went into his defensive mode. He knew he could not pull anything over on Mitchell because Mitchell was a smart man, and full of common sense. Too damn smart for Greg. But still Greg continued on with his delusional defense for striking his wife. "I asked her if she liked my shirt. She said, to tell the truth, she didn't much care for it? Ain't that something? I paid a lot of money for this shirt." He pat himself on the chest as if to prove to Mitchell the shirt warrant a better approval than what his wife was willing to give. "Look at it man, pure silk, pure silk; and this thing is Italian print, too. I don't get it."

Helen had gone into the boys' bedroom; Mitchell heard the door lock behind her. He pulled up a chair, then Greg start to get up from the bed he was sitting on. "Naw, sit on down, Greg. Don't get up man. I'm only going to say this to you because I feel you need to hear it. I know you came from a family where you saw you dad beat your mother. But man, that ain't right. You can't do stuff like that. It just makes you look bad, man. It makes you look like a real coward, beating on a woman."

Greg tried to say something, but the words were getting stuck. When he got his tongue untangled he said, "What are you talking about. You trying to say my ol' man was less than a man?"

"Naw Greg. Don't go putting words in my mouth. I think you know what I'm getting at. Look, your dad did what he felt worked for him. I'm just trying to say, you and your wife don't have to live like that. You don't need to be punching on Helen. Man, she's a small woman and you out-weigh her by fifty pounds; you can really hurt her."

Greg didn't want to hear another word that came out of Mitchell's mouth. "What make you think you can come into my place and tell me and my ol' lady how we should live our lives. You have nothing..."

Mitchell stood up from his chair. He was tired of trying to talk rationally to the man. All he wanted was some sleep. And that wasn't happening as long as his brother and sister-in-laws were fighting like caged dogs over his head. He let the man have it. "Look Greg, the moment your wife's screaming wakes me up from a deep sleep, and I hear fighting and somebody's body slamming on the floor overhead of me, is when it's my place to tell you what you and your wife should be doing. Fighting is not the answer, man. That's all I'm trying to say. You think about what I'm telling you. You're gonna end up hurting her; might even land in jail. Hey Greg, that's it." Mitchell shook his head in disgust; he concluded, "Man, I got to get myself ready for work." He got up from the chair, stood over the man and gave Greg a concerned look. He just could not understand it. Greg had a great little family, but the man was too selfishly blind to see it. Mitchell walked back down to his apartment and knew it was no sense in him trying to lie back down. He packed his lunch and then sat down and watched television until it was time for him to leave for work. He didn't hear another sound from the upstairs apartment.

His telephone rang; he knew who it was before he answered it. "Hello," he reluctantly spoke into the receiver."

"Hello Mitchell. Look this is Ted," he rushed with his introduction.

"Yeah Ted. I know it's you, man. You supposed to be here already." Mitchell told his friend.

"Yeah, yeah man, I know. Look somethin' came up at the last damn minute. Man, I ain't gonna be able to go in today. Can you catch another ride?"

"Man, do you know what time it is. You are supposed to be parked in front of my house right now to pick me up. Why didn't you call earlier?"

"Didn't you hear what I just said? Somethin's done happened and it's a real 'mergency. I got to take care of it. Do you think I would be lettin' you down for some stupid shit?"

"Alright man. Don't even sweat it." He hung up the telephone, locked up his door and start jogging to work. To keep his mind in the zone as he ran, he reminisced of how he ran cross-country in high school. When he reached the door of Delco Products it dawned on him, he left the house in such a rush, he forgot to grab his lunch.

CHAPTER 4 -- CAR

After three months of bumming rides to and from work, and getting told at the last minute that the person he was riding with wasn't going in for the day, Mitchell decided he was going to buy himself a car. He had his ninety days in and was no longer considered hired on a trial basis. He was now officially an employee of Delco Products. He was at Delco Products working on the line when he mentioned to Rickie, "I'm buying myself a car. I'm going to the dealership this weekend to see what I can find."

"You're getting a car? But I thought you said you didn't know how to drive, man," his co-worker said.

"I don't. But I'm buying me a brand new car and I'm gonna teach myself how to drive it. Hey, I taught myself how to swim; figure I can teach myself how to drive."

Rickie continued putting his grommets on the parts that came down the assembly line. "I ain't never heard of such a hair-brained idea. You don't know how to drive, so you're buying a brand new car so you can learn how? Yeah, sure you are." He was laughing so hard he had to stop the line to catch up.

Mitchell took a swig out of his coke bottle, then said to Rickie, "You can laugh if you want to, but that's exactly what I'm doing. I'm getting tired of depending on other people to get me to and from work. Yeah, I'm sick of it."

His co-worker laughed long and hard. "Man, I got to tell you, you got more balls than I've got. No way would I be buying a new car to learn how to drive. I can understand you teaching yourself how to swim, but teaching yourself to drive, in a brand new car? Now that's fuckin' crazy. Why not buy somebody's old jalopy and learn on that?"

"I don't want an old car. I want a new car to learn on, and I'm getting a new one, Rickie, just as soon as I can."

~ ~ ~

That weekend Mitchell walked to West Main Street to Brown Chevrolet. When he got on the lot he looked at all of the shiny new cars. They were beautiful brand new 1964 automobiles. He was excited and could feel his heart racing. It crossed his mind that he did not have a driver's license, only a learner's permit. That was just a minor problem he would deal with after he purchased the car. He spotted the one he just had to have. The only problem, it was not the color he wanted. He stood at the hood of the car and looked into it. He visualized himself behind the wheel in a cool pair of sunglasses. He was still daydreaming when he heard, "That there's a beauty ain't it, son," He turned around and saw a tall man dressed in a light blue shirt, gray speckled tie and dark gray slacks. He had a slender build and looked to be in his early thirties. The man gave two quick taps on the hood of the car then said, "I certainly can see you in this car. Yes sir, Mister uhh?"

"Lauers, Mitchell Lauers." He accepted the extended hand of the salesman, and the man shook Mitchell's hand as though he was pumping for oil.

"Mr. Lauers, it's good to meet you sir. I'm Vincent McKenzie. You can call me Vinnie. Yessirreee, I can just about see you in this car, buddy. You like it?" Vinnie's sales pitch was on, and he was determined to make a sale today after a dry week of sparse customers.

"Yeah man, I like it a lot." Mitchell wasn't going to lie, he did like the car. He just didn't know how to tell the man he had no license and worst yet, had never so much been behind the wheel of a car, let alone driven one. He didn't dare tell the overzealous salesman any of that stuff, so he decided what Vinnie didn't know, wouldn't hurt him. He continued on, like he had a ton of money in his pocket. "Yeah, it's a real beauty. How much do you want for this car?" he asked, as though he was ready to write a check for it right on the spot.

"Two-thousand, four hundred dollars, Mr. Lauers." Vinnie smiled from ear to ear. He was beginning to feel as though he had the young man right where he wanted him. But what he didn't know, was the fact that it was the other way around. Mitchell had the salesman exactly where he needed to have him; anxious to make a quick sale on the new automobile. Vinnie eagerly advised, "Now don't let the price scare you; we can negotiate the money portion once we sit down in my office. What are you, a Kodak man?"

Mitchell knew what the man was referring to. Most of the dealerships were always happy when Kodak employees got their bonuses. One of Mitchell's co-workers informed him of the big impressive Kodak bonuses. But what he also learned was that the people who worked at Kodak were only getting those healthy bonuses to offset what they should have received in their regular paychecks over the years.

"No man, I work for Delco Products," he told the anxious salesman.

"So, Mr. Lauers, you're a General Motors man, even better. I have dealt many times with Theresa from Lyell Federal Credit Union for you Delco Products employees." He reached into his pants pocket and pulled out a set of keys. He dangled them in front of the young man. Mitchell knew he could not drive the car, but he wanted to put the salesman right at ease. Even though Mitchell hated when people shortened his name, he took his cue from the salesman.

"Vinnie, call me Mitch. Please! Are those keys to this car?" he asked in a most casual voice.

"Yes they are, Mitch."

"This is a real sharp-looking car; I really like it," Mitchell walked around the car as the salesman stood by still holding the key ring looped around his index finger. The young man ran his hand alongside of the car to feel the automobile's smooth texture. He didn't want to show it, but the car excited him. He'd never been near a brand new car, let alone touched one. After he walked completely around the car and was back in the position where he'd left the salesman, he asked, "Vinnie, what is the make of this car?"

With that salesman's smile, Vinnie answered, "Why Mitch, this here is a 1964 Chevrolet Impala Coup. That's what this is. Just rolled off the factory line. Ain't she a pretty thing?"

"Yeah, I like this car, but I want it in black, not blue."

"I'll see what I can do. You want to test drive it, son?"

"Sure," Mitchell admitted. "But I tell you what, why don't you drive it and I ride in it. I don't want to be responsible if somebody run into it. I'll be able to tell if I like it by the way it rides." As Mitchell seated himself comfortably in the passenger's seat the newness of the car's smell penetrated his nostrils. Vinnie got in, turned the engine on and looked over at Mitchell. "Listen to this baby purr. Ain't that there a sweet sound?" He put the car into drive and drove down West Main Street, turning left onto Genesee Street. When he got to Brooks Avenue, he made a right. He wanted to take the customer on nice ride so the young man could take in the luxury of the new car so he continued to drive. He turned onto Thurston Road. When he got to Chili Avenue he made a right-hand turn and headed back to the dealership. Vinnie parked the car back on the lot and soon afterwards Mitchell found himself in the man's small office haggling over the price. When the price of two thousand, one hundred dollars was agreed upon, Mitchell place an order for a brand new 1964, dark green Chevy Impala Coup. It was the closest color to black Vinnie could get for him. When Vinnie asked him for his license, Mitchell told him he didn't have it on him at the moment. He didn't feel bad about saying that because he didn't have it on him. It was no problem for Vincent

McKenzie. He hadn't made a sale all week and this would be his first. He wrote the new car order up and sent it on its way.

Within four weeks Mitchell's new car was delivered to his apartment. His chest protruded proudly. He practiced all weekend, driving the car on Genesee Street and the surrounding Avenues, Plymouth, Jefferson and Bronson. That Monday he drove the car to his job. He felt good, knowing he now had control over his way to and from work.

As he pulled into the B-Shift parking lot, he spotted his co-worker, Rickie. He pulled up alongside Rickie and said, "Hey Rickie, how you like my new car?"

Rickie looked in the direction from which he heard the voice but nothing computed in his brain. He did not recognize the car but he saw his friend, Mitchell, sitting behind the wheel of the brand new car. He rubbed his forehead with his fingertips trying to figure out why what he was witnessing did not make sense. Then it came to him what Mitchell told him four weeks ago about purchasing a new car to learn how to drive. Finally, when things start clicking in his brain, he jokingly said, "Well I'll be damn. Man, whose car is this you done stole?"

"It's my car, man. I told you I was getting a car. Remember?"

"Would you look at this? I can't even believe you really got yourself a new car." Without asking, he opened the door and got into the passenger side. He played with the radio, looked into the glove compartment, turned around and looked at the back seat. "Man you is too much. You said you was gonna get a new car. Well, I'll just be damn. And look at you, you drivin' this thang. Did you really teach yourself how to drive it?"

"I'm still learning, but so far, so good. Hey! I haven't had any accidents yet. What do you think? I'm doing pretty good, huh?"

"Man, when you say you're gonna do somethin' you don't jerk around. This is really great. Like I told you before, man, you got more balls than I got to pull off a stunt like this. What did they say when you told them you didn't have a license?"

"Rickie, I couldn't tell them that I didn't have a driver's license. I just told the salesman I didn't have my license on me right at the moment. I told him the truth; I didn't have a license on me right at that time." They both laughed at the humor they found in Mitchell's play on words. The new driver pulled his wallet out and proudly showed his friend the only driver's document he had, a learner's permit; then added, "Hey Rickie, got the insurance just by giving the insurance company my learner's permit number."

"Get the hell out of here."

"That's right, man. I told you I was going to buy me a new car and teach myself how to drive."

Rickie got out of the vehicle and walked around it to inspect the brand new car. He stood back and gave it another once-over look, then shook his head. There was a serious look upon his face as he stood with his arms crossed just staring at the car. For a few uncomfortable seconds he said nothing.

Mitchell became concerned. He asked, "Is something wrong, man?"

"Aww, hell naw," Rickie answered. "I was just thinkin', that's all. Man, I just want to know one thing. Do you think you can buy one of them small airplanes and teach yourself how to fly? I bet the hell you could. Mitchell, you could fly us all over the U. S." The men both burst into laughter. "Look man, I'm gonna let you park this baby," Rickie said. "I'll meet yo' smooth-talkin' ass in the plant." He gave the car a gentle tap, then added, "Man, congratulations. This is one beautiful car."

PART TWO

CHAPTER 5 -- HOME

    Mitchell was proud of his new car. He received a lot of praise about it from his brother-and-sister-in-laws. He even took the little family for a spin in it. Helen packed sandwiches and sodas and put the lunch in the trunk of Mitchell's car. With Greg sitting in the other bucket seat and Helen in back with their boys, Mitchell drove them to Hamlin Beach where they enjoyed the day. While Helen took the boys to the swing sets, Greg bragged about his two new girlfriends he had on the side. Though this offended Mitchell because it showed a complete lack of respect for the man's family, Mitchell did not let it show. He was somewhat relieved when the evening was over, and even with Greg's lack of morals he was still happy he'd taken them out on the little picnic, just because it got Helen and the boys out of the house.

~ ~ ~

    Now that Mitchell self-taught himself to drive he knew he must go on with his life. He had waited patiently for Brenda to return to him; but it was to no avail. When his estranged wife turned eighteen years old, the law considered her as an adult, able to make her own decisions and care for herself. Mitchell filed for divorce; by law he no longer had to wait for Brenda. He moved out of the apartment and found a two-bedroom apartment on Genesee Street. Once he was completely comfortable with his new car he put the Chevrolet Impala on Route 15 to head for Cresaptown, Maryland.

~ ~ ~

"Son, you must be doing pretty good up there in New York. Why look at you, you got a nice big fancy car and everything. What kind of car is that anyway?" Mitchell's mother asked.

"It's an Impala Coup, mom," he told her in a voice filled with confidence.

Matilda Lauers was very proud of her boy. And even though Brenda left him for another man, Mitchell's mother didn't too much worry about it. Now he could come to Cresaptown even more. His mother knew her son was lonely and missing his wife. She hadn't too much cared about him getting married to the young lady in the first place. Matilda wasn't the type to throw it up in her boy's face by saying *I told you so*, but she sure was thinking it. Look what happened to her son. He had married Brenda in hopes of making a better life for the lady; and what does she do? She thank him by running off with some man, a man old enough to her father. It was better for him to find out sooner than later the young gal wasn't worth his time anyway. Now Matilda Lauers had her boy partially back for herself and that made her happy.

Jeremy, Jr., inspected the car, inside and out. "Hot damn, I ain't never seen a brand, spankin' new car before. How much does a car like this cost?" Jeremy, Jr. asked. He married his high school sweetheart, Carla, a week after Mitchell and Brenda had tied the knot. And now he and Carla had a little girl whom they named Judith, and another baby on the way.

Mitchell beamed as he answered, "It didn't cost too much, just a little over two-thousand dollars. I special ordered it because the dealership didn't have the color I wanted."

"What do you mean it didn't cost too much. Why two-thousand dollars is a fortune. You can't be making that much money up there in Rochester," Jeremy, Jr. exclaimed as he puffed on his cigarette. "And you say you special ordered it? Hell, I didn't even know you could special order a car." He shook his head, wishing it had been him who had come into such luck. But it wasn't; and even so, he was not about to give up his job at the body and fender shop to go following Mitchell to Rochester. He was the oldest, and he certainly did not want his mom and dad thinking Mitchell made better decisions than he.

All of Mitchell's brothers gathered around the car. His father wasn't too impressed about the vehicle. He was more concerned about his daughter-in-law. What was she going to do up there in Rochester, New York without her husband? No, the brand new car didn't mean a thing to him. He felt when a man takes on a wife he must do everything he can do to keep the union together. Why, he and his Matilda had been married for over thirty years and he knew if Matilda left him, he would walk through fire to win his wife back. Kids today; he just didn't understand them.

Mitchell always wanted to do the right thing. Even when Brenda was bent on leaving him, he tried to save the marriage; but she was not interested. What was he to do? He could not force her to stay with him if she did not want to. She proved she wanted nothing to do with him when she ran off with the older man and got pregnant by him.

Jeremy, Jr., though he would never show it in the presence of his parents, gloated on the fact that Mitchell's life wasn't as perfect as he would lead people to believe. Look at him; he couldn't even keep his wife up there in the big ol' city of Rochester. Even so, the oldest brother felt a spot of envy with all of Mitchell's other accomplishments. He would not show any of his contempt because everyone else seem to looked upon Mitchell as a young successful man. Here Mitchell was off on his own with a great job, his own apartment and a brand new car. He hadn't even been away from home for a good six months and he had accomplished way more than they could ever dream of achieving. But all the time Mitchell looked upon his married brothers as dutiful, loving husbands and fathers. He wished his marriage had worked, and the fact that it hadn't, and his brothers both still had their families intact, made him think of them as successful young men. He felt he could help make their lives even more complete, if only they would move to Rochester. He was sure he could get them both jobs at General Motors.

CHAPTER 6 -- LANDLORDS

Bert and Charlotte Jacobs got into the landlord business five years after they had married. Bert worked for Kodak and Charlotte had a job at the Xerox factory. After many test for both, it was determined that Bert's abnormally low sperm count deemed it virtually impossible for him to impregnate Charlotte. So when they both realized having children would not happen for them, Charlotte suggested they save their money and in a few years purchase a fourplex apartment building. With them being childless, becoming landlords would be a perfect business for them to delve into. So that was exactly what they did; and in the fifth year of their marriage they became landlords.

Bert and his wife had owned the property on Genesee Street for a couple of years when Mitchell approached them about renting an apartment from them. Mitchell was impressed when Bert showed him the apartment. It was so much larger than his place beneath Greg and Helen. The rent was seventy-five dollars a month, plus he had to pay for his utilities. He knew he could afford the place so he gave Bert the first month rent plus the security deposit.

~ ~ ~

Bert and Charlotte Jacobs were unconventional landlords. Instead of insisting upon a strictly professional relationship with their tenants, they presented themselves as friends. It was not a good idea, but being new to such an endeavor, they did not know there were boundaries that should never be crossed. Their tenants did not refer to them as Mr. Jacobs or Mrs. Jacobs. By the encouragement of their landlords, all of their tenants addressed them by their first names, Bert or Charlotte. And it was not uncommon for the landlords to socialize with their tenants. The young landlords participated in water-balloon fights in the yard, cook outs on the grill; and intertwine their business of being landlords with the friendships of the tenants. They never thought anything wrong could happen with such an inappropriate combination.

Bert worked a full-time job from three-thirty in the afternoon until midnight at Kodak. Charlotte gave up her Xerox job to stayed at home and oversee the property. Because Bert worked both inside and outside of the home, with the money he made from his full-time job at the Kodak facility, he felt it was alright to use it however he saw fit. So with that money from his full-time job, he gambled most of it away.

It was not uncommon to hear the husband and wife landlord-team squabble amongst themselves. Sometimes, in the heat of their arguments they would ignore their tenants and have their loud disagreements right in front of them. Bert was a gambler at heart, and it was well-known that he screwed around on his wife, too. One night around three o'clock in the morning Mitchell awoke to screaming and yelling from Bert and Charlotte's apartment. Charlotte was breaking dishes and drinking glasses as she threw them at Bert; and screaming nasty words to him as well.

"You son-of-a-bitch! I am sick of your fuckin' gambling and staying out until the wee hours in the morning. This is the last damn time you're going to do this shit to me, Bert. You hear me? It's the last time." She threw another plate at him; he ducked, but didn't duck enough. The plate grazed the side of his head. "You bastard, we have bills that's got to be paid. You know this, and you still gamble away the money." The fight lasted for hours, and though Mitchell felt like calling the cops on the couple, he did not. It was best to let his landlords do what they wanted to do. If he was in Cresaptown he would have called the police. But he had witnessed the brutality of the Rochester Police Department when it came to responding to the colored population of Rochester, New York. Mitchell liked the couple and did not want to place them in danger. Besides, he was impressed they had their wits about them to purchase such a fine piece of investment property, so he learned to let their spouts go. Charlotte always seemed to have the upper hand on her husband; so Mitchell knew she was definitely in no danger. If anyone needed help, he was sure it was Bert; and that did not concern Mitchell at all.

~ ~ ~

It had not always been like that with the landlords. Mitchell remembered thinking how great of a couple he thought they were when he first rented the apartment. He liked them as landlords. They were an attractive couple who took on the venture of being landlords. They didn't seem too much older than he was; maybe about five years older and that was it. That thoroughly impressed Mitchell and he was happy to have one of those apartments. And though he felt the couple must really have it together by owning the rental unit and keeping it in tip-top maintenance, it was anything but the truth. There was constant bickering amongst Bert and Charlotte. Their fights had started off quiet and the tenants never suspected any disharmony between them. But they were having marital problems and it was getting harder and harder for them to maintain decency towards one another.

It was Bert's obligation to make the repairs on the apartments and maintain the outside perimeters of the property and make sure the property was up to city code. Charlotte's job was collecting the rent monies, taking care of the paperwork and screening the applicants. She also made sure the deductibles for filing income tax were accurate as well. That was what the couple agreed their responsibilities would be upon purchasing the unit. It was not unusual for Bert to receive a phone call about changing a light bulb or snaking out the drain to a sink of one of their tenant's apartment. His wife never went with him on any of the maintenance jobs. Though he had some flaws which drove her crazy, Charlotte never had any reason not to trust her husband around the tenants; nor did Bert have to worry about his wife. They trusted one another when it came to the responsibilities of their unit. But that was as far as Charlotte's trust went with her husband, Bert.

CHAPTER 7 -- FAMILY

In order to obtain an inexpensive divorce Mitchell re-establish residency in the state of Maryland. He did this by having his mail sent to his parents' address and going to Cresaptown every other weekend to pick it up. During one of his runs to his small hometown, his younger brother Andrew asked about employment. He asked at the right time because Delco Products was hiring. So Mitchell had cleared it with his landlords about letting his brother and his brother's family move in with him. Bert and Charlotte gave him the go-ahead, with no increase of the rent. His new apartment was certainly big enough. It had two bedrooms and Andrew's family could stay in one of them. Seven months after Mitchell arrived in Rochester, New York and got his job at Delco Products, he returned to Cresaptown and moved Andrew's family to Rochester. One week later Mitchell procured a job for his brother at Delco Products. Andrew, Ethel and their toddler boys lived in the apartment with Mitchell, and all seemed to be going well. Andrew split the expense of the apartment with his brother, Mitchell.

~ ~ ~

Mitchell had many problems with his older brother, Jeremy, Jr., when they were growing up, but now they're grown men and Mitchell never forgot what his mother taught him about family.

Thinking of his mother's teachings, he felt he owed it to her to mend the fence which had slightly separated he and Jeremy, Jr.'s brotherhood. Six months after moving Andrew and his family to Rochester, Mitchell went down and brought Jeremy, Jr., his wife and their little girls to Rochester.

When the older brother followed Mitchell to Rochester, he was happy he made the move to the big city for his family. Within a couple of weeks Mitchell found a job for his brother at Rochester Products, one of the sister plants of General Motors. The plant produced carburetors and other items for the General Motors cars.

"Gee man, now I can make some decent money like you and Andrew," he boasted to Mitchell.

"Yeah, I think you and your family will do pretty good here. It's a little different from Cresaptown, but I'm hoping you'll get used to it." And get used to it, the little family did. Mitchell allowed Jeremy to use his year-old car for two months to get back and forth to work, while he bummed a ride to his job at Delco Products. Mitchell continued to look out for his older brother, always making sure the family was doing alright in their new environment. As soon as Bert and Charlotte had an apartment for rent in the rental building Mitchell informed Jeremy; and soon Jeremy, Jr. and his little family moved into the building with his other two brothers. So even though Mitchell lost the love of his wife, he replaced it with the love of his brothers and their families. He did everything in his power to make life wonderful for them.

~ ~ ~

Life was good for Mitchell. He and his two brothers now lived in the same apartment building. Andrew and his little family shared Mitchell's apartment, so his portion of the rent was thirty-seven dollars and fifty cents each month, plus half of the utilities bill. Jeremy, Jr. and his family had an apartment upstairs. With all three of the brothers working for General Motors they were pulling down good wages.

One day while the two men's wives were out shopping with their children, Mitchell sat in his apartment and talked business with his two brothers. Mitchell presented a business proposition to them. "You know, I saw a Laundromat for sale on the corner of Genesee and Brooks Avenue. If we pool our money together, I'll bet we can make a go of it." He looked at them for an affirmative acknowledgement. But he could tell by Jeremy's nervous habit of shaking of his left leg, he was not too keen on the idea.

Andrew, who rarely made a decision on anything, simply sat by and let his two brothers figure out a plan. He was sure if their oldest brother, Jeremy, thought it was a good idea, they would all go for it. And as he had always done, he would go along for the ride. But if his two brothers could not come to a solid decision, he knew there would be no venture for him to worry about pooling his money into, and that was just fine with him.

~ ~ ~

Jeremy, Jr. was the oldest of the five boys in the family. He was named after his father; consequently, he had always been called Junior when he was growing up. Early on it was quite obvious that even though Junior was the oldest, he certainly was neither the most ambitious nor the smartest.

Secretly Jeremy, Jr. hated the fact Mitchell was more motivated than he. And even though he was the oldest and things pretty much went his way, he couldn't help notice his brother seemed to thrive with success. He despised the fact Mitchell was the first to get married, the first to move to Rochester, New York and find a high-paying job, the first to get a decent apartment and the first to buy a brand new automobile. That bugged him the most. Here he had always been the favorite son; but when he saw his mother go on and on about how great Mitchell, the second-born son, was doing, inside he seethe with anger.

Of course he would never admit he had grown distant from his brother. How would that look if he showed the disloyalty hidden within his heart? It would look as though he was jealous of Mitchell. And he was not about to let people, who didn't understand the situation, even think he, the oldest and the most favorite of the Lauers' clan, had an ounce of resentment towards Mitchell. Here he was, the eldest son, depending on Mitchell for his most vital needs. Why couldn't it have been the other way around? Why couldn't he have been the first in all of those fine achievements? But the truth of Jeremy, Jr.'s universe was, had he been the first, he would not have been as generous as his brother, Mitchell. Had he had the opportunity to move to Rochester, New York, land a good-paying job at Delco Products, he would not have helped any of his brothers in pursuing a better life in the new city. He would have kept the spoils of success all to himself. And so it was, even though he hated the fact that Mitchell was wise beyond his years, he would do everything he could to take full advantage of what Mitchell offered him. But he would not be a part of making his brother look any greater than he already looked. There was no way he would agree to going into joint venture with Mitchell on any of his ideas. He wanted his family, including parents and siblings, to regain their belief that he was the wisest of the Lauers boys; not his brother, Mitchell.

Jeremy took a drink of the beer and said to his two brothers, "I'm sure that's a good idea, but I think we could do much better fixing up cars. Hey we're already working in the automotive industry; we might as well expand on it."

Andrew grabbed his beer and sucked out of the bottle. "Well I think they both sound like a good idea," he offered. He was never a great help as far as getting things started or even in the promotion of any project. "Look like you two might have to flip a coin to figure out what we should do." He took the last gulp of his beer, swung his legs from the coffee table, and then went to the refrigerator to get another. "Hey, either one of y'all want another beer?"

"Yeah, bring me one of them beers. In fact, grab the whiskey bottle and bring it too," Jeremy, Jr. said. He continued, "Mitch, me and Joey made a lot of money in Cresaptown as mechanics. This is a big city and we can rake in the dough here."

Mitchell wondered if Jeremy made so much money in Cresaptown doing body and fender work, then why did he happily make the move to Rochester? Mitchell was inclined to say something about his brother's work ethic as he had remembered it to be when they were teenagers; again the brother held his tongue. Maybe Jeremy had grown into a more responsible person. From what Mitchell could see, the man was working hard at Rochester Products and Mitchell was pretty sure Jeremy was bringing his money home to his little family. He felt since his brothers were grown men with great responsibilities of caring for their families, they were mature enough to go into business with him. He'd seen other families in Rochester bond together and run extremely successful enterprises. Mitchell wanted him and his two brothers to be amongst the group of elite entrepreneurs.

Andrew returned with the beers and bottle of whiskey. Mitchell, who was a non-drinker, got up from his chair and grabbed a Pepsi-Cola, then returned to the discussion. "Look Jeremy, I understand you are good with body and fender work, but think about it. If we go into body and fender, we will be putting in long hours, and then we will be too tired to go to our regular jobs, which gives us all fat paychecks and great benefits. Working together as a family with the Laundromat we can all have some peace in our lives; peace for our families and peace for ourselves by obtaining even more stability for us all. If we do this for the love of our families, it would be like having peace in paradise throughout our lives."

"How do you figure man," Jeremy, Jr. countered. "You ain't got no family. Sure, this is easy for you to come up with, all of this stuff 'bout more peace in our lives. Me and Andrew don't see you with no family, taking your chances with your money on this here thing. If it fails, it's no money out of your family's mouth 'cause you ain't got no wife or kids. I say the body and fender shop is the way to go." He tried to emphasize his point. He took a long drag on his Marlboro. When he released the smoke, it hovered and lingered amongst the three men until it finally dissipated into the air. Then he added, "Look, there's three of us. With the three of us we can take shifts working the body and fender shop."

Mitchell knew what the oldest brother was trying to do. If he had said let's go into the body and fender business, he knew Jeremy, Jr. would have said the Laundromat business would be better. Mitchell questioned his brother, "How do you think we can work in shifts at the shop? It's going to take all of our time and we will be pulling down long hours between the two jobs."

Angrily, Jeremy, Jr. blasted, "You're just not seeing it my way. You don't ever take into consideration I might be on to something. You think you know everything."

Mitchell could see this was not the way he wanted the presentation to go. Yet still he let his oldest brother have his say. When he was done, he restated his case. "Man, I'm just saying, we buy the Laundromat and then we clean the machines, make sure the money changers and detergent dispensers are filled. Your wives can do general upkeep on the Laundromat every day; wiping down the machines and so-forth. We don't even have to be there most of the time. Think about it. It would even give your wives something to do, and it won't take up much of their time. Why, I think it would be a nice little responsibility for them."

At one time their youngest brother, Bill, was living with Mitchell and Andrew's family. He even took on a job at the pizza shop down the street. But he didn't really like the city, so within weeks he returned to the safety of their hometown. But Jeremy and Andrew had good jobs. And Mitchell knew they were there in Rochester for the long haul. With two brothers staying on permanently Mitchell looked forward to the three of them running a family business. But no matter how much Mitchell tried to convince his older brother the Laundromat was the way to go, the more Jeremy, Jr. let Mitchell know the potential venture was a no-go for him. Andrew remained neutral. It didn't matter which way the decision went so he never obliged either of his brothers by giving his opinion. He drank his beer, kept his mouth shut and waited to see which brother would win out.

~ ~ ~

Even with Mitchell's Laundromat dream being nixed by his oldest brother, he did not give up his ambition of having an extraordinary life. He felt God placed him on His Earth to help others. He had a kind heart, and a determination to do good by people. The man remained focused with a strong ambition of not only helping others, but to be successful in his life as well. Mitchell remembered the teachings of his mother, and one of the lessons he learned was to help his siblings. But apparently Mitchell was the only one of Matilda's sons who had taken that particular lesson to heart. This is surmised because of the way his other brothers were; filled with themselves and always attending to their needs first and foremost. It didn't bother Mitchell none. He figured just because they came from the same mother and same father did not necessarily mean they would hold the same ideas or values. He realized they were free to do and be whatever they want, and act however they like. He would not impose his values upon them, for he certainly would not like for them to force their beliefs upon him. If they did not think the Laundromat business would be a good investment for them, then so be it. He would no longer present the proposal.

CHAPTER 8 -- SOAP OPERA

As the months passed, Mitchell noticed the boredom of working at the plant wasn't the only thing that caught his attention. He discovered being an employee of Delco Products was like being a character in the drama of a soap opera. Many times he saw couples split up because the man couldn't keep his zipper zipped, or a woman couldn't keep her legs closed when it came to being faithful in their present relationship. Marriages broke up; women fought one another over somebody else's man. Men plotted with any women of whom they wanted to have sex with to meet them at dingy motels. It was ongoing. Mitchell found the older women were always quick to approach him. They had nothing to lose, especially if the men in their lives did not work there. And with him being young, handsome and now single he could pick and choose from a vast assortment of ladies, young or old.

And it wasn't just the sexual immorality that went on in the plant. Mitchell witnessed men losing their jobs because of theft. One of his friends bragged on how he'd thrown an expensive power tool over the fence of the plant, then later drove onto the 490 Interstate, next to the plant, to retrieve it. Theft was so prevalent at one time that Willie the Guard was ordered to inspect lunch pails and purses as the people left their jobs. Bernard Taylor's lunchbox didn't have to be checked, because no sooner than he got to the guard the handle of his lunchbox gave way and the box fell to the pavement. Willie bent to pick it up and grab the thermos that rolled out. The guard found the thermos to be extraordinarily heavy. He opened it and found it filled with copper chips. Bernard was detained, then fired on the spot.

Many cars had been vandalized and the supervisors felt the need to add more guards onto the present staff. They hired Kathy and Patti. When the crew of security guards met, the supervisor, Ted Wilson, asked, "Have any of you seen anyone breaking into cars, or looking suspicious? Keep in mind, these thefts could be one of our employees. So even if someone looks anxious or out of place, you should investigate." Most of the guards shook their heads, indicating they had seen no strange happenings during their shift.

Patti, rubbed her chin, then said, "I did see something that seemed odd. I questioned the operator of the flat-bed tow truck, and he showed me the paperwork."

Ted Wilson could feel his face getting heated. He inquired, "What tow truck?"

"The tow truck that came to get the repossessed motorcycle," she answered. She heard murmuring from the other guards. The mumbling didn't sound good and she had a deep concern she might be in trouble. She wished she had kept her mouth shut.

"When did this happen?" the supervisor was now extremely frustrated. He didn't know if the tow truck had legitimate reasons to be on the property, or if it was part of a highly organized theft-ring.

"About five o'clock this afternoon."

"And you didn't think maybe you should get Willie involved in making the decision of letting the tow truck driver leave our facility with someone's motorbike? You figured you were experienced enough to make that call?"

Patti became fluttered. Generally, she had it together, but now she was not so sure she had made the right call. She wanted to portray herself as a strong woman. But her faltering at the supervisor's interrogation left her frustrated. Her voice became louder than normal. Patti erupted, "What are you talking about, Ted? We were just told to watch out for people prowling around the cars. Nobody, not none of y'all said anything about challenging tow trucks drivers with repossession orders."

"Wouldn't you think by being new on the job it would be common sense to contact one of the other guards before you let the tow truck driver remove the bike off of Delco's property?" the supervisor asked in a level-headed tone. There was stone silence.

Then the head guard, Willie, interjected. "Look Ted, Patti's new to the job. We should have given her more detailed instructions as to what we wanted her to do when a situation like this one happens. It's not her fault."

"Yeah, but she should have had sense enough…"

Patti nervously ran her fingers through her dirty blonde hair; "Oh, so now you're saying I don't have no sense? Huh." She stood up from her seat, took her badge and arm patch off and threw it onto the floor. "You put my ass back on the line. I ain't gotta take this shit." She angrily rushed out of the supervisor's office. Patti was hot and furious about the whole thing. She didn't know how to handle problems when she was the one being accused of doing something wrong. She would gladly go back on the line. As far as she was concerned, they could stick somebody else on the job. She quit.

When the B-Shift was over, true enough there was one employee whose motorcycle was not in the parking lot. It was Dale Benton. And just as the security supervisor had suspected, the bike was not repossessed; it had been stolen.

That night the Rochester police officers came to the plant. Dale gave the policemen the information concerning the description of his customized motorcycle. The following day he went to the police department with proof he owned the bike. Once it was determined the bike hadn't been up for repossession, an all-points bulletin was placed into action. For months the police department searched for the person or persons responsible for the theft. Word around the plant suggested the bike was stolen by one of Dale's co-workers. The person who took the bike was said to be extremely jealous the man owned such a beautiful bike and hired a friend with a flatbed to steal it. And though word got back to Dale who the thief was, without proof Rochester Police Department could not do anything about it. Dale Benton's motorcycle was never recovered.

CHAPTER 9 -- AMWAY

Mitchell had been working at the plant for a year and a half when he met Harold Rienardi. Harold was transferred from Department 215 to the Machine Pool Department. Mitchell knew the machine pool like the back of his hand, so he took time to teach Harold the intricate skills of performing many of them. This gave Harold an extreme appreciation for the young man. Not only had the new man been pleased with Mitchell's knowledge regarding the machines, but he especially liked his friendliness. Thursday night, after the paychecks were handed out, Harold offered to drive Mitchell over to Casa Leon's to cash their checks. He wanted to show Mitchell his new truck. When Mitchell climbed into the vehicle, he was surprise at all of the bells and whistles it was equipped with. Harold was proud of the truck and his jubilance showed through as he pointed out each feature. When they got to the club and cashed their checks, the men sat at the bar. Mitchell treated himself to a steak sub and a soda, while Harold got a couple of beers, two cheeseburgers and a basket of french fries.

"Man, how you like it at the plant?" Harold asked his new friend.

"Pretty good," Mitchell said with real pride. "Man, I remember when I first started at the plant; I didn't think I would last any time. God, the boredom was killing me." He laughed, and so did Harold. "But hey, what other place can I work pulling down money like this; and with great benefits? None that I can think of."

Harold took a swig of his beer, then said, "You sure are right about that, Mitchell." He shook his head and laughed.

"What you laughing at?" Mitchell asked his friend.

"Aww man, it ain't nothin'. I was just thinkin' six dollars an hour, yeah, that's good money." As he leaned in closer to Mitchell, he whispered in the man's ear. "It's good money, but I know how you can make more."

"Yeah, I know too. That's why I got me a second job at Technique and Wood."

Harold pulled away from his friend and laughed hard. He grabbed his beer and finished it, then slammed the empty upon the bar. And though Harold did not share with Mitchell what he found so funny, Mitchell felt it was best to leave it be.

~ ~ ~

One evening while they were on their break, Harold said, "Hey man, what you doin' over the weekend?"

"Nothing. Why?" Mitchell asked.

"The reason I'm wonderin' if you're free for the weekend is 'cause I'm havin' a barbeque. Figured if you're not busy, maybe you would like to come join us."

"Sure man, what do you need me to bring?" Mitchell asked.

"Not a thing, just be prepared to have a good time and meet some good people." Harold grabbed the piece of cardboard he saw lying on the floor, then went over to the foreman's desk and searched in the drawer for an ink pen. He wrote his phone number, address and crude directions down for Mitchell. "Hey, if you can't make it, don't sweat it. We'll be havin' cookouts all summer long; you're always welcomed." He scratched his head with the tip of the pen then stuffed the implement into his shirt pocket. With a quick slap on Mitchell's back, he left the young man to think about the invitation as he headed back to his machine.

Mitchell thought about Harold's invitation. He had planned on making a run up to Canada to be with his friend, Agnes. But she called him the night before and told him she had to go and help her sister out with some problem she was having. She promised they'd catch up with one another in a few weeks. With nothing planned for the weekend, he took Harold up on his invitation to attend the barbeque.

That weekend Mitchell found himself following the basic directions Harold had written on the piece of cardboard. When he pulled up to Harold's long graveled driveway he found it to be filled with cars and motorcycles. He had a feeling it would be a good party and was happy to be there. Mitchell noticed Harold and a small blonde lady walking towards his car. He was a brawny man, six feet, two inches tall and two hundred and seventy pounds. The long stringy black hair laid slick to his head. His large frame overshadowed his little wife. His wife was under five feet and her strawberry blonde hair was neatly pulled into a ponytail. The couple greeted him as he sat in his idled car trying to figure out where to park it.

"Hey buddy," Harold greeted. "Me and the missus here are glad you could make it." He looked at his wife, then back at Mitchell. "Mitchell, this my wife, Lois." He looked down at her, then explained, "Honey, this here is the guy I been tellin' you 'bout, Mitchell." He squeezed onto his wife's shoulder, pulling her close to him. "He's a good guy, real good guy," he confirmed. Then Harold's attention turned back to Mitchell. "Hey man, this a good lookin' car you got here. Yeah, mighty fine car. I see you like the better things in life." Not knowing how to take Harold's comment, Mitchell chuckled at the unexpected statement. Harold put the Genny Light to his lips and finished off the half bottle of beer, then handed the empty to his wife. "C'mon man, just pull the car onto the grass, anywhere you find a spot. We got a lot of people here so wherever you park is good. Hurry up; you got a lot of catching up on the booze to do."

Mitchell was very impressed with Harold's property. The house looked to have been built in the early 1940's. It was a large ranch, made of brick. As he walked towards the house, he paid a compliment to the owner. "You have a beautiful place here," he said to Harold.

Harold opened the door to the house. "Hey, come on in; let me show you around the place." As he walked in, his wife excused herself and headed back to the crowd of people who were hanging out in their oversized yard. In the kitchen Harold pride himself as he showed off the beautiful wood cabinets, the ceramic flooring and the newly installed built-in oven. Then he took him into the living room. "How do you like this livin' room set?"

"Nice. Really nice," Mitchell acknowledged.

"Come here, I want to show you my pride and joy." He opened a door and turned on the light. Mitchell followed him down the stairs. There was a bar from wall to wall lined with leather swivel chairs. "Go ahead, look behind the bar." He did and found it to be completely stocked. Mitchell noticed the pool table and not one, but two televisions, one on each side of the huge room. Mitchell was lost for words. He didn't know how the man and his wife could afford so much stuff. And when Harold took him outside he showed Mitchell the collection of toys in the garage. There were jet skis, motorcycles and what he perceived, Harold's wife's Mustang.

He was so astonished, he said to Harold, "Wow. You've got some nice stuff here, Harold. Geez man, how long have you been working at Delco?"

"Ahh, just a couple of years longer than you," Harold admitted.

"Man, you must have worked a lot of overtime."

"Nope. Overtime hardly ever came my way. Well, maybe every now and then I would get a chance to make some overtime money. But it didn't happen too often." Harold smiled.

The way Mitchell figured, Harold and his wife must be knee-deep in debt or somebody left a fortune to them in their will. They had a beautiful home which sat on at least five acres of land and there was even a large pond on the property which Harold claimed to have filled with fish.

After the grand tour Mitchell joined the crowd. He found most everyone to be very friendly. There was plenty to eat and beer of every kind. Since Mitchell was not a drinker of hard alcohol, he picked up a can of Millers to go with his ribs, and side dishes of macaroni salad and baked beans. There were a handful of people from Delco Products, and even though he didn't know some of them, they seem to know him.

A short man with freckles, by the name of Bruce, asked Mitchell, "Have you ever thought about selling Amway?"

"Amway? What's that?" he asked.

"It's different cleaning products you can sell. Yeah, you should talk to Harold. He's big into Amway. You can make a lot of money in the business," Bruce explained to Mitchell.

"I don't know, I'm not really a person who likes to sell things."

"Okay," Bruce said with a hint of disappointment. "But you should really talk to Harold about Amway when you get a chance?"

Mitchell excused himself. He moved around and socialized with other people. He walked around the property, making small talk with the different people he'd come across. Mitchell figured the Amway business must be very good for Harold to be able to afford all of the things he was seeing on the property. He stayed for a while longer and then informed the host he was about to leave. That was when Harold told Mitchell if he ever wanted to make some extra money just let him know and he could help him out.

"I like you Mitchell. I like you a lot. Look, I really appreciate you comin' to the cookout; hope you had some fun."

"Yeah, I did. I enjoyed myself; thanks for inviting me; and thanks for the tour of your house. It's a great looking place, man." And Mitchell was not just saying the home was beautiful, just to be saying it. It really was gorgeous; everything about it.

Harold leaned into Mitchell's ear, "Hey, you interested in fattening you pocket? You can make a lot of money, man."

"Harold, Bruce already told me about the Amway venture. I'm looking for something; been thinking about buying a Laundromat business. Start out with one, see how it goes; then maybe get a couple more."

"Laundromat, huh? I know where you can get your hands on the capital to get it goin'. You interested?"

Mitchell hoped to get away from the co-worker before he started to try and encourage him on becoming an Amway Distributor. Anxious to get out of a hard-sell he said, "Look, I already told Bruce and his wife, I ain't too much on selling things. I'm just not interested in promoting the Amway products; though I do appreciate the consideration."

Harold walked Mitchell to his car, and now the two of them were leaning their butts against the Impala. No one was near them so Harold felt free to talk in a normal voice. "Look man, I'm not talking about selling any Amway. I just use the Amway stuff as a cover; you get what I'm sayin'?"

Mitchell scratched his head, then answered, "No, not really?"

"What would you say if I told you I could make it possible for you to financially afford to put a nice-size down-payment on your first Laundromat?"

Mitchell's attention was on point. "What do you mean?"

"Say you had two-hundred dollars, no let's say it's five-hundred dollars, you give it to me, and I can turn it into a thousand dollars for you. I can literally double any dollar amount you give to me."

Mitchell, still not knowing where the conversation was headed, asked, "And who do I have to kill to get a deal like that?" He wanted to laugh, but he didn't trust how the laughter would be perceived by Harold.

"That's the beauty of it, Mitch, you don't have to kill or hurt anybody." He laughed as he slapped Mitchell on his back. "Like I explained, whatever you give me in cash, I can double it in counterfeit bills." Harold pulled out his cigarette pack. He offered Mitchell a smoke, but the man declined. He lit one for himself and sucked long and hard on it. Smoke furl out of his nostril, and he took another drag before he continued on. "You can quickly get the money you need to put down on the Laundromat you want."

The word *counterfeit* was still ringing around in his head. Suddenly, all of the things he'd seen at Harold's home made sense. He wondered how the man owned so many expensive possessions on his General Motor's salary. He wanted to know just how long Harold had been into the counterfeit con. The next thing Mitchell knew, Harold pulled out his billfold. He leaned in close to Mitchell and showed him the different denominations in the opened wallet. "Go ahead, take it out." Mitchell did; he examined the hundred, the fifty, and the twenty. The man could not believe how real the money look and felt. "So what do you think? You think you might be interested? I like you; I like you a lot kid. I've been in this gig for over three years. I've never offered this deal to anyone, not nobody, but you? You know kid, I don't mind showin' you the ropes. How to make the money clean, you know, turn it into legal money."

There was no way Mitchell was going to pass on Harold's offer right then and there. He said, "I appreciate the offer, Harold; honest I do. Look, let me think about it." With that, he handed the fake money back to Harold, thanked him once again for the fun day and drove away.

~ ~ ~

It was natural for Mitchell to be around Harold at work as though the counterfeit conversation never took place. But even though Mitchell tried to put it out of his mind, Harold was not going to let it happen. That Monday, on their break, Harold mentioned the illegal opportunity to Mitchell once again.

Mitchell said to Harold, "Man, I really appreciate you giving me this chance to get in on the action, but I'm going to pass on it."

"Okay, I'm not gonna to ask you again, Mitch. Let's just say you're passing up a once in a lifetime opportunity coming from me."

Mitchell slowly eased away from the friendship of Harold Rienardi. He didn't know how many more people at the plant knew about the counterfeit deal. There was no way he was going to get himself tied up in a federal offense; even worst, the mafia. If it worked for Harold then it was well and good. Mitchell knew to keep his mouth shut. He was not about to let anyone know his conversation about the counterfeit scheme Harold had going for himself. And if anyone asked his opinion on why Harold always carried a wad of money on him, he would tell them about them the man's Amway business; plain and simple.

It was almost four months to the day of Harold's cookout that the tall guard, Willie, came walking into Machine Pool Department. By his side were two men in black business suits. Behind them were two men in blue FBI jackets. Their side arms were showing and the people in Machine Pool Department were all craning their necks to see what was going on. When Willie the Guard went up to the foreman's desk, the boss man looked over towards, Harold Rienardi, then pointed him out to the suits. The group of men all walked over towards Harold. The two men in the back moved up close to the men in suits. Each one had his hand on his unsnapped-holstered gun. Once Harold was in custody, he was walked out of the plant in break-neck speed.

The buzz was all around the department about Harold's arrest. Many people wondered what was it that caused Harold to be taken out by the FBI. Had he kidnapped someone, had he robbed a bank, what had Harold been up to? His co-workers gossiped about the chaos Harold had found himself in. At break time when they asked Mitchell what he made of the feds taking away the big man; with a sincere look upon his face, he said, "Maybe it had something to do with all of that Amway he was selling."

CHAPTER 10 -- SALUTATIONS

Sometimes things happen with no rhyme nor reason. Mitchell never thought about how his divorce would affect him. He loved his wife, Brenda, but she made it quite clear she only loved him like a brother. The marriage was over, the divorce was filed. Since Mitchell filed for divorce, Uncle Sam placed Mitchell Lauers in the drafting category. Upon receiving his Greetings and Salutations letter, Mitchell accepted the fact that he would be drafted into the army.

Mitchell waited and waited for the government to contact him about reporting to the army. He turned another year older and figured maybe Uncle Sam had forgotten about him and no longer was interested in inducting him into the army. At twenty-three years old and no longer worried about going into the military, Mitchell ordered a brand new Riviera automobile. But the new car would not materialize for him. Shortly after ordering the car, the government sent orders for him to report to Fort Gordon, Georgia for basic training. He had to cancel the Riviera. Mitchell contacted Delco Products' personnel department to inform them of his induction. He also sent out letters to his creditors to let them know he would pick up on the repayment of his debts once he was discharged from the military in two years. There were also a few co-workers from his job he wanted to say goodbye to; mostly people whom he had grown to like over the three years he had been there.

His younger brother, Andrew, and Andrew's little family, had been living in the apartment with him for two and a half years. Now Andrew would have to pay the full seventy-five dollars a month for rent, plus all of the utilities. Mitchell knew his brother would be able to handle the expense because Andrew was receiving good pay from Delco Products. The man was pleased to know he had the two brothers situated in decent apartments with Curt and Charlotte as landlords. And happy they would do fine working their General Motors jobs. He would leave for the military with it in mind he had done all he could do to enrich his brothers and their families' lives. They would be okay while he was doing his two-year army stint. And even so, he noticed with all he had done for his older and younger brothers, not one time had either Andrew or Jeremy thanked him for changing the course of their lives. Had it not been for him, the two would still be in Cresaptown, Maryland, making mediocre wages. But he could not worry about their lack of gratitude now; he was going into a different phase of his life.

~ ~ ~

His two sister-in-laws, Carla and Ethel, put together a little surprise dinner party the Sunday before it was time for him to report to his training post. And though his brothers were busy with other things, Carla and Ethel were determined Mitchell was to have some type of farewell party. Ethel fixed sweet potato pie, string beans, potato salad and fried pork chops, Carla cooked fried chicken, scallop potatoes and macaroni and cheese. Both of the Lauer families gathered at Mitchell's decorated apartment for the celebration. Mitchell was happy to see such a wonderful gesture his family had done for him. He never expected they would give him a farewell party. He was honored. When Bert and Charlotte knocked on the door and walked in with a pineapple upside down cake, it completed his celebration. "You guys knew about this party?" Mitchell asked his landlords.

"Yes, and we didn't want to miss it." Charlotte handed the cake over to Carla, and the sister-in-law immediately took it to the table and sliced it.

Mitchell, loss for words, shook his head. "My goodness, this is wonderful," choked out of his mouth. He could feel himself becoming emotional, so he said no more, less he would start tearing. He had to compose himself; he took a break and went into his bedroom. He was happy, and there in the privacy of his room he allowed the emotions to surface. He blew his nose and took a deep breath. He felt a little strained from the surprise celebration. He left his room and went into the bathroom. Mitchell dampened a clean washcloth, folded it in half and placed it over his forehead to calm the tension. Mazie and Daisy, his Canadian friends, once told him it was the best way for a person to de-stress. Mitchell laughed at the thought of him doing such a thing, but when they made him try it, he was surprised to find it really worked. He felt himself calm enough to go back to the party. Somebody played James Brown's, *Papa's Got a Brand New Bag* on the stereo and the children were on the floor dancing along with their parents.

"So, were you surprised, Mitchell?" Charlotte asked. Bert reach pass his wife and shook Mitchell's hand. As they shook hands, Mitchell responded, "Yes! Yes I was and I still am surprised. How long have you guys known about this?"

"Ever since you told us you got your orders. Your sister-in-laws put this whole thing together. Me and Bert just had to show up with the cake."

"Wow," was all Mitchell could say.

With all of the excitement going on, kids' laughter, his brothers drinking and clowning around, the music on the stereo and the women talking up a storm, no one heard the knock on the door. When the person at the other end got no response after knocking four times, he opened the unlocked door and walked on in. In a loud, commanding voice he said, "IS ANYBODY HOME? YOU REMEMBER ME?" Everybody stopped and looked at the tall, fair-complexioned man who stood in the living room.

"Well I'll be," Mitchell was the first to recognize his cousin. But he looked so strange being out of Cresaptown, Maryland and in Rochester, New York. It just seemed odd for him to be there in his apartment. Everyone greeted the cousin.

"Nathan, what are you doing here," Andrew asked his cousin.

Mitchell said, "What, you guys didn't plan this? You mean you really didn't plan for our cousin to be here for this party."

"No we didn't plan it," Jeremy, Jr. admitted. Then he added, "Hey, if we had planned for somebody special to surprise you, it sure wouldn't have been this bum." And then he laughed at his own sour joke. But no one was in the mood for his stale joke, so the one-liner was ignored by everyone as the fuss over Nathan continued.

After the excitement simmered over Nathan's arrival, Mitchell introduced the newly arrived cousin to his landlords. Charlotte, who was astounded as to meeting yet another family member of Mitchell's said, "My goodness, Mitchell, how much family do you have?"

Before Mitchell could answer, Jeremy, Jr. said, "Lem'me tell you, you don't got to worry 'bout how much family we got. All you got to do is know who the best lookin' one is."

In order to sidestep the cocky man's humor, Charlotte asked, "And who might that be? 'Cause I know damn well it ain't you."

Everyone, including Jeremy, Jr.'s wife, Carla, start laughing. His face reddened. He said nothing more as he headed for the whiskey bottle in the kitchen.

Mitchell was happy to have the big apartment. His family and friends, and even one of his neighbors who had dropped in, were all comfortable in his place. The atmosphere of the party was a happy one. The music on the stereo was going and the drinks were flowing. Even Bert and Charlotte enjoyed a couple of drinks. And though Mitchell didn't want anything alcoholic, he took a beer and drank it slowly with his family and landlords. The little table which Ethel had the children eating was cleared away. A can of Legos were placed on the clean table for the kids to play with. Carla and Ethel were in the kitchen cleaning the dishes. Ethel put a new pack of playing cards on the clean table so the brothers and their cousin could play a friendly game of tonk.

By one o'clock in the morning the party was over. Mitchell decided he would talk to his cousin, Nathan, when he got up in the morning. Mitchell gave Nathan a sheet and bedspread and told him that the sofa was a sofa bed, he could pull it out whenever he wanted to. Right now, it had been a long day for him; he needed some sleep.

CHAPTER 11 -- COUSIN

It had been four months since Mitchell left for the military. The day after his farewell party he got a chance to talk to his newly arrived cousin, Nathan. The cousin informed Mitchell and Andrew he'd just come for a week's visit. He would be returning to Cresaptown in six days. Mitchell relayed the information to Bert and Charlotte. They didn't have a problem with him visiting for a week. As long as it wasn't a month like Ethel's mother managed to do the year before. The following day Mitchell left for the army.

~ ~ ~

People don't always do what they say they are going to do. When Nathan discovered his cousin, Mitchell, was drafted into the military, and would not be at the apartment for a couple of years, the cousin decided to stay. Nathan felt since Mitchell wasn't there, he'd take his place. So the one-week visit turned into a residency for Nathan. And soon he was running the household instead of Andrew and Ethel.

Bert didn't have a problem regarding Nathan replacing Mitchell; he liked the guy. But did Charlotte like him? Now that was another story. However, the rent was still being paid on time and the apartment was always clean and decent. And Nathan found an evening job at Saint Mary's Hospital as a janitor.

~ ~ ~

One evening when Bert left for work, Charlotte heard a faint knock at her door. When she opened it, she was surprise to see her tenant's three and four year old sons standing in the hallway. "Miss Charlotte, we gotta use the bathroom," the oldest boy said.

"Where's your mother," the landlady asked both of them.

"She's in the house. She won't answer the door," the youngest one complained.

"She won't? She must be asleep," Charlotte offered. "Come on in." She swung the door opened for the little boys and led them to the bathroom. For the life of her she could not understand why the woman was unable to tend to the supervision of her sons. It was five-thirty in the afternoon; no reason for Ethel not to have been outside watching them. After she fed the children some cookies that they saw on her countertop and milk to wash the chocolate chips down, she walked the little boys across the hall and knocked loudly upon the door.

It took Ethel a while to answer the door; and for a moment the landlady was beginning to think the children's mother was not at home. She placed her hands upon both boys' shoulder and began guiding them back to her apartment. Suddenly she heard the door open. **"Here I am,"** the mother's musical voice sang to her little boys, as though she had been playing a game of hide-and-go-seek with them. The boys ran to their mother and Charlotte followed.

As Ethel was about to close the door, after retrieving her sons, Charlotte stopped it with her hand. "Where were you? Didn't you hear the children knocking on the door?" she asked the woman.

"I was in here. No, I didn't hear them knocking," Ethel explained in a defensive tone.

At this point Charlotte was peering inside of the apartment. She saw Nathan, sitting at the table drinking a beer and reading the newspaper. She gave Ethel a wicked look. Then said, "You say you didn't hear them knock? Humm, I wonder why?"

Ethel noticed how Charlotte looked at Nathan, as though she was disgusted about something. Charlotte yelled into the apartment from the doorway, "I thought you were working this evening, Nathan. What, you got the day off?" Nathan didn't say anything; he continued to sit at the table and drink his beer. Charlotte, irritated by his non-responsive attitude added, "When Mitchell said you showed up on his doorstep, me and Bert thought nothing of it. But since you made a point of staying, I've noticed in the four months Mitchell has been in the military, things have gotten a little bit strange around here." She rolled her eyes at him, then added, "I don't know what's going on, but I'll tell you one thing, Nathan, I don't like it."

She said no more; and as she was turning to leave, Ethel said, "You should mind your own business, and stay out of ours. Besides, haven't you ever wondered why your upstairs tenant, Darlene, has so many repairs Bert have to take care of?"

"What are you insinuating?" Charlotte's eyes bucked wildly.

"I ain't insinuating nothing, just asking you a question; that's all."

Charlotte cut her eyes at Nathan, then turned and stormed across the hall. She had long ago suspected something was going on between the cousin and her tenant, Ethel. This evening, with her taking the little boys to their apartment, she knew her suspicion proved to be true. Since Mitchell had been gone, the family he left behind was falling apart.

~ ~ ~

When Charlotte received the phone call at nine-thirty that night she answered, "Hello," in a casual voice. She was not surprised to hear Nathan's voice on the phone.

"I'm on my way over, is it okay?"

"The side door's unlocked; just walk on in," she said, in an uncaring tone.

She heard him walk out of his door. He walked down the corridor, went out the back door and headed for his landlady's side door. She stoodby anxiously awaiting him. When he came in she grabbed him and began kissing him passionately. Then she pulled away from him and began acting snide towards the man. When Nathan asked her what was wrong, Charlotte lit into him, "I did not know you'd be fuckin' your cousin's wife, Ethel. Does your cousin know what's going on?"

He pulled her back into his arms, then said, "Don't be stupid, Charlotte. There's nothing going on between me and Ethel; not a thing."

"Then why didn't you let me know you would be staying home from Saint Mary's tonight. And why did it take so long for her to answer the door. I wasn't expecting you to be there with her." She pulled herself away from him again, then asked, "What did she mean about Bert and my up upstairs tenant, Darlene?"

"She said that just to be mean to you. That's what you women do," he assured her.

He leaned in to kiss her and she let him. She was feverishly hot for the man and was happy to have him to herself for the moment. He led her into the spare bedroom, the usual spot where they'd been having their affair. But there was something about Ethel's statement that jabbed at Charlotte. All she could think of was her husband and the upstairs renter. "No; not in here. Let's go into my bedroom."

Nathan looked at her in disbelief. He said, "You want me to screw you in the same bed you and Bert sleep in?"

"That's exactly what I want. You got a problem with that, Nathan?"

"Hell naw," he exclaimed as he scooped her up and carried her into the bedroom.

After they finished having sex, Nathan kissed her belly which barely showed her pregnancy. He asked, "So when are you gonna to tell him you're pregnant with my baby?"

Charlotte squint her eyes, and warned Nathan, "I've waited for so long to feel a baby inside of me. I will never tell him I'm pregnant by you. And what makes you think it's your baby anyway?"

Nathan slapped her on her butt, then said, "Oh sure. Right! It's not mine! Your ol' man is shooting blanks, least that's what you told me, and I'm the only lover you got. How are you gonna explain it to hubby, who is dark like you, when you have a fair-skinned baby? What you gonna tell him, that his miracle child just happened to come out bright-skinned?"

"Don't you worry about what I tell him. You just continue to pretend to everyone, that I'm the landlady from hell, and as far as you're concern, I'm a real nasty bitch. Got it?"

"Yeah, I got it." Nathan matter-of-factly replied. He laid with her for another half hour. With the darkness of the night as his shield, Nathan slipped out of the side door, reentered the front door of the building, then let himself into his apartment.

CHAPTER 12 -- HAPPINESS

Over the many years of Bert screwing around on Charlotte she had taken their vows serious and never betrayed him. No matter how much she'd argue, fight and let him know what he was doing was wrong, still he continued to do as he pleased. He felt as though he could do whatever he wanted with the ladies who threw themselves at him. And why shouldn't he feel that way. He was incapable of making a woman pregnant. His wife had always wanted children, at least one. Even though Charlotte knew Bert could not give her a child, still she stood by him. But his insincerity of their marriage over the years began to wear her down. She decided to move forward with her life. She would become pregnant. Bert was doing his own thing and he seemed fine with it. It was time she did hers.

~ ~ ~

Charlotte noticed Nathan Lauers the day he arrived at Mitchell's going-away party. She came off as annoyed the man was there; especially when he decided to stay. She treated him cold and was nasty and mean in front of his family and Bert. When Bert told her to check herself, she'd turn on him. According to Charlotte, there was no reason the man should be there. He was not on the lease and he was taking advantage of the situation. But Bert did not see any harm in letting the man's cousin share the apartment with Andrew and his family.

That was exactly what Charlotte was hoping for, because deep down in her soul, she was just putting on a front. The landlady had found the man which she wanted to be pregnant by. She would become involved with Nathan. True, he had a rough edge about him; but he was single, very attractive, and she noticed his funny sense of humor. And even with his ruggedness, it impressed the landlady that the man was generally easy going. She liked him; she could tell Nathan saw right through her act. He had a thing for her as well. She played up to him; and after only a couple of secret attempts she enticed him into the spare bedroom in her apartment. For the first time in her marriage, she cheated on the cheater and it felt wonderful.

~ ~ ~

The stress of the gambling, drinking and womanizing of her husband had taken its toll on Charlotte. She knew he still had lots of girlfriends. There were too many tell-tale signs. She remembered when they first married. She was cleaning out his satchel when she found a love letter he had written to a woman who was fifteen years older than he. In the letter he confessed he was married but still had feelings for her. As time went on, so did his irresponsible behavior. When he told his wife someone stole his money, then another time claimed he lost his wallet, she discovered he had gambled the money away. Out of anger, she put sugar in his gas tank. When he took a trip for his company and she found receipts for sexy lingerie upon his return, after a loud argument with him she slashed his tires. There had been many other affairs in between. Nothing he did came as a shock to Charlotte. It seemed as though Bert loved putting it in her face that he was cheating on her. So when five or six of his girlfriends called, and were brazen enough to brag about having sex with him, Charlotte wondered how they had obtained their telephone number. At one point she believed Bert might have given it to them so they could make her look even crazier. She did not fail to deliver; on the front lawn, she burned up his music collection. The latest incident that had done it for her was when the women start showing up in front of their building. They wanted Charlotte to know they were a part of Bert's life, too. It was the straw that broke her. All of her faith in her husband had finally been destroyed.

As a wife, she'd done all the right things. She helped him with the purchase of the beautiful property. When his own family said he would never mount to anything, it was Charlotte who encouraged and motivated him. Why did he have to be so disloyal to her? And why did he have to put it out there in front of family, friends and tenants? With the accumulation of his atrocious affairs, Charlotte decided she would look for a way to hurt him as much as he had hurt her. She tried to deal with most all of his indiscretions without making herself look like she had gone off the deep end. She had already done enough craziness for her family and tenants to wonder if she was really all there. *Strange*, she thought, *he does the deviant crap and because I retaliate I'm the one who appears to be the bad person.* Did he want her to look like a monster in front of family and renters? Maybe he wanted their sympathy so his running around on her could be justified. She knew she might end up losing her marriage, such as it was; but she was not going to just walk silently into the night. She was out for vengeance. And the new tenant, Nathan, had planted the seed for her sweet, sweet revenge.

~ ~ ~

Charlotte's love affair went unnoticed. None of the tenants knew she was involved with Nathan; and it was for certain Bert didn't have a clue that all of his affairs might very well come tumbling down around him at the cost of his marriage.

Charlotte was three months pregnant when Ethel's sons showed up at her door to use the bathroom. She found it to be absurd to believe Ethel's tale of Bert's involvement with the upstairs tenant. Of all the things Bert had ever done to her, screwing around with the tenants had never been one of them. Whether it was true or not, the fact that she was now pregnant reinforced her happiness. And she was even happier it wasn't Bert's baby, though she knew that could never happen. She was pregnant by someone who did not resemble her husband. Charlotte didn't have any intention of letting her husband think God had given him a one-out-of-a-million blessing of becoming a father. When it was time for the baby to be delivered, she wanted Bert, and everyone else, to know there is no chance in hell that the baby could possibly be his. That was just how much he had killed her love for him. After nine years of being married to her cheating husband, Charlotte was done with the man. She was making her own happiness; and now she was carrying a baby inside of her. She let the unmarried tenant, Nathan Lauers, become involve with her for one purpose only, to make her pregnant. She did not want him as a lover; she did not want him for company, she didn't even want him as a friend. She just wanted to have a baby; and he successfully impregnated her. And since she was now pregnant by Nathan sometimes she would lay with him to simply comfort herself, not him.

~ ~ ~

But the rumor of Bert having a fling with the upstairs renter bothered her. She wondered if he had really stooped that low to start having sex with their lady tenants. She was furious at the thought of him and the attractive Darlene having sex. In a sense, it made her happy she was having an affair with Nathan. So if Darlene really was Bert's new thing, then big deal. Her husband could not hurt her any more than he already had. Soon she would be proudly showing her pregnancy. He could stay with her and accept her baby, or they could divorce. She really didn't care. Life with Bert Jacobs was only mediocre as far as she was concerned. They owned a beautiful rental property,

Bert worked at Kodak, and each had their own automobile; but what was that supposed to do for her miserable life. She was not happy with Bert's lack of love and respect towards her. If she had to throw in the towel, then so be it. She would gladly walk away from everything they owned in order to regain her dignity.

~ ~ ~

Darlene had a six month old baby and Bert was always on top of any repairs pertaining to her apartment for the sake of the infant. Charlotte was determined to find out what was going on with Darlene and her husband. She knew the twenty year old was on welfare with no job. She was also aware the attractive lady had no boyfriend. Charlotte kept her eyes and ears opened.

One Sunday afternoon Darlene called their apartment. Bert answered the phone. When he hung up he said, "That was Darlene."

"Yeah, what did she want?"

"Said she didn't have the stopper in the drain and her bracelet fell down into it. I got to go and remove the trap so I can retrieve it for her."

"Oh, I see. And she can't wait until in the morning for you to do that?" Charlotte asked with squinted eyes.

"No Charlotte, she's nervous about losing the thing for good. Says it's a bracelet her great-aunt left to her."

"Umm umm. Okay. You sure you don't want to hire a plumber for that?" she tried to give him an out.

"Don't be foolish, Charlotte. I've removed many a traps. I'm not paying a plumber fifty dollars for that?" Bert, grabbed his tool belt and tool box and left his wife sitting on the sofa watching *The Dick Van Dyke Show.*

~ ~ ~

Ten minutes after Bert left, Charlotte went into their bathroom. Darlene's bathroom was right above Charlotte's head. The landlord's wife strained her ears to listen for metal on metal.

She should have heard something; at least the wrench on the drain pipe. But there was no racket; not one sound of plumbing work being done upstairs.

It was five minutes later that Charlotte quietly climbed the stairs. Charlotte placed her ear to Darlene's apartment door. She could not hear anything, and this alarmed her. Maybe they were already in the bedroom. She quietly slide the pass key into the lock of Darlene's apartment door. She peered her head into the apartment. She saw the baby's bassinette in the living room, but no baby inside of it. The television was on but the sound was turned completely down. She crept farther into the apartment and was by the small bedroom, she pushed the door opened; the room was filled with baby crib, dresser and a small blue chest of drawers. She was at the second, and largest bedroom, carefully she opened the door but all it revealed was an unmade bed and a cluttered room. Finally she was back by the bathroom. She could hear talking, but couldn't make out what was being said. She shove the door opened, expecting to catch Darlene bent over the sink and Bert humping her wildly. All she saw was the attractive tenant sitting on the seat of the commode, bottle-feeding her infant son while Bert was lying on his back underneath the sink, struggling to loosen the slip nut.

Darlene was startled when the woman burst into the bathroom. But when she realized it was Charlotte, she said, "Oh, hello Charlotte; I didn't know you were coming up to help Bert."

Bert bent his neck to look up at his wife. "What are you doing here, honey?" he asked; he was just as dumbfound as the tenant.

"I thought you might need this." She showed her husband the big flashlight; it was her excuse to be there.

Darlene always locked her door to make sure she and little Jimmy were safe inside of their apartment. She figured they hadn't heard Charlotte knock so she must have let herself in with the pass key.

"Man, that's just what I need. The lighting in here is terrible. Remind me to get a hundred-watt bulb for this bathroom. That seventy-five watt just ain't hitting it. I might as well change the other bathrooms to the same wattage." He wiped the sweat off of his forehead, then said to Charlotte. "Baby, can you shine the light right here for me?"

"Sure honey." She proudly aimed the light onto the spot. "How's that?"

"Much better. This slip nut is on so damn tight." He clamped down on the wrench and gave it another hard jerk. "Ah hahh, it's about damn time." He looked up at his wife, smiled and then said, "You must have brought me some luck, baby. I been working on this thing seems like forever." He went back to his work, dumped the water from the trap into the bucket and grasped onto the bracelet as it slid out. "Here you go, Darlene. I'll get a drain strainer to insert into that hole so you won't have this problem again."

~ ~ ~

He and the missus picked up their tools and left the young lady's apartment. Charlotte was happy there was nothing going on between the tenant and her husband; she was disappointed she'd fallen for Ethel's lie. She now realized that the woman made the whole thing up to cover her and Nathan's transgressions. When they got back to their place, Bert complimented, "We make a pretty good team, baby. I think I like you working with me."

Charlotte, anxious to start a new and happy life blurted, "Well, don't like it too much, I'm pregnant, Bert. And it's not your baby." A look of sadness engulf his face. He lowered his head, then shook it violently as though he was trying to fling out the words she had shot into his ears. Charlotte could see the hurt in his face. Wasn't that what she wanted? He'd hurt her so many times before. But why didn't this feel good to her; why wasn't she happy to see him feeling screwed over, and why was there a pain in her gut? She couldn't imagine that Bert would want her anymore. She asked, "I take it you want a divorce now?"

Her husband screamed at her, "No Charlotte, I don't want a divorce. I ain't never wanted a divorce; but you might, seeing how you're pregnant." He dropped his tool belt into the kitchen chair, went to the refrigerator and got himself a Genny beer. "You want a beer?" he yelled into the refrigerator. He didn't even have the stomach to look at her.

"No, I don't, Bert. I don't want anything but some happiness. You got a bottle of happiness in there? 'Cause if you do, then I'll take a couple bottles of that. God knows I ain't had any in years."

Her comment made him even angrier. Did she think it had been easy on him knowing he was the reason they didn't have children. It hurt him the day they both found out. So what does he do to make himself feel like a man, screw every woman who would lay down for him. Now that his wife was tired of taking his infidelity year after year, he discovered he didn't like tasting a dose of his own poison.

He grabbed a bottle of beer for her anyway, opened both beers then slid one over to her. After he guzzled half of the twelve-ounce beer, he put the bottle down and twirled it around. He looked her in her eyes, then abruptly said, "I been waiting for this day. Yes, I have." He nodded his head in affirmation.

"What do you mean, Bert? That's an odd thing to say when your wife tells you she's pregnant and you're not the father."

He finished off the beer. "I guess you're pretty damn proud of yourself. You found somebody else to do my job." He nodded. "Yeah, I guess I fuckin' deserve this. Instead of me trying to figure out how to solve our problem I stick my head in the sand." He reached over and grabbed the bottle of beer sitting in front of his wife. "I was so mad when I discovered I was the reason we didn't have children. I didn't care anymore. I figured if I couldn't make you pregnant maybe if I made you hate me, then you would walk out of my life and find someone you could make a baby with. I ain't never expected for you to be so fuckin' committed to our marriage. You must have really loved me to put up with my shit for so long."

"I still love you, Bert. I just don't like the way you treat me. Bert, you treat me like shit. I worked my ass off at Xerox. We pulled out our savings that we squirrelled away to get us this property. In return, you suggested I give up my job and take this building on as my job. I did it too. I helped you get this income property, I help you run it and I do everything else I'm supposed to do as your wife. But what do I get out of the deal, not a fuckin' thing but heartache with you screwing every woman that opens her damn legs for you. I give you all the support I can give to you, but it don't mean anything to you, because Bert I'm just a buddy to you. A roommate that you have sex with every now and then and it ain't that fuckin' good, anyway."

Hearing his wife tell him what he already knew, hurt him. He hadn't been putting forth any effort in sexually pleasing her. He was too busy trying to figure out how to keep his many affairs going; so there was nothing left over for Charlotte. "This is all my fault. Ain't nothing I can do to fix it. If I told you I love you, I really do love you, would you even begin to believe it?"

"Are you telling me you actually do have feelings for me, Bert?"

"Yes Charlotte. I do love you. I just thought you didn't want me anymore because I couldn't give you babies."

This infuriated Charlotte. "And how long have we known we couldn't have babies, Bert. Huh? How long? After the second year that we went to the doctors and found out about your sperm count; that's how long. So for seven damn years, Bert. And how long have I been standing by you as the woman who loved you, no matter what? Nine years, since the day we married. Not one year did I ever give up on us." Bert opened his mouth to say something but Charlotte put a finger up, warning him she was not done. "Why would you run around on me with all of those women, knowing it would make me crazy, knowing I would do stupid shit to get you to be a decent husband to me?"

Bert sat fuming as Charlotte told a truth he did not want to hear. In retaliation he belligerently yelled, "Why would you go and get yourself pregnant when people know I can't give you a baby?" He gulped down the remainder of the second bottle of beer, slammed the empty bottle down, then pounded his fist so hard onto the table that the two empty beer bottles rattled around, one fell and rolled onto the floor. Bert snatched up the standing bottle; grabbing hold of it by the neck. He leaned over the table, bottle neck in his hand and said, "I hate you did this to us Charlotte; you getting pregnant and all. You didn't have to go and do that? I would have rather you just go ahead and left my ass." His grip tightened around the neck of the bottle; he added, "At least I wouldn't be looking like a fool."

That was it for Charlotte. She could see the anger in his eyes. She would not take the chance of her husband wanting to beat the baby out of her. There was no way she was going to risk having a miscarriage of the baby growing inside of her; the baby that she loved so much. She knew the marriage was over. She got up from the table, looked down at the man and told him, "You know what Bert, I didn't do this to us; you did this to us. And I don't care how this is gonna make you look. A baby wasn't that important for our marriage to work. I've always loved you, baby or not. But you chose to show me no love; you chose to give your love to other women and to gambling and drinking too. And when I finally look for something to take away all of this pain you have placed in my heart, what do you do, worry about people knowing that you didn't make me pregnant. Well you don't have to worry about it. I won't even be around anymore. So you are getting your wish, Bert; I'm leaving." And with that, she went into the bedroom, threw a few things into an empty shopping bag and grabbed her purse. In a show of defeat, Bert placed the beer bottle on the table. When Charlotte walked back into the kitchen, Bert was sitting at the table with his head in his hands. Charlotte stopped in front of him; she could see his tears dropping onto the table. It was too late for him to cry now. They could have stayed together and raised her baby as a family. She dealt with his misgivings for so long, yet he could not understand why she had gone to such drastic measures. She was leaving him. As he slowly lifted his head and stared a look of self-pity to her, she informed him, "I'll be back tomorrow with the police to gather up the rest of my things. Any further conversations which I might have with you will be communicated through my attorney." She turned away from him and walked out of the door.

PART THREE

CHAPTER 13 -- JULIA

Julia Holton was the oldest child of Jake and Eleanor Holton. The family lived in the projects in Philadelphia, Pennsylvania. Piedmount Projects was one of many projects in the large city. One year Martin Luther King stopped in the Piedmount Projects to spread his words of peace and equality. There were many projects for the poor people to live in, and they were all segregated. The poor whites had their projects, and the impoverished coloreds had projects as well. It made for interesting living. Because even though their living communities were segregated, their schooling and churches were not. The one thing the separation of races in their different projects had in common was the fact that they were all very poor; though the children never knew it. They lived their lives playing hop-scotch, double-dutch, jacks and shooting marbles with their friends. Never did they ever have in their minds that their parents only made enough to pay the bills and put food on the table. They were too busy riding their bicycles and skates and playing with their hula-hoops to worry about something as insignificant as money. There were hundreds of families in the projects, some people liked their neighbors and would chat over the clothesline, and some couldn't stand their neighbors, nor anyone else for that matter. Those individuals had that *don't bother me, and I won't bother you* attitude; or *you keep you kids off of my grass, and I'll do likewise* assertiveness.

Jake and Eleanor Holton lived in the projects with their many children. And because the family was large, income was small and patience of both parents extremely short, they lived miserable lives. Being the oldest child, Julia's responsibility was to make sure things were clean and neat for the family.

In spite of Eleanor's discontent with her husband the two of them stayed together. It was common for Julia to witness them fighting during the day and into the night. Why had God placed her in the care of two people, who not only displayed destructive behavior amongst themselves, but passed their discontentment onto their children as well? Holidays were the worst for Julia because the cops were sure to come. When they showed up, everyone in their section of the projects knew it was because of that crazy Holton family. And then there was the cursing; *fuck-this*, *muthafuck-that* and *that muthafuckin' cocksucka* were words that spew from Jake and Eleanor Holton's mouth straight into the ears of their children. The filthy language fell from the parents lips like a flurry of hail falling from the sky. These curse words and many more were everyday language used by the unashamed parents. When one of Eleanor's children complained to her about the harsh language, Eleanor was quick to reply, "You can't tell me how to talk. I cuss whenever I feel like cussin'. If you don't like it, then that's just too muthafuckin' bad." The Holton children were of little importance to Jake or Eleanor. Many times, Eleanor angrily said to her children, "I shoulda gotten rid of you lit'le muthafuckas before you was born." And then she would go about her business as if what she said was a perfectly normal statement to say to a child. Whenever the two parents fought and she was very angry after a brutal bout with her husband, she would blame her children for the predicament she was in. Nastily she'd tell anyone of them that was handy to assault with her anger, "I should walk off and leave you lit'le bastards fo' the state to take care of." Julia hated her mother's smoking and her father's drinking and the filthy language which ejected from both their mouths. The teenager detested when Eleanor would refer to she and her siblings as little black bastards, bitches or whores. But Eleanor did not care what her oldest daughter felt. She was the one stuck raising them while her husband worked and drank up most of his earnings. She let all of her children know she hated they were in her life. She was only doing what she must do to get them to the age of eighteen so they could leave the fire-pit of a home.

But it hadn't always been that negative of a life with her mother. At one time Eleanor Holton had been decent to her children. Before anger and resentment invaded Eleanor's soul, the mother would enroll her three girls into tap dancing and let them join social events such as the Brownies and the Girl's Club. Often times she would let the girls go to the movie house and once she even let them go roller-skating. When the stress of the large family became unbearable for the woman, she created an environment of ratchet hate for everyone in her life.

There were too many children, not enough income and the sound of a nagging wife to send Jake Holton towards the whiskey bottle to mask his frustrations. When he drank, he beat up Eleanor and cursed her. And even though they had a lot of children, they did nothing to protect themselves from unwanted pregnancies. That is why they had so many children. All boys after the three girls; which created a lot of work for Eleanor and her three daughters to clean. When Jake cursed his wife and gave her black eyes and burst lips, it stole what little love she had for her children away. Eleanor Holton was lost. And even though Julia knew something was wrong with the family, she was smart enough to know there was nothing she could do to fix it.

Julia's only sense of sanity was her mother's sister, Jackie Mae. The aunt came almost every weekend to visit with the family. The attractive woman brought laughter and smiles for all of the Holton children whenever she came over. She was two years older than Eleanor. Jackie Mae was concerned about her sister because Eleanor had so many children and didn't want any of them. She, herself only had two boys and she dearly loved her sons. Often Jackie Mae would hear the crude words hurled at her nieces and nephews and she would warn her sister. "Eleanor, don't you know you are killing these children's spirit when you talk to them with such hateful words." But no matter how much Jackie Mae tried to encourage the mother of the large family to do the right thing, the more the mother cursed and berated her offspring.

Eleanor was light-brown in complexion; her hair was black and hung pass her shoulders. No hot comb touched her beautiful hair until she became bored and decided to press it like the other mothers of the projects. Her sister, Jackie Mae, was fair-skinned with shoulder length reddish course hair. Eleanor and Jackie Mae had two other sisters. They were Mattie and Tee-tie. Their skin was the pretty peach color as Jackie Mae's but both had silky hair like Eleanor's. Jackie Mae had two sons, Mattie had one daughter and Tee-tie had no kids. Eleanor was the only one from her family who had given birth to nine children. This made Julia wonder if there was pinned-up resentment within her mother because she had so many more children than her sisters.

Once when Jackie Mae heard Eleanor call one of her boys a little black bastard, she asked, "Eleanor if you didn't want black children, then why did you marry a dark-skinned man? You knew Jake was black as night when you married him."

In an angered voice Eleanor looked Jackie Mae dead in the eyes and said, "You think you're so smart Jackie Mae. You don't know half the shit about Jake Holton that I know. For your information, the bastard raped me when we was on a date. When I told him I didn't want to, he forced his black ass on me anyway. After that I went my way and he went his. That is until I found out I was gonna have a damn baby; here I was, just eighteen." She rolled her eyes at her sister; then added, "I hunted his ass down 'cause I wasn't gonna be raisin' no brat by myself. I made him marry me, even though he was still married to his crazy-ass wife. What else was I supposed to do, Jackie Mae? Huh? What would your smart ass have done?"

"Eleanor, what is wrong with you? You could have turned him in to the authorities."

"Yeah? And tell the cops what? That he raped me? And what do you think Jake Holton would have told them? We was on a date and I gave it to him; that's what he would'of said. He ain't even my type; but it look like I just got stuck with his black ass. How did I know I would be having a fuckin' baby year after year by him; just because I wanted him around to take care of just that one? I should have cut my muthafuckin' losses and gave the brat to somebody who wanted a baby. I sure the hell didn't want it." She became sickened by the thought of how she made the worst critical choice by dating the black man. And when she became pregnant she made yet another bad choice; hunting him down and forcing him to marry her. It was the beginning of her hellish life. She had straddled herself with a drunken bully that kept her pregnant and miserable. Not to mention she hated his guts.

Jackie Mae fussed with her sister, "Eleanor, you should've taken him to court and made him pay child support. If you knew his cup of tea was too black for you, then the last thing you should have done was want him back in your life. Now you got all of these children, and because you hate Jake and his darkness, you hate your children too. It just ain't fair to these kids, Eleanor. It just ain't fair."

Jackie Mae found no reason to continue arguing the dynamic in the strange turn of events of her sister's life. The sister knew Jake was separated from his wife with a toddler son when the pregnant Eleanor went looking for him. When Eleanor told Jackie Mae she was going to make Jake marry her, Jackie Mae reminded her that the man was already married; just separated. Eleanor did not care. She was determined he was going to be around to help raise the little black baby growing in her belly. How ironic; she's wasn't fond of him because of his dark color, but each year after they marry she has a baby every year by the abusive man. Not one of the children picked up Eleanor's pretty caramel color; they were all as black as her husband, Jake. Jackie Mae was worried for Eleanor. She realized with no love in her sister's heart and nine children, who all resemble the man she hated, no wonder Eleanor was an angry and bitter woman.

CHAPTER 14 -- PREDICTION

The other children of the projects made fun of the Holton brew. They were always the brunt of many jokes. *"Here come Jake Holton's gangbusters"* or *"Let's get a ringside seat for the Holton fight."* Life as a kid for Julia Holton was not easy. Many times she would go to sleep crying as she heard her father beat her mother. And when Eleanor got tired of Jake giving her bloody lips and black eyes, the woman found the courage to start stabbing him. Often Eleanor would get angry at her children for not jumping in to help her fight Jake Holton. But they were just children; and Julia wondered how a mother could want her children to fight their father. It was just the sort of craziness her mother would try to manipulate her children into doing. At the age of twelve Julia was a nervous wreck; and whenever someone slammed the door or yelled at her she would jump. The pre-teen had very little self-worth and knew she would not amount to anything if she listened to the beliefs of her unhappy mother.

When Julia was thirteen, her aunt, who didn't even have a daughter, had to explain to Julia about the menstrual cycle and where babies came from. Up until that point Julia thought whenever her mother had to go to the hospital, the doctor would give the woman a baby as a gift to take home with her. Julia thought it was strange her mother could not tell her about the menstrual cycle and babies, yet the woman could curse her and her siblings with no hesitation and without shame. It was not her aunt's responsibility to have that conversation with her; it was her mother's. She always felt it was up to her mama to educate her daughters. Now she knew why there were so many kids she had to oversee and it disgusted her. She recalled the countless times her parents fought during the day; then she would hear their headboard banging against the wall at night. She was happy her aunt took the time to tell her how babies were created. She knew of a few girls who had been known to do it with the boys. It was a miracle they hadn't found themselves pregnant.

During Julia's teenaged years her mother decided to make some money on her own. She picked up small jobs cleaning offices for downtown companies. The woman was trying to become more independent and less abusive to her children and Julia could see a slight change for the better. On Eleanor's good days she would stressed the importance for Julia to graduate from high school. Eleanor dropped out when she was in the tenth grade and Julia's father, Jake, only made it to the fourth grade. But when Eleanor found herself depressed, the hateful words would resurface. "You gonna be just like me. Marry some black bastard and have a houseful of sorry-ass kids. And because you're such a scaredy-cat, he's gonna beat the shit out of yo' ass every chance he gets. At least I fight this muthafucka back," she'd tell Julia; indicating she wasn't afraid to protect herself against the abuse. It was her mother's prediction of how horrible her life would be that made Julia realize she had to leave the home. If it was one thing the young teenager knew, she would not live the same type of life she was witnessing as a child. She was determined no boy would put his penis inside of her for the very fear of ending up like her mother. That would surely make her mother's prediction become her reality and she could not let that happen. She didn't know what type of job she would have as an adult, but it was for sure she would have to earn money to take care of herself. If her parents' marriage was an example of love and devotion, she would never become someone's wife. When Julia turned fourteen she worried about how she was going to make it on her own.

In the summertime her brothers would craft together skate-a-mobiles and wooden shoeshine boxes. They'd go to the business sections of Philadelphia and shine the shoes of men in nice suits and fedora hats. Sometimes they would make as much as seven dollars after shining shoes all day. Since Julia and her two sisters were the three oldest girls, they had to help Eleanor with cleaning house, doing laundry and child care. Sometimes after cleaning the living room and kitchen Julia would sit on the sofa and admire the spotless apartment. She wondered if she would ever have a place as nice as her parents' when she became a grownup. But that was far off in the future. She had to get herself through junior and senior high school first. By the age of sixteen, Julia still didn't know what she would do to make a better life for herself. She had to find a plan that would get her out of the city of Philadelphia.

CHAPTER 15 -- NAVY

Julia was seventeen and in her last year of high school. A lot had happened in her crazy family during that year. Her twelve year old brother, Clifford, ran away from home; and her sister, Jenny, got pregnant, left school, then married a boy from the projects. And her father was thrown in jail for disorderly conduct.

~ ~ ~

One day in study hall Julia was sitting with her friend, Anita Bryant. Anita asked Julia, "Have you ever heard of the WAVES?"

"The WAVES? What's that?" Julia asked.

"It's a woman's organization affiliated with the United States Navy." Anita snatched out a piece of notebook paper, then she boldly wrote the letters W A V E S. She quickly pointed at each letter and explained what it stood for. "Women Accepted for Volunteer Emergency Service," she rattled off to Julia. She pulled out a pamphlet from her history book and showed it to her friend. The brochure had a picture of a woman in a navy uniform and all Julia could think of was how much she wanted to be in that uniform. The leaflet listed all of the criteria which must be met in order to sign up for the navy; must be eighteen years old, must be a high school graduate, must be physically fit and a have the sense of adventure. *Join the Navy and See the World*, that brochure was calling her name. Julia liked what she saw and she was sure it was her ticket out of the state of Pennsylvania. She had just turned eighteen a week ago; next month she would be at her graduation celebration, receiving her high school diploma. As for the physically fit qualification, she was skinny but maybe they could fatten her up once she joined. And she certainly wanted to experience adventure.

As soon as she graduated from high school, she went downtown to sign up for the Navy. Everything checked out to her advantage for acceptance into the navy, except for her weight. She weighed only ninety-five pounds. The enlisting officer informed her, "You are five pounds below our weight criteria. If you are still interested in being in the navy, then come back when you've gain the weight." Julia wondered, *What does he mean, if I'm still interested? Of course I'm interested.* She ate and ate and ate; not even a pound was added onto her thin frame. Determined to get out of the unstable home, she put on her girdle that held up her cinnamon-colored stockings, she stuffed it with every small knick-knack she could find in her mother's display case. Two small iron bulldogs, those will do, a decorative cast iron cooling tray; that was sure to add some weight. Once the girdle was loaded up she wore a baggy empire dress to camouflage the deception. She returned to the recruiting center and was relieved when the scale tipped in her favor. She signed her name to the contract and left the federal building feeling ten feet tall. She now belonged to the United States Navy. It was the beginning of a brand new life for her.

~ ~ ~

In boot camp she had to learn a whole new way of communication. In navy lingo, the bathroom is called, the *head*; the uniform hat is referred to as a *cover*, a rumor is known as *scuttlebutt,* and the cafeteria is referred as the *mess hall*. There was so much she had to get used to; who to salute, how to march and how to hold herself to the high navy standard.

In Company Seven, right before graduating boot camp, she was asked to list three naval stations which she would like to be stationed. She was born and raised in Philadelphia, Pennsylvania, so her three choices were all in California. Those were her prime choices. Upon receiving her orders, she was very disappointed to find out the navy assigned her to Patuxent River, Maryland. She thought. *I've taken my boot camp training in Bainbridge, Maryland, and now I'm stationed in the state of Maryland too. That doesn't seem right.* Many times it ran through her mind, if she had only written her three choices as Patuxent River, Maryland, Baltimore, Maryland, and Annapolis, Maryland, maybe she would have gotten a naval station somewhere in California. But though she was not stationed anywhere in the state of California, she was still happy to be at her assigned base.

~ ~ ~

Upon reporting to Patuxent River, Naval Air Station, Seaman Apprentice Julia Holton was assigned to work in the Air Traffic Control Tower Building. Her office was a deck below the air traffic control tower. The first day Julia reported to Operations Admin, Lieutenant Kadowski gave her some memos to type. She was use to typing; she had taken three years of typing classes and Gregg Shorthand in high school. There were five memos to be typed for her lieutenant. She whipped through three of them with ease on the electric typewriter. As Julia was completing the fourth memo there was a loud explosion. It was so great in volume, it sounded like a bomb. Seconds later a cloud of black smoke rose upwards and could be seen as it reached the third floor windows. Everyone in the office jumped from their desk and ran to the oversized windows to see what caused the explosion. They saw reminisce of a crashed jet on the landing strip. **"Crash Crew, Crash Crew,"** came echoing throughout the whole building. Sirens filled the air traffic control building from top to bottom with the urgency of the accident. Sailors ran outside to get a glimpse of the tumultuous crash. Sirens and alarms blared fiercely. The tar-mat was filled with crash crew personnel, fire trucks and an array of hoses all in disorder and shooting foam onto the wreckage of the jet. More and more crash crew trucks roared out of the station towards the burning jet to put the inferno out. A pilot died that day and Julia was very concerned. Through her upbringing she'd always been a basket of nerves and when she witness remnants of the fatal accident she was beginning to believe she may have to be reassigned to another department away from the air traffic control tower.

When she could no longer stand looking upon the fatal plane crash, she naïvely turned and asked Yeoman Cross, "Does this happen every day?"

"No, not at all. I've been here for two and a half years and there has never been an accident," Yeoman Cross explained. "Don't worry Holton, this is just a fluke."

Julia was sadden, but she knew she should show strength, not weakness. "Just my luck," she said to Yeoman Cross, "My first day on the job and a jet has trouble and crash upon the landing strip." She hoped there would be no jets dropping from the sky tomorrow.

The yeoman gave the new wave a pat on the back, and said, "Welcome to the Air Traffic Control building, Holton! Welcome aboard!"

The only positive thing that came from the jet crashing on Julia's first day of her job was the fact that the following days could only get better. She had typing the memos down to an art, and whenever she thought she was through, Chief Hill would come with more memos to type. She didn't mind. She loved typing. Earlier that day the wave joked to Yeoman Cross that taking the years of typing classes was her ticket into the navy. But deep down, she knew even if she didn't know how to type the navy would have figured out a trade for her, and then sent her to school to learn it. But as it was, she already had a valuable skill and she was so good at it the navy didn't have to improve upon it. After Julia's first week, Commander O'Shea told her he was pleased with her work; that was when the seaman apprentice knew she was born to be in the navy.

CHAPTER 16 -- GREYHOUND

In basic training Mitchell Lauers impressed his commanding officer so much he was appointed as a squad leader. This authority placed him in charge of making sure the barrack was clean and the men of his unit were ready when needed to be. Once he completed his six weeks of basic training he was sent to his assigned army post, Fort Dix, New Jersey.

When Mitchell reported to Fort Dix he gave one hundred percent, his very best. Mitchell was a much liked soldier in the army; and within weeks he earned the approval of his Sergeant Major for his outstanding demeanor. One Thursday evening Mitchell said to the Sergeant Major, "I'd like to go home this weekend, but I know we can't go out of the two-hundred mile radius."

"Where's home, private?" Sergeant Major asked.

"Cresaptown, Maryland, sir."

"Tell you what, bring me a bottle of Wild Turkey and I will make sure you're marked present and accounted for during reveille call come Monday morning."

As soon as he got to his mother and father's home in Cresaptown he made sure he went to the liquor store and purchased the bottle of booze Sergeant Major requested. His visit was great and he took in every moment of it. His parents and friends fussed over him when they saw him in his uniform. He felt proud, almost as proud as he was when he got hired at the General Motors facility in Rochester, New York. There were neighbors in and out of his mother's house. His father, who rarely fussed over the sons, made it a point to invite Mr. Harry over to see his second-born son in uniform. Though the old man never wanted to admit it, he was more than pleased with his boy. Why he, himself, had never been in the military; so as he stole glances at his son, his heart beamed. Every now and then the son would catch the senior Lauers looking his way; and during those moments Mitchell realized his accomplishment was something great. Today he saw his father smile. He had not seen happiness in his dad's eyes since he announced to the family he was divorcing Brenda.

When Mitchell's weekend visit was over, he prepared himself to head back to his post. He packaged all of his belongings; the Wild Turkey for Sergeant Major was safely wrapped in his civilian garments and tucked into his satchel. "Son, please be careful," his mother told Mitchell. She kissed him on the cheek.

"Do you need any money, Mitchell?" his father asked. Though Jeremy, Sr. was not much on saying goodbye to any of his sons, he found himself giving the soldier a fatherly handshake. The elder man knew Mitchell would make a great life for himself. Jeremy, Sr. and his Matilda did all they could to prepare the Lauers boys to do their best. He was happy three out of his five boys were pretty much self-sufficient. "How much do you need, Mitchell?" His dad dug into his pants pocket and pulled out his wallet. But Mitchell would never take money from his parents.

Mitchell said to them, "I don't need anything; I have enough to see me through." Mitchell took some bills out of his wallet and pressed them into his mother's palm. "Here mom, you take this and use it for whatever you and dad need. It ain't much, but I'm hoping you can use it." That was just like Mitchell, always looking out for everyone else with little regards for himself; always willing to make things better for others.

Mitchell's mother and father took the cab with him to the small Greyhound Bus Station. It was a beautiful sunny day and his parents were filled with pride as their son exited the taxi cab.

He was tall and muscular. The paleness of his face could easily confuse the average person into thinking he was of another race, rather than Negro. The mother and father looked at their son with respect as he retrieved his satchel from the cab. Mitchell's mother worried; and though she tried not to show it, she was sad to see him go. The Vietnam War was going on and she feared Mitchell would be caught up in it. It even crossed the father's mind he may not see his son again. All of Matilda's life she tried to teach her boys how to be fearless. From her teachings Matilda Lauers believed Mitchell was the one who took the lessons to heart. No one, no thing, no creature did the young man fear. And though he was courageous, he had a giving and compassionate heart.

As he and his parents walked into the waiting room of the small Greyhound Bus Station, they saw a young lady sitting on her red, hard-shell suitcase. She was a skinny thing dressed in a navy uniform. She sat nonchalantly on her suitcase reading a magazine. Mitchell noticed the young lady. He asked his mother, "Mom, do you know her?" When his mother admitted she didn't know the lady in uniform, Mitchell told his mother that he would sit with her on the bus. His mother said, "Go ahead son." As soon as he spotted the Greyhound pull into the station he bent down and gave his mother a final kiss on the cheek. Proudly, he stood tall and gave his father a firm handshake. "Be safe, son. Call us when you get a chance," the father advised. The son promised he would and then boarded the bus.

~ ~ ~

As the lady in uniform sit down in a vacant section towards the middle of the bus, she thought how happy she was to get out of the small town. She'd never seen a city like it; and it was surprising to her such a tiny place existed. Things were alright now; she was on the bus and more than ready to get herself back to Patuxent River Naval Air Station. When she was comfortably seated, Mitchell, who had sat in front of her, turned around and asked, "Is it alright if I sit in the seat next to you." She was so flattered the soldier showed a liking to her, she told him he could. The eyeglasses made her look homely so she quickly removed them and put them into her military purse. As Mitchell seated himself next to Julia, he felt pleased the lady in uniform had said yes. He looked out of the window, nodded and tipped his army hat to his parents to let his mother know he managed to sit next to the young wave.

"Hi," he said. "I'm Mitchell Lauers."

"I'm Julia Holton," she told him.

"Are you from Cresaptown?" he asked.

"God no, I'm not from this desolate place," the young lady said with attitude. Mitchell was taken aback by the lady's attack on the small city; a city which was his birthplace and where he spent many fond memories as a child.

"So if you're not from Cresaptown, then what brings you to our town?" he questioned.

"I came to visit my friend's twin brother and her family. I promised her I would after we graduated from boot camp."

"Who's your friend?" Mitchell inquired.

"Ruthie York. We graduated from the same company. Company Seven."

"The Yorks. I know the Yorks; they live on the south end of town. They're a pretty nice family. Did you have a good time visiting them?"

"I like the family, just don't like this town," the skinny wave said in a matter-of-fact tone.

Even though the lady was quick and to the point, Mitchell got a chuckle out of her. Someone else would have been offended, but not Mitchell. He saw something redeeming about the immature lady and her unfiltered statements. As she rambled on about how miserable her stay in Cresaptown was, he was sizing her up. He looked at her features. Her facial complexion was a pretty brown tone; and her skin was smooth. She wore only eye mascara and lipstick. Her hair was short and curly; and if Mitchell had to guess her weight, he would have guessed she weighed about ninety pounds soaking wet.

He liked Julia; he liked her spunk, and he wanted to know more about her. "So what is it that you don't like about Cresaptown?" Mitchell thought there must to be some great feature she had discovered about his town.

"Don't get me wrong, I like the Yorks. They were all very nice to me. I promised Ruthie I would visit her twin brother, and I did. I met all of her family and they were really great."

"Well that's comforting to hear," Mitchell acknowledged. He figured the young lady hopped back onto the subject of the Yorks to keep from putting down Cresaptown again. Thinking she was trying to spare his feelings, he smiled as he looked at her and listened.

"I just didn't like her twin brother, Reggie, taking me to a boring high-school football game; and I had to pay fifty-cents to get in." She rattled on, "I hate football. I mean, what's the big deal; bulky high-school football players fighting over a ball. And it's not even a real ball. Balls are supposed to be round." She sighed to show her distain for the sport. "And why does it take so long for them to play four innings of the game? All of that stopping the clock and starting it up again. Gracious me; I don't know why people even like such a long drawn-out sport."

"My goodness, you did have a rough visit," the soldier didn't want to laugh at the young lady confusing the game's quarters as innings; but he had to admitted he was amused by her.

Instead of asking Mitchell something about himself, the unimpressed wave continued to let off steam. "And whoever heard of streets and sidewalks made of brick. Why, if those bricks were painted yellow, I would have sworn the Greyhound dropped me off in the Land of Oz." She shook her head; just venting her one-day ordeal to the soldier made her feel a little better. She looked down at her shoes. "Aww shoot!" she said with disgust. Thinking she had dropped something, Mitchell looked as well. "My poor heels," she said in a sad tone. "They got stuck between the cracks of those bricks." As she examined one of the black heels, Mitchell controlled the laugh that wanted to escape. He looked at her heels to access what type of damage Cresaptown's bricks could have possibly done. He noticed how tiny the lady's ankles were, but he did not see anything that looked out of order regarding the lady's high heels.

"**HAGERSTOWN**," the bus driver yelled as he pulled into the terminal.

Mitchell wanted the navy wave to continue on to Washington, D.C., then catch another bus to get herself back to her naval air station. He said, "Look, why don't you ride the rest of the way with me to D.C. Maybe I can convince you into coming back to Cresaptown to visit with me and my family for Thanksgiving." He knew it was a long shot.

Trying to decline without hurting the soldier's feelings, she said, "Umm, I have to get off here in order to transfer. I appreciate the offer, but I'll probably be going home for the holiday myself." She could tell he was a little disappointed, but she had no intention of ever returning to the town. She hated making promises she really didn't want to honor. The wave had fulfilled her promise to Ruthie; that was it for her. She would not oblige the army man by coming back to the old-fashioned town for a second time.

He asked, "Then can I have your address?"

Even though she did not feel comfortable giving the soldier her address, hesitantly, she gave it to him anyway. In turn he jotted his information down on a sheet of her notepad. She looked it over, then tossed the paper and pen into her purse. He knew the lady was a little harsh to take at times, but he felt she was just a naïve eighteen year-old, away from home for the first time and new to being on her own. The soldier could sense the wave was desperate to get herself back to someplace familiar; he was right. That someplace familiar was her navy base.

Julia was happy when the Greyhound Bus pulled into the Hagerstown's terminal. Mitchell got up to let the wave depart the bus. Taking the opportunity to stretch his legs, he followed Julia into the depot. As they walked into the Hagerstown's bus station, he asked Julia if he could treat her to anything. She declined and assured him it was nice meeting him. Mitchell went into the restroom; when he came out he noticed Julia purchasing a comic book. Though he really wanted to pay for that item for her, he could understand her declining his offer. He smiled, walked pass her and boarded his bus. He had her address; he would write to her.

~ ~ ~

The moment Julia got back to Patuxent River Naval Air Station from the tiny town of Cresaptown she was relieved. She remembered why she had made the promise to Ruthie. While Julia was in basic training she had a hard time adjusting to the new life. She failed the health portion of the military course and that set her back two weeks. She had to leave Company Six and reported to Company Seven. In that company, Ruthie York helped Julia by taking her under her wing. With Ruthie's guidance Julia passed all of her military studies and was able to graduate from boot camp. So when Ruthie asked Julia if she would go to her hometown, Cresaptown, Maryland, and meet her brother and family, Julia felt an obligation to do so. It was the only reason the wave found herself in the small town. Now that Julia fulfilled her promise to Ruthie, she was happy to finally be back on her base.

CHAPTER 17 -- SIMPLE NOTE

Julia tossed the man's address in her nightstand and got herself ready to go out with Natalie and Jasmine to the mess hall for dinner. When they asked how her visit with her friend's family went, she told them it went well, but she was happy to be back where she belonged.

Five days later, to her surprise, she received a letter from the guy she had met on the bus. If someone asked her if she thought the soldier would really write to her, she would have told them *not a chance.* Many times people will ask others for their address or their telephone number, just to make passing conversation. And many times people will gladly give the information. But more times than likely the requestor had no intention of writing or calling. This was not the case with Mitchell. He hated when people made promises and would not keep them. If he said he was going to do something, he prided himself on doing it. Julia opened the letter, she was curious as to why the good-looking soldier would write to her. In the envelope she found a picture of the man in his uniform. He was very handsome; too handsome, and she wondered why he sent his picture to her. Julia was sure the army man had many beautiful ladies clamoring to be by his side. And though she felt this, still she was excited that he had written to her. The letter read:

August 15, 1966

PFC Mitchell Lauers
Radio Morse Code School
Barrack #C-497
Ft Dix, New Jersey 08640

Dear Julia,

    It was very nice to meet you on the Greyhound Bus. You are an extremely charming person. I found it quite amusing that you visited my hometown, Cresaptown, Maryland, and it didn't meet your standard of what a city should be. I can assure you that Cresaptown is a beautiful place. The reason I know this is because I was born and raised there. I don't reside in the town anymore, but I do return to visit my parents.
    I am hoping you have given some consideration to revisiting Cresaptown for Thanksgiving. My invitation is still opened to you. If you come I will make sure you have a wonderful time.

Sincerely,

Mitchell Lauers

    Julia never really expected to hear from the soldier. What should she do? Should she answer the letter or just ignore it. She wasn't sure she would write him back. She got herself into trouble once before by writing to her ex-boyfriend. But this guy was a soldier; he seemed to be a nice guy. This guy, this soldier guy, did not come across as someone who would do anything vile to her. Julia was confused. She made a huge mistake that truly disturbed her, now she no longer trusted her own common sense when it came to the opposite sex. She would have to think long and hard about answering his letter. She couldn't afford to make another wrong decision. She put the letter in her top drawer. And even though she tucked his letter away, she propped his picture up against the mirror. She dug back into the drawer and admired the letter. She picked it up and examined the man's handwriting and even lifted the letter to her nose in case there was a scent of cologne sprinkled on it. She'd seen the other waves do it when they got letters from friends. The envelope was unscented; she smiled. It didn't matter if the letter wasn't scented. It was just a simple note from a guy she had met on the bus. It was not like he was a friend of hers. She looked at Mitchell's photo propped against the mirror. She bit her lip and mumbled, "I don't know if I'll write him or not. I just don't know."

CHAPTER 18 -- REFLECTION

    Julia loved being part of the navy family. The life was so exhilarating; for the first time ever she had a sense of belonging to a people who cared about her. An organization which not only wanted to see her succeed, but was there to help her if she stumbled. Being a military member was completely different than being a civilian living at home with her parents. She wanted to distant herself from the turmoil she left behind, so rarely did she contact her family. When she didn't stay in touch as often as her mother thought she should, then her mother would write scathing letters to her, telling Julia of how much like her father she was; and how she hated the son-of-a-bitch with each passing day. In the letters she's point out how selfish the young lady had been to run off and join the navy. Julia wondered if her mother would ever get over the fact she had left Philadelphia behind. In between the nasty landmines Eleanor would plant in her letters, she would often add, *oh, by the way can you increase the allotment money by a few more dollars*. Julia wondered how her mother expected her to send more money home when her military pay was only one-hundred dollars a month. Whenever her mother's letters arrived, that same nervous feeling she had when she was being raised would resurface in her stomach. Never did she want to read any of them. They were always filled with negative news from home. And somewhere in Julia's soul she felt her mother might actually enjoy writing the awful letters to her. Somehow, she felt her mother's depression was not genuine and she came to the conclusion Eleanor Holton sought out anything sad or depressing to draw attention to herself. And if there was nothing dismal within the course of the woman's day, then she would manufacture it. Determined to keep her own wits about her, Julia would only read her mother's letters when she felt her system was strong enough to handle the negativities which were encased by the envelopes.

She pulled the letter from her purse which she tucked away two days ago. When she opened it she was surprised to see the greetings: *My Dearest Daughter*. That was a switch; normally it started out with just her name, *Julia*. Then her mother would go on about how much she has done for her and her brothers and sisters. She would bring up the fact that Julia owed her big time, from the time she gave birth to Julia until when Julia had the nerve to leave home. But this time as she read into the letter, she was surprise to see some sort of change in her mother's information. She continued to read the letter. It read: *I know I ain't been that great of a mama to you kids, but when you have a sorry-ass, good for nothing husband and a house full of kids, then you have to do the best you can. That's why I tried to steer you and your sisters in the right direction. I didn't want you to fall in the same trap as me; marrying a good for nothing bastard and being stuck in a miserable life. I don't want that for you girls. Anyway, I didn't write this letter to ask you for no money, I just want to let you know that I was thinking about you and I always wanted the best for you. If you think you can make it home for Thanksgiving I will try to have that favorite sweet potato pie you like. Remember I always had faith that you would be somebody special. I knew it. Believe me I'm a little bitter cause I could of made something out of my life, like you done did for yourself. But no, I had to get stuck with your fuckin' daddy. I could kick my own ass for chasing after him. Now I got a housefull of damn kids, just because I wanted to make sure he was around to take care of your little ass. Trust your mama girl; you don't want to wish this on your fuckin enemy. Well Julia.*

I am hoping you come home for the holiday. It sure would be good to see you again. Take care of yourself.

Your mother, Eleanor

Julia folded the letter and tucked it in a shoe box she used for miscellaneous items and slid the box beneath her bed. She didn't want to run across it again and she didn't want to discard it just yet. She thought about what her mother wrote. It must have been hard for the woman to see her daughter go off and make something of herself, when she, as a mother, predicted a miserable existence for the teenager. In so many words, her mother admitted she was jealous of her. It shocked Julia because she didn't think God meant for mothers to be envious of their children. Weren't mothers supposed to teach and guide their kids? At this point in Julia's life she knew this to be true, all she had was herself. She was the only one she could truly depend on now. If she made mistakes, it would be because she knew no better. It bothered her that her family was not a normal, loving unit. That is why she never talked about her mother, father or siblings to anyone. Even she did not believe the type of childhood she lived. To alleviate the pain her heart held, she would concentrate on the few fun times she did have as a child with her school friends. And oddly enough she could even remember times with her mother and father that were not always so bad. She reflected on the happier times when she didn't see her father and mother fighting. How things almost seemed okay in the Holton household. She liked those days. Then there were the days her Aunt Jackie Mae would come to their house for a visit. And how her mother and aunt would sit and drink beer while Julia combed her mother's hair. They both were gorgeous women, but somehow Eleanor Holton never thought of herself as beautiful, whereas Jackie Mae never took her beauty for granted. In fact, Jackie Mae did everything she could do to celebrate the loveliness the good lord bestowed upon her. And those were the lessons Jackie Mae felt best to pass on to her nieces, especially Julia. Though Julia was the oldest of the Holton brew, she was the most timid and softest of the girl children. When Julia thought about it, maybe that was why her mother was always so blunt and unaffectionate towards her. Maybe it was Eleanor Holton's way of making the girl become tough. If that was what she wanted to do, it didn't work. Instead of the mother taking time to talk to her daughters and explain how things and people worked in the world, she only put her girls down whenever she found the opportunity to do so. So when Julia left for the navy, she was on her own. She knew nothing of what she should look out for; she knew nothing about bad people being in the world. Julia thought the bad people were inside of her home, her father and mother. She thought the outside world consisted of other families such as the ones on the television shows like *The Donna Reed Show, Father Knows Best*, or *Leave It to Beaver*; good wholesome people. But now she was out on her own. Now she would find out what the real world was like. She came through some tough patches while away from home, but she learned to get over those patches and continue on. She had been stuck into the Holton family; if she could get through that rough phase then she knew she would be able to get through anything that awaited her on the outside world. Would she be going home for the holiday to appease her mother, out loud she spoke her answer, *"Thanks, but no thanks. I will not be going home for Thanksgiving. I will go to visit my grandmother instead."*

CHAPTER 19 -- WEIRD MAIL

The WAVES Barrack was the best place Julia had ever lived. Why? Because it represented the beginning of her life as a young lady. Being in the navy gave her self-esteem, just like the brochure said it would. Before joining the navy she didn't even know what self-esteem was. But now that she was a navy wave she felt filled with esteem because the military made her feel so alive. She accomplished something wonderful; she was a member of the United States Navy. She had everything to look forward to with her new home in the military. The navy provided her with the things she needed to become someone exceptional. She had beautiful uniforms, beautiful comrades, beautiful employment and benefits, a beautiful base on which to live, and a beautiful room in the barrack.

When she initially reported aboard at the WAVES Barrack, Julia was assigned to room 112. She became the roommate of Natalie Avery. Natalie was a colored wave, brown in color with long black pretty hair. She was a little shorter than SA Holton and just as skinny. Julia was Natalie's roommate for only a month; because when an empty room became available, Julia requested it and the room was given to her.

The young wave loved coming home after the end of her day at the Operation Admin Office. It felt good getting off of Jim's bus right in front of the WAVES Barrack and walking down the long walkway to get into the quarters. She loved going pass the quarterdeck, saying *hello* to the duty officer, and walking down the hallway towards her room. Life was sweet for the young lady and she knew it.

~ ~ ~

There were four other colored waves stationed at Patuxent River Naval Air Station. They were Natalie Avery, Jasmine Fredrick, Lucy Platts and Carolyn Litton. They all lived in the WAVES Barrack. And though they worked in different facility on the base, they ate chow together when they could, and sometimes on the weekend went to The Dance Spot. They were friends who seemed to get along very well. But though they socialized with great vigor at the Enlisted Men's Club and the Dance Spot somehow Julia always felt like the stranger that couldn't fit in so it was only occasional that she joined them.

The base, Patuxent River Naval Air Station, which is a mouthful of words, was shortened by the military; it is referred to as *Pax River*. Surrounding cities or towns located on the outside of any naval facility, by navy terminology, is always referred to as *the beach*. When the weekend came, the waves would venture outside of the base, onto the beach. Once on the beach they found themselves in the small city of Lexington Park, Maryland. There was only one or two night clubs in the town of Lexington Park. The one night club that the colored people went to was called The Dance Spot. Located almost two miles up the road from the naval base, it was a fun place to go. The community could listen to music, dance, drink, and shot pool. Many weekends, when the waves did not have duty, they would go to the Dance Spot and dance the night away. Once in a while Julia would join them.

~ ~ ~

For almost a month Julia received mail from the army guy. She remembered when she received the first letter from PFC Mitchell Lauers. It came as a surprise when Yeoman Cross placed the letter on her desk. She recalled reading his first letter. It was just a basic letter stating how nice it was to have met her. But as his letters continued, she could tell by the contents he was a man who knew what he wanted out of life. As she read his words, she believed him because Julia had an innate feature of trusting people. It was wired within her being. Today when Yeoman Cross came by her desk and dropped an envelope off to her, she was excited to get another one of the soldier's letters. But when she looked at the envelope. She knew from the handwriting that it was not from him. The return address made no sense to her; it was a name she did not recognize. It read:

D. A. Johnson
#896590
Attica, New York 14011

She scratched her head and wondered who sent the letter. She opened it; the return address gave no clue as to who the person could be. She only knew one person in high school by the last name of Johnson but that person's first name was Mary. And no way did she live in Attica, New York. Julia pulled the letter out of the envelope. It read:

D. A Johnson
#896590
Attica, New York 14011
November 17, 1966

Hi Julia,

That's a strange name for a colored girl. How's bout if I just call you Jewels. I like that name. It suits you. It was nice of you to visit with me. It's been a while since I had a fine lady like you to even give me the time of day since I been in my situation. Maybe sometime I can get together with you and we can have a good time. You know things are really starting to look good and I feel like I am just on top of the world since your visit. My ex ol' lady dump me because of my problems, she just stop believing in me and I don't get it at all. I mean everybody makes some mistakes and I know I have made my share of them, but so did my ex. Well look, it's been really good knowing you are in my corner, and I really look forward to seeing you visit again. Anyway if you get a chance maybe I can call you sometime. You didn't give me your phone number before you left the visiting area. You do have a telephone don't you. I can call you collect if you send me your number when you write to me. Don't forget to take care of your sweet self, babycakes.

P.s. If you got a friend that is needing some loving and you're not interested in what I got to offer, then give her my address. I don't have time to be wasting.

D. A. Johnson

"What the heck kind of letter is this," Julia mumbled. Having no clue as to who the person was or what he was rambling on about in the letter, she tossed the letter in the corner of her dresser. She quickly changed so she could meet Virginia at the mess hall. At the last moment she retrieved the weird letter from the dresser and put it in her purse.

~ ~ ~

Virginia was an attractive white girl with fair skin who wore her brunette hair in a shoulder length pageboy. Her eyes were brown and they sparkled when she smiled; and she walked as though she was playing an elegant role in a movie production. Julia met Virginia upon the fourth day of reporting aboard the base. The white lady noticed Julia at the Navy Exchange. There was something about the colored wave that captured Virginia's need to want to befriend her. She walked over to Julia and said, "It seems as though you are looking for something. Is there anything you might need my help in locating?"

Not being familiar with the store's layout, Julia said, "Yes, there is. Do you work here?"

"No I don't, I'm a wave; same as you. My name is Virginia Payne and I'm a third class photographer's mate."

"I'm Julia Holton, seaman apprentice. I'm sorry, I thought you worked here, you're so well dressed."

"Yes, that's alright. I try to get out of my uniform as soon as I can. After wearing it all day, as soon as I get to the barrack I'm ready to change into my civilian clothes." She smiled at Julia, then said, "I see you're still in your uniform. It tells me you're mighty proud to be in the navy."

"Yes, I am."

"So am I. But trust me, between three to six months, you'll be like every other wave and sailor, anxious to shed the uniform after their day's work." Virginia laughed, then asked, "What are you looking for?"

"Hosiery and a garter belt."

"Right this way," and Virginia walked the new wave over into the appropriate department.

"Thank you for showing me." Not wanting to end the conversation with the new friend, Julia asked, "How long have you been stationed here, Virginia?"

"I've been at Pax River for going on two years now. Where do they have you working on this base?"

Julia told her, "I'm at the air traffic control building. In the office right below the tower; Operations Admin. I'm the only wave in the office."

Virginia smiled, "Julia, that's how it pretty much is in any unit on this base for us waves. There's only fifty waves on this base, so don't feel like you're by yourself. Look, if you have dinner at the mess hall, I'll meet you there tomorrow after work. I get off at 1630 hours. I'm generally at the mess hall by 1645 hours." Julia agreed to have dinner with Virginia and the two developed a great friendship from that point on. Often after their work day they met up at the mess hall and discuss what went on at their places of work. If for some reason they could not make dinner generally they would call one another to let them know, because neither of them liked eating alone.

~ ~ ~

When Julia got to the mess hall she spotted Virginia standing at the end of the chow line. As they inched closer to the chow area to make their selections Virginia said, "Julia, I had the best job today. My unit assigned me to go to the base hospital to photograph the newborns of the navy wives. It was so great." Julia's work day was nothing as spectacular as Virginia's. And though photographing babies excited her friend, any mention of babies sent Julia into a tailspin. She dealt with babies all her life; photographing them was the last thing that sounded remotely interesting to her. Her day consisted of typing documents for Chief Hill. And since she knew typing and editing correspondence to be what she truly loved to do, she was happy with that.

The waves found a table and sat their trays upon it. One thing they could say about the mess hall, the food was delicious. Even so, Julia could only eat so much, so she took small portions of the foods she liked best. She hated waste. Besides, she noticed the sign on the mess hall's wall, TAKE ALL YOU CAN EAT, BUT EAT ALL THAT YOU TAKE.

Julia finished eating her mashed potatoes; she was taking bites out of her meatloaf when she remembered the letter. Instantly she grabbed her purse and dug it out. "What do you make of this, Virginia? I have no idea who this person is; never heard of him." She placed the letter on the table and her friend picked it up. As Virginia read the letter, she raised an eyebrow, then both brows furrowed. Julia could tell by the way Virginia was holding the letter she'd finished it. But then she noticed her friend reading the letter for a second time. When she finished her forehead crinkled. She placed it back into the envelope and placed it in front of her. Her hand cupped her chin as though she was deep in thought. Virginia stared at her friend, then shook her head. Breaking the awkward stillness, Julia asked, "So what do you think? Isn't that strange?"

Virginia's eyes widen, "Yes it is," she loudly answered. "You say you don't know this person. How did he get your address? People don't just write strangers out of the blue, professing their feelings for them; especially if they have never even met you. He said you visited him, is that true, Holton?"

"Wow! Holton, you're calling me by my last name. You've never called me by my surname since we've met. No, I've never visited him; are you kidding?" Julia ate a small forkful of peas.

"Well whoever this person is, he seems to be pretty sure you visited him. You need to be careful, Holton, sounds creepy to me. I'm telling you, if you never met him and have no clue as to why he sent you this letter then you should definitely not answer this." Virginia positioned the letter for Julia to take. But as Julia grabbed it, Virginia held tightly onto it. Before Virginia relinquished it, she warned, "I'm telling you, just be careful. There's too many nuts around and you don't know what people are capable of; especially if you don't know them." She released the letter and Julia took it. Then Virginia mumbled, barely loud enough for Julia to hear, "Sometimes, even if you know them, you don't know what harm they may bring to you. Don't be so damn trusting." Julia understood. She stuffed the letter back in her purse; and though Virginia tried to lighten the mood, Julia could not get the letter off of her mind.

The two waves left the mess hall. As they waited at the bus stop for Jim, the bus driver, Julia spotted the trash receptacle. She took the envelope out of her purse, balled it up and tossed it into the trashcan.

"What are you doing?" her friend asked.

"No sense in me keeping the thing if I don't know the person who wrote it."

"True, you don't know the person, but don't throw it away. What if something happens to you? No one will ever know you got this crazy letter from a strange person. You have to keep it. What I was trying to tell you back there is just don't encourage this guy. Something ain't right about him. If it were me, I would not be answering his letter." Virginia dug into the receptacle and retrieved it. She smooth it out best as she could and then gave it back to Julia. "Write a quick memo on the back of the envelope, that you do not know this person, date it and sign it; then put it in your bottom drawer." Julia reluctantly took the letter. As they waited on the bus to take them back to the barrack, Virginia could tell the whole incident unnerved her friend. She decided to take her friend's mind off of the stranger's letter. "Hey kiddo, what do you say if we head for Washington, D.C. in a few weeks? This weekend is not good. Thursday is Thanksgiving and I've got that day off, and Friday too."

"Me too," Julia answered. "I'm taking the train to go see my grandmother during those four days. Plus my lieutenant gave me Monday and Tuesday off to cover travel time."

Virginia knew she had distracted Julia from the mystery of the letter. That was her intention. She said, "Look, I just thought of something. We can go in a few weeks, and then again in the springtime. The cherry blossoms are simply gorgeous in the springtime. You'll love them. D.C. is really beautiful that time of year. Is that okay with you?"

Julia smiled, "Heck yeah," she said with excitement. She was thrilled upon hearing Virginia's invitation. Plans immediately swirled into her head for the D.C. trip coming up in a few weeks and then possibly again in the spring. What suit would she wear; should she get new shoes from the Navy Exchange? She knew she wanted to look her best when she and Virginia, exploded upon the monuments, museums and cherry blossoms of Washington, D.C. She'd been in D.C. once before; though it was not to explore the monuments. It was just to pass through to get to her newly assigned duty station. She was looking forward to the trips with her friend, Virginia Payne.

CHAPTER 20 -- GRANDMA

Julia had to call home to get her grandmother's neighbor's phone number. The elderly woman didn't have a telephone. The wave was hoping she would not have to talk to her mother in order to obtain the number; because she had already informed Eleanor Holton she would not be coming home for Thanksgiving. She was in luck when she called home; it was her father who answered.

"Hello daddy, how are you doing?" she asked

"Julia, is that you; why girl, how is you doin' is what I should be askin' you."

"Why you say that, daddy?"

"Yo' mama seems to think you is mad at us. Says, you ain't comin' home for Thanksgivin'. She out now; her and yo' sista, Josephine, shoppin' for Thanksgivin's Day dinner. How come you ain't comin' home Julia?"

It was just what Julia was trying to avoid; explaining why she did not want to be home during Thanksgiving. The holidays at the Holton household always started out alright but ended up with drunken brawls and vulgar language and then somebody might ended up getting hauled off to jail. That was her past and she certainly did not want to bring it into her future. She was living her future; there was no room for what she had left behind.

Apparently she'd taken too long to answer her father's question, so he asked again. "Is it somethin' I done did, Julia. Is that why you not comin' home for Thanksgivin'?"

There was something strange about the conversation with her father; and then she realized what it was. Her father was sober. On rare occasions she had seen him sober. To ease his mind, she said, "Of course not daddy. What would even make you think such an awful thing?"

"It's yo' mama, Julia. She says I'm the one who done chased you away. I'm the reason you done up and joined the military. She even says she's thinkin' 'bout leavin' me too; maybe join the Foreign Legion, and stickin' me wif all these kids. I don't know what I'll do if she go and do a thang like that. I jist don't know."

Julia, for the first time in her life, found herself feeling sadness for her father instead of embarrassment. She tried to put his mind at ease. "Daddy, please know this one thing that I am going to tell you. You are not the reason I joined the navy. I joined to make a better life for myself. You can't have me living at home forever. Don't you and mama want me to do good in this world, to be someone honorable now that I'm eighteen?"

"Yes, Julia, we do."

"Then that's what I'm doing; so please don't ever think that you or mama or anybody else for that matter, is the cause of me going off to serve our country. I'm doing it because in my heart I believe this is what I am supposed to do," she assured him.

"Julia, I'm so happy you done explained that to me. I stop drankin'; honest, I have. I'll do anythang to hold onto yo' mama. Jist that I get so jealous ev'ry time some other mens be lookin' at her. I go crazy. That's why I drink so fuckin' much. I can't take it knowin' other mens be wantin' to have they way with her."

"Daddy, I know you've done the best by me and my sisters and brothers that you could do. Please know I appreciate every single thing you and mama have done in the course of raising me from a baby to a grownup; the good and the bad."

She could hear a strain in her father's voice, and she felt he was on the verge of tearing up. "Oh baby, do you really mean that? Even those times I was drunk and actin' stupid, beatin' on yo' mama. I know. I'm a sick man, Julia. I jist cain't help myself when she make me do those thangs to her. And you really think I did my best tryin' to raise you kids?"

"Yes daddy. I think how you and mama raised us was the best way that you could. Seeing everything that was going on just made me realize how precious life really is. Believe it or not, I learned a lot from you and my mama." She did not want to stay on the telephone for too much longer. Already, one of the waves had walked patiently by the telephone booth twice. She knew she must cut the conversation short. She asked, "Daddy, can you please give me Miss Trina's telephone number? You know, grandmama's neighbor across the street from her."

"Yeah, yeah, sure baby. Hold on." It was about forty-five seconds before she heard his voice on the phone again, and he sound a little more upbeat. "Here you go suga; the area code is 859 and here's the telephone number." He rattled off the number, then asked, "Is that all you need, Julia?"

"Yes daddy. That's all I need. I do have one more thing to tell you." She took a deep breath, and then in her sweetest voice she said, *Daddy, I love you."*

She could hear her father choked up. His voice cracked as he sniffled and tried to hold back the tears; "I love you too, Julia." He slammed the phone down so she would not hear his loud sobs of sadness. They were tears of regret. Regret of poor behavior he and his wife displayed around their children. Regret because they could have been better parents, but were so caught up in themselves that their kids never mattered. Regret because Julia was a grownup and on her own; he couldn't take back all the anger and abuse she had witnessed. Regret because a baggage of crap was dumped upon his oldest daughter. She didn't deserve it. None of his kids did. Regret! Yes, Jake Holton had much to regret. But within his heart there was a glimmer of rejoice. Rejoice because deep down in his soul he knew Julia turned out okay in spite of it all. Rejoice because he knew she would be somebody special. Rejoice because his number-one daughter told him she loved him. Rejoice in knowing it was her way of saying, *Daddy, I forgive you and mama.* And for those reasons, his heart held great rejoice. Rejoice!

~ ~ ~

Julia contacted her grandmother one day prior to let her know she would be spending some time with her. The sun was beaming down as Julia took the Greyhound Bus from Lexington Park to D.C. When she got off at the Greyhound Bus depot in Washington, D.C. she took the cab to the train terminal. Julia was on her way to Covington, Kentucky to visit with her grandmother, and she was excited.

Before going to boot camp Julia was told to bring twenty-five dollars to cover personal items. Her parents did not have the money so her grandmother sent her the funds. Julia wanted to honor the grandmother by visiting her and showing the woman her uniform. It was her way of letting the elder woman know how much she appreciated the money she sent. Now she sat waiting in the D.C. terminal for her train to Covington.

Julia had a three and a half hour wait before boarding the train to Covington. She was at her wits end because she didn't bring any reading material. She didn't know how she left the barrack without at least a <u>Reader's Digest</u> in her military purse. As she was sitting and checking out how ragged her nails were, a blonde lady, about the same age as Julia, noticed her uniform. She asked, "What branch of the military are you in; the air force?"

Julia, who was happy for the conversation, got up and moved to the seat next to the young lady. "I'm in the navy?" she proudly stated as she pointed to the anchor emblem on her hat.

"Ahh, the navy. Do you like it?" she wondered.

"I do like it. I like being in the navy a lot. It's the best thing that's ever happened to me," she explained with a wide smile.

"They would never accept me into the armed force. I have no right hand," the attractive lady admitted.

"Huh? No right hand; that's weird. What happened to it?" Julia, hadn't caught the comment before it left her mouth. "Sorry, I didn't mean to say that," she said, trying to rectify her crude question.

The lady laughed, then said, "Don't worry about it. I'm use to that reaction."

"Yes, but you shouldn't have to be. I meant no disrespect by it; honest I didn't. I apologize."

"No apology needed. I was born with no right hand. My mother told me the doctors didn't know the exact answer as to why. Their theory is that it could have been some medication she took while she was pregnant with me. But since I never had a right hand to start with, I really don't miss it." She saw Julia's eyes divert down towards her hands. The blonde moved the arm which the prosthetic hand was attached to, then said, "Most people can't even tell it's not real." She took her left hand and placed it next to the artificial hand. "See, almost look real, don't it?" Then she smiled, "That wasn't fair of me to blurt that out to you, but I always feel it's best to get it out of the way, before people are quick to point it out to me." Then she gave a giggle of a laugh, and added, "As if I don't know the darn thing is a prosthetic."

Julia gave a nervous smile. She didn't know what to say, so she simply sat and listened to the woman talk about how caring her parents were and what loving support she received from her four older sisters. She told how protective they were of her because she was the baby of the family and she'd been born without a hand. Julia was intrigued by the prosthetic. She mentioned how natural it looked and the blonde let Julia touch it. Julia noticed even though the fingers on the implement did not move, all in all, it did look real. And she was about to ask the lady how long had she had the prosthetic when a loud announcement came over the PA system. The lady said, "Well, that's my train; nice chatting with you." And just like that, the lady was gone.

Julia looked around at the other patrons in the union station to pass the time. When she tired of people-watching she took her fingernail file out her purse and start filing her nails. She was almost done when she felt the presence of someone approaching closely towards her. She stopped her filing and looked in the direction; almost next to her stood a man a bit taller than she. "Hi, you look like you can use some company," he said. And before Julia could answer, the man sat right down in the seat next to her. He was a medium brown man, with short hair. He reminded Julia of her twenty year-old half-brother and that made her feel comfortable. "Oh, I see you're in the military. Navy. What rate are you?" he asked.

"E-2," the wave told him.

"I see; you're new in the navy, just an E-2. How do you like it so far?"

"Fine," Julia told him.

"That's good; my sister is in the military too. She's in the marine's though."

"The marines? Wow, sounds like a real tough branch to be in for a lady."

"Yeah, I thought so too, but she's handling it pretty good. She's been in for one and a half years now. In fact she's left some stuff at my house. Told me I could give it away." At that moment he gave the wave a hard look, then said, "Stand up a minute." And like a little puppet, Julia stood up.

"You know what, you're the same size as my sister. There's a coat she left, it would look perfect on you. I think she would love for you to have it; being you're a military person, same as she." Julia smiled, but said nothing. "What time does your train leave?" Julia told him. The young man added, "That's plenty of time. Look, my place is down the street, just three houses from here. We can go get that coat and be back in time for your train all in fifteen minutes." His smile was friendly and Julia felt she would be doing his military sister a favor, taking the coat as a gift. From one military lady to another she thought it was an excellent gesture. She picked up her red suitcase and naively left the safety of the train station. She followed the man three houses away from the union station down the street. He walked her into the brick apartment building. In the hallway of the building he led her into an apartment. Once he closed and locked the door, he said, "There is no coat. I can't believe you believed me." He took her into a tiny bedroom and made her take her uniform and underwear off. He forced her onto the twin bed and climbed on top of her; Julia laid motionlessly. As he fucked her with his big penis, he complained, "Move around; don't just lay there." She tried to do what the man asked even as fear tightly gripped hold of her.

As he was on top of her, she was so scared. She found herself in such an awful situation all because of a coat he said would look good on her. He seemed so nice while he sat and talked to her in the union station. She fell for his bait. She tried to take note of what he looked like. He was about five feet, seven inches tall, brown in complexion with no facial hair. He was not handsome, but he was far from ugly; he was just an average-looking colored guy. Julia had trusted the wrong man. She was disappointed in herself for being so gullible. When he was done with the wave he got off of her little body then ordered her to get dress. As he walked Julia into the living room of the apartment, there upon the coffee table she saw a letter opener. She knew something bad had happened to her. When he convinced her there was a coat, she never thought he would force himself on her. Now she had to live with it. In a nasty voice he warned, "You should never follow a stranger; didn't you mama teach you that? It could get you killed, you stupid bitch." He gave a snarly grin and looked her up and down; he said with a sound of distain, "It won't do any good for you to go to the police; they won't believe a word you say. Besides, you were lousy anyway; can't fuck worth a damn, you dumb-ass bitch. You'd think somebody in the military would be smart enough to know not to believe everything they hear."

The man turned his back to look into the small room they'd just come from. He learned to double-check the room because one of his previous rape victims left her panties under the dresser and his roommate found them. He had a tough time coming up with the reason the underwear were there. Ever since that incident he doubled check when it was time to get the victim out of there. He was down on his knees looking beneath the bed when he felt a sharp pain in his neck. It stunned him, and for almost thirty seconds he could not get his bearings. When he finally did he saw Julia with her red suitcase in tow unlocking the door. Quickly he got to his feet to try and grab her. But with each step he took a pain shot through his neck, slowing his step. The letter opener which was on the coffee table was now impaled in his neck. Julia had been raped before and now she was raped again. She felt as though she was in the Twilight Zone and couldn't find her way out. Why would this happened to her, yet again? She figured if she must go through this pain and humiliation, then he was going to feel some pain too.

As the agony in the rapist's neck intensified he became fainter. His eyes bulged from their sockets as he felt the pressure of the stab. Desperate to relieve the distress he pulled the letter opener out. Blood gushed all over the tan shag carpet. After stumbling a few more steps, the rapist start losing consciousness and fell, hitting his head on the marble coffee table. The letter opener partially severed his carotid artery; he laid on the floor bleeding. He could feel the life draining from him as his eyes glazed over. His raping days were gone.

~ ~ ~

Julia's heart pounded as she quickly walked back to the train station. It was a straight shot down the street and she couldn't get there fast enough. She was in her uniform and she looked out of place walking quickly down the street clutching onto her red suitcase. She was hoping no one was paying any attention to her. As she was heading towards the station, she wondered how badly she had injured the man. What was she thinking; and why did she follow him. During her walk back, she scolded herself for trusting the man. He had no right to lure her from the station. He must have felt pretty proud of himself knowing he was going to rape a lady in the military. The man saw her in the uniform, yet it did not deter him from gaining her confidence and walking her out of the train station to degrade her. She was sure she had badly injured him; she used a lot of force when she jabbed him. Her brain said to her, *It'll be a long time before he trick another girl into following him into that little apartment.* She continued to talk in her head to herself, *Calm down Julia, calm down. This is not your fault; this is not your fault.* She took a deep breath, slowed her walk and entered the building at a normal pace.

Now she focused on survival. Afraid, she sat in the train station and said nothing to anyone. It was a lesson she needed to learned, not to believe everything people tell her. She was so naïve and such a trusting person. Why was she like that? She was very embarrassed by her stupidity and she could not bring it upon herself to tell anyone what happened to her. She sat quietly on her suitcase against the wall and waited for the train. When her train arrived she boarded it and took the long journey to her grandmother's house. Once in the safety of her Grandma Sarah's house she cleaned herself to wash away the rape. She cleansed her body best she could because her grandmother had no bathtub, nor shower in her home; only a tiny room with a small sink and toilet. She was happy to finally be at her grandmother's house, but the visit had been made at the expense of her innocence.

~ ~ ~

In spite of being raped, Julia knew she must try to put it behind her, just as she had done when her ex-boyfriend forced sex upon her when she returned from boot camp. Both times that she'd been raped she felt she bought it on herself. With the ex-boyfriend, she had been so overwhelm in boot camp that she wrote telling him how rough of a time she was having and how happy she would be to see him when she came home. When she arrived home for her two-week vacation she was proudly wearing her uniform when he picked her up from her parent's apartment. He took her to his place and casual conversation turned into the young man forcing himself on her. When she was resistant to his sloppy kisses, he pushed her onto his bed. He insisted on having sex with her. When she told him she did not want to, he called her a cheap tease; then pinned her to his bed and forcibly removed her military skirt and her underwear. He projected himself into her body. That was her first time experiencing a penis inside of her. After the rape, she never saw nor communicated with him again. When the stranger in the D.C. Union Station lured her out of the terminal and raped her, she felt ashamed of herself for being so easy to fool and falling for his lie about the coat. She was so traumatized by the incident that she totally blocked the man's face from her memory. If she came face to face with the rapist at that very moment, she would not even know it.

It was there at her grandmother's sanctuary, though she never told a soul but God, she vowed to put both incidents behind her. She would not be raped again. Julia Holton learned a valuable life lesson on the second rape. She must be more cautious with her life. And once she learned that life lesson, she knew she would have to let it go. She would not give up on people because of the two bad men that she innocently allowed to intrude her life. She used terrible judgment, plain and simple. And though it was the two men who had taken it upon themselves to rape her, she blamed herself for being so senseless and getting into such degrading situations. Both rapes had tarnished her dignity. Julia knew she had to put them behind her. She had a bright and shining future ahead of her and she would not let the violations deter her from going after it.

CHAPTER 21 -- THANKSGIVING

Her visit with her grandmother, Miss Sarah, was a very nice. She could tell the elderly woman was proud of her because she invited all her neighbors and relatives over to visit. She paraded the young lady throughout the neighborhood; stopping at each of her friend's house to show her granddaughter off. She was so happy Julia came to see her. The elderly woman financially came through for Julia and the wave never forgot it. That was why it was so important for her to go and visit the elder. It was Julia's way or showing appreciation.

~ ~ ~

"See my granddaughta; she is in the navy now. Why, don't she look darlin' in her uniform?" Julia let her grandmother brag on her to Miss Trina right before they headed to the store. After they made their way through the weeded trail to get to the little country store, Julia marveled at how resilient the old lady was. When the two of them finished picking out the items they needed in the store, Miss Sarah unloaded her cart and boasted to the old man behind the counter, "Mr. Teddy, this is my granddaughta, Julia. You rememba my daughta, Eleanor?" The clerk nodded that he did, "Well, this here's her chile. She named Julia."

Mr. Teddy extended his hand and Julia shook it. "Why, Miss Sarah, you got a granddaughta old enough to be in the military?

Miss Sarah, you too young to be havin' a granddaughta in the service." He gave a wide toothy smile at both the ladies and Julia could see her grandmother blushing. Mr. Teddy started ringing up the items on the counter on his push-button cash register. As he rang up the item he placed it into a big brown paper sack. Once completed he looked at the register's total then said, "That'll be four dollas and fifty-two cents. You want me to put it on your tab, Miss Sarah?"

"I don't know, Mr. Teddy. How much is on it already."

He pulled a tablet from beneath his counter, turned a few pages until he came across her name, then added the numbers up in his head. "Nine dollas and twenty-two cents, Miss Sarah."

"Naw, don't put it on my tab. I don't want that thang gettin' any higher than it have to."

Julia pulled out a twenty-dollar bill and attempted to hand it to Mr. Teddy. "Here you go, Mr. Teddy. This should take care of it." He looked at Miss Sarah for her approval to accept the payment from her granddaughter.

"No, Julia. I can't have you payin' for my debts. No indeedy." But Julia was determined so Mr. Teddy took the money.

"Please use that to pay my grandmother's purchases and her debt to you." The store owner nodded and did as Julia requested, then gave the navy lady the change. Julia slipped the change into her grandmother's coat pocket, as Mr. Teddy gave Miss Sarah a nod and wink.

"That's some granddaughta you got there, Miss Sarah. Yes indeedy, it ain't ev'ry day you find a relative, willin' to pay yo' debt for you. You must be mighty proud of this young lady."

The old woman smiled back at the clerk. "Now Mr. Teddy, I mean t'tell you, 'deed I am. Yes indeedy, I be proud of this here young'un." As Julia picked up the bag of groceries Miss Sarah gently pinched Julia's cheek. "I'm awfully proud of this gal. She's gonna make somethin' of herself. You wait and see."

He nodded, "I believe you, Miss Sarah, 'deed I do. Y'all have yo'selves a tee-rific Thanksgivin' Day. Miss Julia, it was awfully nice meetin' you. You's a fine young gal. And you look so purdy in that there uniform."

Miss Sarah and Julia said goodbye to the clerk then left the store. The cold wind pushed them with a bit of force as they walked the dirt trail through the overgrown parcel back to Miss Sarah's shack. Once in the house both ladies warmed themselves up by the wood-burning stove, to take the chill off, then they removed their coats. Grandma Sarah and Granddaughter Julia sat at the table in the warmth of the kitchen embracing the moment. Somehow they knew neither of them may never enjoy the tenderness of one another's company ever again. Sarah got up from the table and continued to converse with her granddaughter as she warmed up milk for two cups of hot chocolate. She added a marshmallow to each cup, sat the cups on the table and joined Julia in warm cocoa and more sweet conversation. It was a moment that Julia knew would stay with her for the rest of her life.

~ ~ ~

The smell of turkey cooking in her grandmother's cast iron, wood-burning stove danced into Julia's sleepy nostrils. She had slept well on the old thick bed which sat inconspicuously in Grandma Sarah's living room. Her arms flung upwards as a strong, loud yawn bellowed, announcing she was awake. Her grandmother came into the living room. "Why I see you done slept pretty good, Julia. You musta been mighty tired from that train ride, yesterditty."

"Good morning, Grandma. I did sleep good. Why didn't you wake me so I could help you finish the holiday dinner?"

"Naw baby, I loved lookin' at you whilest you was a'sleepin'. Don't reckon I'll get a chance to see you again. I'm old and it jist does my heart good to know you is a young lady now."

"Aww grandma, I'll try to come and see you whenever I can."

"Chile, you say that now, but you is grown. And you is a military lady at that. Yo' life is jist startin'; mine is almost over. That's why I am lettin' you know, whilst I'm still here and you're here with me, that I love you."

Julia was touched by the words of her grandmother. She longed to hear loving words from her own mother, wrapped in warmth and affection. Deep down, she knew her grandmother was right. Chances were, she would not get an opportunity to get back to Covington to see the elder woman. She hugged her grandmother then kissed her on the cheek. "Grandma, I love you and appreciate everything you have done for me."

"Now, now, Julia, I think we betta finish up this here cookin'. Now I done ate 'bout six-thirty this mornin'. I jist now finish fixin' you some eggs and grits and bacon. Oh, there's buttered toast out there yonder on the stove if you would like some. And the apple-butter's in the icebox, chile."

Once Julia was washed and had her dress on, she went to the kitchen and ate the breakfast her grandma prepared for her. Then she busied herself with helping her grandmother with the dinner. Since she knew nothing about cooking, her grandma showed her simple things like making dough for the sweet potato and blackberry pies. As she saw Miss Sarah pour the blackberry filling into the unbaked pie crust pan, it brought back memories. She hadn't tasted her grandmother's blackberry pie since she was fourteen years old. She remembered how she, her sisters, and their little Kentucky friend, Inez, used to pick bowls and bowls of blackberries and her grandmother would whip up blackberry pies for them. Their fingers and tongues would stained from the blackberries as they picked some and ate some. After the pie crust was done, Miss Sarah showed her how to cut up celery and onions and make gravy from the drippings of the cooked turkey. With the little bit of help Julia managed to give, between the both of them, they fixed mash potatoes, collard greens, cornbread, sweet potato and blackberry pies to go with the turkey and dressing.

Miss Sarah prepared the little table the night before. She set the table with her best white-laced tablecloth, china, crystal and flatware. And while the food was still on the hot cast-iron stove, Miss Sarah insisted they dress up for the dinner. "Now I know you didn't pack much, so if you want to wear your uniform and that pretty hat that they done gave you that'll be fine with me."

The both of them left the kitchen area, and when they returned, Julia was dressed in her uniform, complete with hat, which in military jargon is called *cover*, instead of hat, to please her grandmother, and Miss Sarah wore a black suit, silk white blouse beneath the jacket, little black pumps and her Sunday-best hat.

"Grandma, you look beautiful. But why are we all dressed up? It's just the two of us."

The elder took her granddaughter by both hands then said, "Julia, I jist want you to always remember how much I love you. I know we lived hundreds of miles apart, but I always think about you. This is the only way I have to show you how much you mean to me, chile. I want you to remember this day, and the time we are sharing together right now. Jist you and me." The old lady took a step backwards and looked at Julia. "My, my, aren't you a sight to behold. You're just a ray of sunshine to me, honey-chile."

Julia blushed, and as she hugged her grandmother, she could smell the woman's perfume. Then she remembered she packed her instamatic camera and flash cubes in her suitcase. "Grandma, I'll be right back." She got her camera and flash cubes and asked her grandmother to sit at the dinner table and pose for the photograph. She took four pictures of the woman, replaced the used flash cube with a new one and then showed her grandmother how to use the camera so she could take a photo of her in her uniform. When they were done taking pictures, Miss Sarah said, "Chile, I cain't wait to dig into that turkey and mashed potaters. Let's have a seat and bless this food. This is truly a day for us to give the good lord his proper thanks."

~ ~ ~

When it was time for Julia to leave, the old lady packed a big lunch of turkey sandwiches for her to take aboard the train.

She was happy her granddaughter came to visit; even happier she got a chance to show the girl off to all of her family and friends. Julia took the cab to get to Covington's train station. Within ten minutes after she was seated in the terminal a young attractive brown man came and sat next to her and said *hello*. Julia did not move to another seat, she sat there and listened to the man talk about how professional thieves stole all of the furniture from his apartment. She had never seen the man with a train ticket in his possession; but it could have been in his coat pocket. When he talked about his apartment being burglarized, for some reason Julia took it that the man lived right there in Covington, Kentucky. She knew in her heart, though he seemed like a nice person, there was no way she was going to trust him. As they made small talk, the young man decided it would be nice to offer her something to snack on. He asked, "Hey, would you like to go and grab a bite to eat before your train comes." When she declined, using her grandmother's packed lunch as her reason, he stayed and continued to talk. Even though Julia Holton had been raped, she refused to close herself off from people altogether. She did not think God wanted her to do that. And though she could not figure out why God wasn't there to prevent both of the rapes, she knew she must take ownership of each of those situations. She was going to sit her butt right on that bench until it was time to board her train. The man continued to talk to Julia up until the moment her train for Washington, D.C. arrived. And when she headed to get onboard, he walked her down the corridor and to the entrance of the passenger car then wished her a safe trip. Once Julia was seated on the train, she thought how odd that each time she was at a train station, a young man had approached her. The first one raped her. Was the second man who had befriended her, there to take advantage of her as well? She was thankful that she would never know.

PART FOUR

CHAPTER 22 -- SECRETS

When Seaman Apprentice Julia Holton returned to Patuxent River, Naval Air Station, she felt safe and secure. The experience of the D.C. train station had made her change the way she viewed any man who came into her life. She was on her own now, no longer a child who could run to her mommy and daddy to address problems she may have. Because even though they were abusive and mean-spirited amongst themselves and often time to their children as well, they would do what they could to help their kids whenever they were in their right senses. Julia was sinking into a place she had never been before. What she thought would be a breeze for her to get over, the raping of her body, she discovered it was not.

Two weeks after visiting her grandmother she fell into a depression. When Virginia insisted she get herself out of the barrack and go to Pax Movie Cinema, to see a Bob Hope movie, Julia declined. The wave did not want to go anywhere. Virginia could sense something was not right with her friend. The two waves made plans to meet at the mess hall for dinner. But when Julia didn't show up and did not call to cancel out, Virginia became worried.

That evening the brunette went to the Navy Exchange. She purchased some Pepsi-Cola, a large bag of potato chips and french onion dip. She returned to the barrack and knocked on Julia's door. When her friend opened up, Virginia noticed how bad she looked. Her hair was uncombed and matted together. And Julia's eyeliner was almost worn off. Her eyes were red and mascara trailed down both sides of her face. Virginia smiled at Julia and walked into the room, closing the door behind her. "Figured you might like some company," the brunette said. Then as she stood facing Julia, who now was sitting on her bed, she added, "What's going on, Julia? I thought you said you were going to be okay?"

Ashamed to admit she was down in the dumps, she replied, "Virginia, there's nothing wrong. I am okay. Can't you just let me have some time to myself? Please? Just let me be alone for a little while."

Virginia opened up the bag of chips and went to Julia's all-purpose drawer and pulled out two plastic cups, two small paper plates and a silver spoon, and then proceeded to divide the snack up for the both of them. "No Julia. No I can't just leave you alone. You need somebody to talk to. This thing is too heavy for you to handle by yourself." She placed Julia's snack portion on her side of the desk along with a cup of soda.

Virginia worried about Julia ever since she returned from the trip to see her grandmother. At this point Julia knew there was no getting rid of Virginia. Her friend was going to keep her company, whether she wanted it or not. There was no sense in denying that she obviously was having a tough time; she was happy Virginia was there. Reluctantly, she admitted that her friend was absolutely right; she did need to talk, to rationalize things that were going on in her mind. She pulled her pillow onto her lap and hugged tightly onto it. Tears welled in her eyes as she began. "Virginia, I don't know what I'm supposed to do anymore. I thought I could sort everything out." Though she told Virginia about being raped in D.C. she was too ashamed to tell her of how her ex-boyfriend forced himself upon her. Who would believe she had been raped twice by two different men? She was having a hard time believing it herself.

Virginia hated seeing her friend in pain; she consoled, "Julia, I'm telling you, if you just get pass this rough patch, you are going to be okay. I promise you that."

Julia wiped tears from her eyes, she hated feeling sorry for herself, but since the trip, that was all she could feel, pity for what happened to her. She looked her friend in the eyes and said, "Look at me, I'm eighteen years old and don't even know how to take care of myself. How could I have been so stupid?"

Virginia wanted to let Julia talk as much as the lady needed to. She knew it was the only way her pain was ever going to have a chance of healing. When she saw Julia was not going to say another word, just sit and hug the pillow, she encouraged. "Julia, this thing that happened to you, well, what I want to say is, it wasn't your fault. You're more a kid than a grownup. You believe what people tell you and you don't question anything. Please know this man is the one at fault, not you."

Tears were upon Julia's face. She could not hold them back. Virginia went to the dresser and grabbed the box of Kleenex. She placed it on the bed near her friend. Julia was mentally hurting; as much as she tried to rationalize what happened to her, she still could not figure out why it happened. The sad wave grabbed a couple of tissues and dabbed the tears which ran down her cheeks. She rubbed the tissue across the mucus dripping from her nose. She told Virginia, "I thought it would be fun to be eighteen and on my own; but it's not. Maybe I should have stayed at home instead of running away from my family. I think it's God's way of punishing me."

Virginia's belief in God was strong. She did not want to sit and comfort her friend by giving her the notion it was God who had a hand in her rape. She gently said to her, "Julia, God loves you. He saw what was happening to you. I am so sure He wanted you to realize on your own the man was up to no-good. And when you didn't, He made a safe passage for you to get out of the situation with your life. Believe me; He was with you all the way. You're not stupid, by any means. You're just an eighteen year-old who is trying to find her way through life. That's all.

God will always be there for you; He always has been. Believe that."

Julia began to sob some more. She knew her friend was right. She dabbed her eyes, and calmed herself by taking a deep breath. When she felt she could talk to her friend without tearing up again. She said, "Virginia, you're beautiful, strong-minded and very sophisticated. Not to mention you come from a rich family. I don't deserve to have you as a friend. I come from nothing but a miserable life and a dreadful family; my life is nowhere near as graceful and perfect as yours."

Virginia was surprised to hear her friend tell her this. She knew people thought of her in that light, but the truth of the matter was, they did not know her, or anything about her. She questioned, "And why are you saying all of this?"

"Because it's true. Look at you and look at me. I didn't deserve what happened to me; but it did." she said as she wiped another tear from her cheek. "Why Virginia? Why did I have to go through that?" Though Julia had stop crying, Virginia could tell she was hurting. She watched Julia place her head onto the pillow in distress. Virginia had never seen her in such a state.

Virginia touched her hand; Julia grasped onto Virginia's manicured hand and looked sadly at her friend. Quietly Virginia said, "Julia, I know you're hurting; believe me, you did nothing to bring this upon yourself. Please stop taking the blame for it. The bastard that did this is lucky you were so naïve and did not know what to do after the awful thing he put you through." She cleared her throat. She thought it was time to let Julia in on a well-kept secret; one that she had protected since joining the navy. She would come clean with Julia. She continued, "I am not by any way any better than you, and you're no better than I. I come from a pretty fucked-up life. I have never told anyone in this barrack that my mother and father are wealthy people. It is an assumption they made on their own." Julia looked wide-eyed at her friend as Virginia continued on. "That's right. They look at me, how I dress, how I carry myself; they admire my exquisite taste and style. And because I don't associate with them, unless it's business, they make an assessment I'm rich and stuck-up. I am neither."

Julia could not believe what she was hearing; she asked, "You mean your family is not wealthy?"

"Hell no. I don't even know who my parents are." Virginia saw the uncertain look on Julia's face, but the question in her comrade's eyes did not slow her pace. The sophisticated lady kept divulging her secrets. She patted the back of Julia's hand, "Julia, I grew up in foster care. Do you know the awful things most all of my foster parents did to me? Especially foster fathers. I've been raped and molested so many times by creepy foster fathers and foster brothers that I've lost count. And whenever I would get put into a good family, I'd be yanked out of it and sent to a family that was mean to me.

"One summer, when I was fifteen, Peter and Valarie Stuple chained me in the closet and would both take turns having their way with me. A neighbor got wind of it and the authorities removed me from the hellhole; only to place me into another foster home. I couldn't take it anymore. When I turned sixteen, I ran away and slept under a bridge. I used a knife I'd stolen to protect myself if anyone dare try to rape me again."

Julia's was shock to hear of Virginia's life as a child. She could not believe the words coming from her friend's mouth; yet she knew they were true. Why would she make up such a story? Virginia confirmed, "Yes Julia, I was homeless; I didn't have a damn place to stay and I scrimmage through restaurant garbage bins to eat. That is until Mrs. Dunn, my English teacher, heard about it and took me in. She's the one who taught me to celebrate each day of my life no matter what obstacle had been or will be thrown my way. Do you know she opened my eyes to realize there actually are good, kind people in the world? But you have to be careful with people, because as you have learned, the deviant ones can fool you. Never feel too proud to ask for God's help. He will guide you and show you the way to a fulfilling life." The brunette drank some of her Pepsi, then grabbed a potato chip and dipped it into her french onion dip.

Somehow listening to Virginia's story totally took Julia's mind off of the rape. Never in her life would she have suspected her friend didn't have a mother or father and at one time she was even homeless. All of this information regarding her friend was overwhelming; yet Julia was curious about Virginia's portrayal of wealth. She took a deep breath, she could not stifle her curiosity. She asked, "But why do you dress like you come from a rich family?"

"Why not? Let me tell you something, Julia, I spend no more money on my clothing than anyone else in this place. Because I know how to accessorize, mix and match my outfits and always look stylish in and out of the barrack, the other ladies tend to think my outfits are high-class fashionable apparel. They are not. I wear my hair in a chic style, and I never go pass the threshold of my door without looking my absolutely best." She paused and looked in her friend's eyes to convey the final point. "It's all in the attitude. And my attitude tells me I am rich; rich in the love of God; which makes me rich in everything else." Julia was beginning to understand and a slight smile came across her face. This pleased Virginia. She continued on. "Julia, if I dressed to reflect the way my young life has gone, I would be wearing rags. There is no reason for the people you work and associate with to know every little revolting detail about your life. You have to portray yourself in a positive light; and that requires a positive demeanor. Like I said, it is all in the attitude. Do you think the navy would have accepted me in this fine organization if I presented myself with the same quality of ineptness as most all of my foster parents had thrown on me?" Before Julia could answer, Virginia said, "Hell no; I would have been bypassed as a navy wave recruit."

CHAPTER 23 -- CONFESSIONS

Julia's thought about her terrible childhood which consisted of an alcoholic father and a mother who hated her children. In a sense, she could relate to Virginia. Meekly Julia admitted, "Yeah, I know. My family was not so hot."

"Did you have a mother and a father, Julia?"

"Yes, but they…"

"*But they* nothing. I don't know how bad you may have thought they were, at least your real mother and father were in your life. You knew who your parents were when you were growing up." Virginia took a drink of her soda, then continued. "How would you feel if you have no clue who your father is, and all you know about your mother is the fact that she was a prostitute who gave birth to you, then sold you so she could get heroin? And the man and woman who bought you thought they had killed you when you were three years old after having sex with your little body. Can you even imagine being thrown out with the garbage?" She glared at Julia. She realized she was taking a risk revealing the beginning phase of her life to her only friend in the barrack. Even though it frightened her to disclose her entry into this world, the brunette continued. "The only reason I survived is because a passerby heard me crying and pulled me out of the trash bin, then handed me over to the authorities." She went limp, as though her body drained. When she looked up, Julia could see wetness in the corners of her eyes.

Virginia summarized, "Holton, that was my life as a child." She shook her head; "It's wasn't a good feeling knowing my life started like that, but I got over it. Do you know why?" She stared at Julia, then blurted, "Because there was nothing I could do about it when I was a kid." She stood up from the chair, tossed her head so her long brunette hair danced and bounced around, then smoothed her dress with her dainty hands. As she proudly stood, she looked at her friend and said with a confident air embracing her, "So I chose to celebrate my life and dress myself up every day; that's what Mrs. Dunn taught me. She told me God brought me through all of the turmoil for a reason; and it was not for me to feel broken nor downtrodden. She formulated my mind to except the fact that every day is a day to celebrate; I did not end up dead for a reason. It is a reason that only God knows. So I honor Him by being the best I can be to show Him how much I value my life here on His Earth." Virginia gently touched her friend's arm. "This is what I want for you Julia. You had no control over what happened to you as a kid, nor what the rapist did to you. You must put it behind you and celebrate your life. For God's sake, Julia; think about it; God made sure you survived. You are really fortunate the man wasn't demented enough to want to kill you or keep you as a sex slave. Have you ever thought of that? I was held captive and used for sex; it takes most all of the life out of you. Thank God you did not have to experience that." Virginia placed her hands together in prayer form, lifted her head and praised, *"Thank You Jesus."*

    Those thoughts never entered Julia's mind. And now that her friend pointed it out, she realized how lucky she was that God got her out of the situation with her life. She was grateful Virginia came by to check on her. Somehow, all of her friend's words hit home and she no longer had a spirit of despair. She knew Virginia told her personal life story for a reason. Because if Virginia could make it out of her troubled beginning, Julia knew she would be alright.

~ ~ ~

A lot of bottled-up pain is what Virginia shared with her friend. Except for their race, the two waves were somewhat similar. They both were navy waves, both small ladies with fine articulation, and both came from abusive backgrounds. Virginia was simply trying to encourage Julia not to wallow in her sadness; to look on the brighter side of living. She wanted her friend to know life had a way of dealing some whoppers, but even still, good things will come if you are opened to them. Life is to be rejoiced through all of the tribulations. The beautiful brunette was passing on Mrs. Dunn's training. Dress the part of a successful young lady, do your best and trust in God. Follow those simple steps and bountiful blessing are sure to come your way. For God will not let you down.

Julia did not want Virginia to think she would misuse her personnel information. She paused and weighed the ramifications before revealing another aspect of her rape. She knew in her heart she could trust Virginia. She felt God sent this guardian angel to her so her spirits could be uplifted. Virginia watched her friend as she tossed aside the pillow, got up from the bed and looked beneath it. She grabbed a shoe box, retrieved a small piece of torn newspaper from it, and handed it to Virginia. "Virginia, read this," was all she said, as she handed the three-inch news article to her friend. Virginia noticed the article's headline; it read: D.C. MAN STABBED WITH LETTER OPENER, CAUSE OF DEATH UNDETERMINED. Virginia continued on reading the article.

> On November 22, Matthew Claivon was found dead on the floor of the apartment he shared with his roommate, Daniel Franklin. The cause of his death cannot be fully determined due to a stab to his neck and a cracked skull. It is presumed the victim was stabbed, then fell or was pushed down, striking his head on the edge of a nearby coffee table. Franklin

reported the death after finding Claivon dead in the apartment when he returned from work.

Upon interrogating all of the neighbors, one individual, who requested to remain anonymous, said, "I've seen Mat bring a lot of young ladies to his apartment. And a quite a few of them didn't look too happy when they left. Anybody could have killed him, jealous boyfriend, angry woman; anybody." Many were questioned, but no one recall seeing anything that was out of the ordinary.

Virginia showed no expression. She simply asked, "Is the man in this article the person who raped you?"

Julia looked sorrowfully into Virginia's eyes. "Yes Virginia, he is." Even though the man raped her, she felt bad the puncture to his neck was the direct factor in his death.

Quietly, almost to a whisper, Virginia leaned close to Julia and asked, "Did you do this, with the letter opener the article is referring to."

Julia could barely be heard when she answered, "Yes, I did." She continued on with the whisper, and said, "But I wasn't trying to kill him. And I didn't push him down, causing the fracture of his skull. I think he fell. I was just so mad he did that awful thing to me. Really, Virginia, I did not mean to cause the man to die."

Still, in a low voice, Virginia, asked, "Where did you get this article from?"

Julia, still in a hushed voice, explained, "I walked through the D.C. train station coming back from Covington, Kentucky. I walked through that train station to get to a cab stand. While I was waiting on a cab to take me to the Greyhound Bus Station, I saw the paper lying on a bench. When I saw the article I read it. That's when I realized the man I jabbed was dead." She scratched her head. "Virginia, I didn't realize I stabbed him so hard."

"Have you shown this to anyone else?"

"No, I couldn't; you're the first person I've shown it to."

"And I'm going to be the last person you show it to." In her quiet monotone voice, Virginia asked, "Why did you save it; I mean what is the purpose of having it?"

"I don't know; I was just compelled to take the paper, when I got off by myself I torn the article out."

Without saying a word, Virginia ripped the article into the tiniest pieces. She watched as her friend's eyes became big with wonder. When she couldn't tear it into any more pieces, she dumped the shredded newspaper into her half-filled cup of soda, poured more soda on top and swirled it around with the spoon. She haughtily placed the contents over on Julia's side of the desk and quietly said, "The man caused his own death. You don't need to be reminded of his kidnapping and raping you."

"But he didn't kidnap me. I went with him."

"Julia, the moment he conned you out of the train station under a false pretense, he kidnapped you. That's a federal offense, Julia Holton. Do yourself a favor, like you're going to dump this trash down the toilet first chance you get, dump the episode out of your mind. Have you learned anything from this horrid experience?" Julia nodded that she had. Virginia reached over and squeezed Julia's hand, then added, "Good, then dump this shit as soon as you can, and erase it from your mind. Thank God it wasn't you who wound up dead on the floor of that bastard's apartment."

The attractive brunette sat back into the chair. She said, "Holton, I've told you about my life to aid you through the horrible pain which was placed upon you. Mrs. Dunn taught me I could rise above my past. With her guidance, I recreated myself into who and what I want to be. I was nobody special for so long. I told you my story because I could see the pain you were carrying and I want you to realize this isn't the end of the world for you. You could have been raped, tortured and murdered. You could have been held prisoner and used for many men's sexual pleasure, or you could have been pimped out as a prostitute and pumped with drugs. Please know how much God was looking down on you and protecting you, even though you were in the hands of pure evil. You made it through that terrible moment of your life. Now you must celebrate being alive, as I have learned to do. I promised myself when I got out of the foster care system, my life would be better because I am someone special. I am now, and I was then as a child. I plan on making the most of this life." She squint her eyes and looked hard at Julia. She asked, "What do you plan on doing with your life. Are you going to let his despicable act define who and what your life can and will be? Or are you going to follow your belief in God, in search of peace?"

It was at that point Julia knew she needed to get herself together. She learned so much from her friend; and she was grateful Virginia shared her story with her. She felt bad for her friend's childhood. But she adjusted her feeling of sorrow for Virginia and start feeling a rejoiced attitude for the lady. Virginia's life was classy now; regardless of how pathetic her life began. This proved to the little colored girl from the Philadelphia projects it's up to you to make your life the best you can; no matter what the circumstances are. It was from that point she vowed to really put all of the sadness behind her and move forward in a positive light. She would reclaim her peace. And with her strong belief in God, there wasn't a doubt in her mind that she would be just fine. Julia took Virginia's hand and looked into the lady's eyes. She said, "I am so sorry the beginning to your life was so terrible; I wish nothing but the best for you throughout your life, Virginia Payne."

"And I wish the best for you and your life as well, Julia Holton. I really do."

PART FIVE

CHAPTER 24 -- GERMANY

Mitchell hoped Julia would come back to Cresaptown during the Thanksgiving's Day Holiday, but she did not. And he was okay with that because during the holiday there was a big spat amongst his family; Mitchell was happy Julia didn't show up. It was not the first impression he wanted to make on the navy lady. Four months passed and he was still interested in the young wave. During those months he exchanged letters with Julia because he found himself becoming attached to her. She was prompt to answer all of his letters and this impressed him immensely.

The soldier made a point of writing to Julia within the first week after she gave him her address. When Mitchell received an answer from her, he was very excited. He remembered his conversation with her on the bus, she was so adamant with him about how much she did not like his hometown. Yet within a week after mailing his initial letter, she promptly wrote him back. Even though she didn't like Cresaptown, she took the time to quickly respond to his correspondence. He figured he would simply write her to pass his time while he was in the army. He wanted letters from his family and friends from Rochester, New York; even letters from his family in Cresaptown, Maryland would have been good for his morale. But none came. So when Julia answer his first letter, then answered his second, third and fourth letter, he felt a sense of contentment knowing the young lady thought enough to continue to write him. He realized she too was in the military. She knew the importance of receiving letters from people who cared. Her correspondence pleased him and brought smiles to his face while he was stationed in Fort Dix and Fort Bragg. General, mild conversations are what they wrote to one another, and that was good enough for Mitchell. But mild conversations or not, as the letters kept coming, Mitchell felt he was slowly falling for Julia. While he continued to write, he kept his feelings to himself. He had completed his Radio Morse Code School and Jump School. He would be sent across the ocean to his new post in Frankfurt, Germany. This worried him; he felt a connection between him and the lady from the bus. He was sure there might be a tinge of a caring emotion she felt for him; though she never revealed it in any of her letters. She wrote to him about everyday things, as a friend would write a friend; and that worried him. Because once he left the states for Germany would she continue to write? He didn't want to lose his pen-pal. Pen-pal? Who was he kidding? He didn't even know how it occurred; or even why it happened at all. He was sure he was in love with Julia. He wondered how he could have such feelings just by writing to her. He had never so much as kissed her or held her hand. Nevertheless it was true, and he knew it; he was in love with her. And in a sense it made him anxious. He thought about her often, and he wondered if she could possibly feel the same way about him. He was five years older than Julia; but he didn't care. He only knew what was in his heart; a heart that no longer felt like it belonged to him, because she had surely stolen it. He wanted her and he wanted to tell her so. It worried him that his plane for Germany would be taking off at 0600 hours tomorrow. Now that he was heading for Germany what chance would he have of ever getting to know Julia. He took her picture out of his wallet and looked longingly at it. He was in love. He kissed the picture then held it close to his heart; he wished she was in his arms. He had a passionate need to lay with her, to touch her, to make love to her. He wanted her and he wanted her heart to belong to him. He turned the photo over to read her signature. Her handwriting was beautiful; somehow, it didn't surprise him. She signed it, *To Mitchell, Best Wishes, Your Friend, Julia*; such a generic signature. He would write her, and in his next letter he would profess his love for her. He only hoped he hadn't waited too long; he prayed that no other man had scooped her up.

~ ~ ~

As the flight headed for Germany, Mitchell tried to get himself mentally prepared for his new post assignment. It was hard with all of the carousing his fellow soldiers were doing on board the flight. And after the soldiers worn themselves out with all of their comradery, Mitchell found himself wide awake thinking of Julia. It was unlike him to pass up what he wanted out of life. He was a gentle person, so he was concerned of Julia's well-being. He did not want to spring his heavy feelings of love on her for fear it might frighten her away. If he lost her and her beautiful friendship, what would he do? But he could not accept losing her due to lack of revealing his feelings to her, either. He needed her in his life, and he wondered what he would do if she was already some other man's woman. He would try his best to win her over. He would admit the love he had deep within his soul for Julia in his next letter. If he lost her because of his confession, then so be it; he would accept it. He wanted to write her while he was on the long twenty-hour flight to Germany, but the noise of the plane and his lack of concentration kept him from putting his thoughts on paper. He wanted to be in a place of tranquility so he could hand pick each word he felt would win the lady's heart.

~ ~ ~

When Mitchell arrived at the post he was in awe of the beauty of the land. He ventured around his new post getting familiar with the surroundings. He and a few of the other soldiers walked to the commissary. There he purchased personal items and some attractive writing paper with matching envelopes and some airmail stamps. He was sure she would like the decorative writing paper.

When he sat on his bunk that evening with his pen and paper, his thoughts were floating in his head. He had many beautiful words which he carefully chose to put onto the flowery paper. They professed Mitchell's love for Julia. He was anxious to send the letter off by airmail to the woman he loved. And he prayed his conveyance of his love for her would be accepted in her heart. She was eighteen, new to the grown-up world. And though he felt there was an innocence about her, he also thought she was keeping her guard up. The letter, he hoped, would open her heart to accept him into her life. When he finished writing, he dabbed some of his cologne onto the two-page letter. He re-read it, underlining certain points he wanted to emphasize to Julia. Then he sniffed the cologne as he knew she would surely do. When he kissed the letter, he envisioned her placing her lips on the same spot where his lips touched. Carefully, he folded the letter in thirds, then at the last moment he remembered a snapshot of himself which he wanted to include. He signed the back of the photograph, *To Julia Holton, I love you more than you will ever know. Your man, Mitchell Lauers*. He already claimed her as his woman. He knew God meant for it to be. Confident and pleased he had poured his soul out to Julia, he placed the letter and photograph into the matching decorated envelope, sealed it, then put cologne on the envelope as well. With the envelope addressed and the airmail stamp attached he would drop it into the mailbox outside of the barrack in the morning. That night Mitchell slept with Julia's picture beneath his pillow. In his dreams they were married and making love; holding, kissing and caressing one another. Needless to say, he started the following morning with a smile on his face.

CHAPTER 25 -- LOVE

It was Wednesday afternoon when Yeoman Cross came into the office with Operation Admin's mail. "Here you go Holton, look like this one is from across seas. Umm, that army boyfriend of yours done got shipped overseas, huh?" He started to hand the letter to her, but then he pulled it back and looked at the envelope. "Wow, looks serious. He done went and bought fancy stationery for this letter. My, my." Yeoman Cross flapped the letter in the air, then said, "Umm, you smell that? Wonder what kind of cologne that is?" He smiled his toothy smile at Seaman Apprentice Holton then playfully tossed the letter onto her desk.

"You're so funny, Cross; just a barrel of laughs, aren't you? How many times do I have to tell you that he's not my boyfriend? We just write to one another." She shook her head at him to let him know he had it all wrong. As she picked up the letter, Cross walked away. Lieutenant Kadowski heard the scuttlebutt of Holton writing to the army man. He bellowed from his desk, "Holton, why are you writing to a soldier anyway? You can't find a sailor at sea to communicate with?" Holton decided to let the Lieutenant's comment slide. She knew what he was referring to. He was making her out to be confused as to which branch of the military she belonged to. Yeoman Hurley and Yeoman Kampschroeder laughed. They all chuckled, but she didn't care. So what if she was writing the army man? Big deal. They couldn't dictate to her who she should write to. She chuckled right along with them as she picked up the letter and put it into her desk drawer. She really wanted to open the envelope and read its contents. But that was all she needed, all eyes upon her as she did so. When the officer and her fellow sailors returned to what they were doing, she opened her desk drawer to get a paper clip. The letter was right there for her to see and admire. Without the office funny-men prying eyes, she quickly examined the envelope. It was quite apparent there was something special about this particular letter. She glanced around at her shipmates; they were all busy with their task at hand. Quickly, she picked up the letter and put it to her nose; she was pleasantly surprised. She smiled as the scent of Wild Country flirted with her nose. The envelope was scented, just as Yeoman Cross said it was. Mitchell never put cologne on any of the previous letters. She would wait until she got back to the barrack and in the privacy of her room to read what Mitchell had written. She slid the letter into her purse, then dialed Virginia's office. When Virginia answered the telephone, she said, "Hi Virginia. I'm not going to be able to meet you at the mess hall so don't save me a seat. I'm going straight to the barrack."

"Can I bring you something back from the mess hall? A couple of apples, or oranges? You're going to need something to eat later in the evening, you know."

"Yes, bring me one of each. Thanks."

"It nothing. I'll see you this evening with your fruit. Bye"

"Bye."

Julia liked that about Virginia. She wasn't the type to want to know what was going on with you unless you invited her into that area of your life. Julia knew Virginia enjoyed her own privacy, which is why the brunette was never the inquisitive type. And Julia, likewise, never probed into Virginia's life. She loved talking to Virginia when there were things she needed to run by her. She didn't even know if she would tell her friend about the letter. She would make that decision when and if it became necessary.

Work went by very slow, and for the last two hours the wave was at her wits end. She could not stand it. She wanted to go downstairs into the ladies room to read the letter; but she knew she wanted to be in the comfort of her room. She would wait. She looked at Mitchell's picture under the plexiglass, rubbed her index finger gently over it and smiled as she thought, *Yes, I'll wait until I get home.*

~ ~ ~

When Julia got on Jim's bus she sat right behind him. His general conversation about his grandchildren and what he and his wife would be doing for the weekend was filling the nearest passengers' ears. Julia hardly paid much attention to any of his words. His voice was like a muffled rumble in her ears. Every now and then she noticed the sailor in the seat off to Jim's right say something to Jim; but she was in too much of a rush to get herself to the WAVES Barrack to pay attention to the conversations. Her mind was on the letter in her purse. Julia was happy when she got off of the bus. No sooner than she walked into her room and closed her door, she kicked off her heels as she sat down in the chair at her desk. Immediately she reached into her purse and pulled out Mitchell's letter. Carefully she slid her nail file into the corner opening of the envelope, gently ripped it open, then pulled the letter out. The picture of Mitchell fell into her lap as she unfolded the letter. She picked it up and looked at it. He looked so good to her and she knew she would replace the picture already on her mirror with the new picture of him. He was dressed in his uniform, standing next to a bunk. Julia put the photograph aside, then looked at the flower-bordered letter; she place the letter to her nose. She could smell the masculine scent Mitchell had placed onto the envelope; she loved the scent. She unfolded the letter and read:

December 18, 1966

PFC Mitchell Lauers
17 Long Range Recon Patrol
Gibbs Concern
APO AE 09008

Dear SA Julia Holton,

   It is with much respect that I write this letter to you. As you know from my last letter I had received orders to be shipped off to Germany. I am proud to let you know my unit arrived in Germany safe and sound yesterday. Germany is a wonderful place and I can only wish that you were here to experience the joy of being in this gorgeous country. This is my first full day on German soil and I want to tell you it is indeed as striking as I expected it to be.
   I must let you know how much I have enjoyed the friendliness of your letters that you sent to me while I was in Radio Morse Code School in Fort Dix, New Jersey and Parachute Jump School in Fort Bragg, North Carolina. Those were tough times, but I made it through. It is because of the motivation and encouragement that I received from your letters. Never did I flounder throughout my studies and physical qualifications because of lack of inspiration. Your letters were very much appreciated, and for them, I thank you.
   But this letter is not about me, Julia Holton. It is about you. I want to let you know how much of a beautiful lady I think you are. You have been so encouraging to me and I truly believe God placed

you on that Greyhound Bus at that particular moment for a reason. I think He knew I needed you in my life. Please do not think of me as being forward with what I am about to ask; but I need to know. How are you doing in the navy? Do you have a man in your life whom you can call your own; a man who is always there for you? And if you do, is he good to you? The reason I boldly ask these questions, is because I so want you in my life, Julia. It is all I ever think of when my mind is free from this military venture. I can only presume there is a possibility that you do have someone because of your beauty and your concerns for others. <u>Yes, you are beautiful,</u> though you always mention in your letters that you feel you are a homely-looking girl because of your thin stature and your small facial feature.

 I would like to correct you on a couple of statements which you have made regarding yourself. I hope you are not offended by me noting these facts. First of all you are not a homely-looking girl. <u>You are a beautiful young lady.</u> And second, please don't take this wrong, <u>your small stature is very appealing to me.</u> Don't you know good things come in small packages? And though you find it hard to realize you have real beauty, please keep in mind that beauty is only skin deep. <u>You have beauty both inside and out; it is the quality of you that I most admire.</u>

 I am hoping this letter does not turn you away from our friendship. However, if you are presently involved in a relationship, then please except my humble apologies. If you are not, then my intent is to have you in my life; that is, if you will have me. <u>Julia, I am in love with you and if you can find</u>

it in your heart to love me, I promise I will never do anything to hurt you. And I promise to always love and protect you. Please let me know where I stand on my request to keep you permanently in my heart, and for you to accept the love I have to give to you. I love you Julia Holton, more than you will ever know. All I ask is for you to love me too. I give my love to you intensely.

With all of my love,

PFC Mitchell Lauers

Julia read and re-read the letter over and over. She occasionally would go dancing at the Dance Spot and Enlisted Men's Club on a few dates. But she certainly had no romantic interest with any of her dates. Many times she had thought about the soldier, but Mitchell Lauers was not an avenue she would pursue. He was just a friend; though Natalie, Jasmine and Lucy felt she was holding out the goods and was secretly in love with the army man. They even enticed Carolyn into putting her two cents in on the matter. "How can he just be a friend," Carolyn asked her. "You keep his picture on your mirror. Don't sound like *just a friend* to me." But Julia always reinforced the fact Mitchell was only a friend. That was all; just someone to write to. His letters kept her grounded; and she didn't want to lose the connection. He motivated her; and actually made her laugh out loud with some of the things he'd write. He told cute, humorous stories; funny things that happened to him when he was a kid growing up in the little country town. His mother and father, though they were poor, loved him and his siblings; and he loved them all; he was very devoted to them. Julia wished she came from a family of love such as Mitchell's. But she learned to accept the fact she had not. She was humiliated knowing her parents were unhappy and vulgar people. That was her past and no amount of analyzing could change her past. Virginia taught Julia it was best to let it go; to celebrate her life as it is now. And now at this very moment she had Mitchell's letter, acknowledging his love for her. He let her know he wanted her for his very own. For the second time in her life she felt joy.

She pulled her pad and pen from her desk. What would she write to him? Would she tell him she is flattered by his affections, but she does not think she is the right one for him? Would she tell him she like writing to him, but only as a friend? Dare she inform the soldier he is a great guy, but she does not deserve him? She was lost as to what to do. Sure, she liked Mitchell. The two of them had written for months. They never visited, nor spoke on the telephone to one another since they'd initially met. She thought it odd Mitchell could claim to love her when he only laid eyes on her just once. She hadn't written anything romantic to the man to lean him toward the direction of being enamored with her. Even though Julia thought the world of Mitchell, she was not expecting him to fall in love with her. Something that wonderful never happens to the likes of Julia. Why would he want her? She did not think she was his type; she didn't even look like his type. He was too perfect of a man. But she knew she owed it to him to answer his letter; she just didn't know what she would say. She decided to write what was in her heart. She wrote:

December 28, 1966

SA Julia Holton
Operations Admin
Patuxent River, Maryland 20670

Dear PFC Mitchell Lauers,

I received your beautiful letter today and was very pleased to hear from you. Thank God you and your unit have made it to Germany without incident. It must be very nice to have that opportunity. Mitchell, thank you for wishing I was there to see what a gorgeous country Germany is. Maybe you can send me some photographs when you get a free moment from the business of the army. I would like that very much.

It has never been a problem for me to write to you. I've always enjoyed our correspondence because your letters gives me something positive to look forward to. I am glad my words of encouragement helped you make it through the tough times. It is the same with you writing to me. I always get a kick out of reading the funny stories you share with me. It sounds as though you have a very fun-filled family. That must be so nice.

Have you had a chance to get yourself settled yet? I certainly hope all goes well for you in Germany. You are such a nice person and I am sure you will have a most wonderful tour of duty while in Frankfurt, Germany.

In answer to your question, I have no one that is interested in me in a romantic sense. It is hard for me to envision you wanting me as someone special in your life. You are so good-looking and there is no way I can see you needing me for anything. By the way, why do you feel as though you are in love with me? I think our involvement with one another is fine just the way it is. It is so safe with you writing to me and my answering your letters. Neither one of us have to worry about becoming involved. Why would you want to change that? Besides, you know nothing about me or the life that I have lived. Please do not be annoyed

if I ask you to let me digest this new turn that you want our friendship to take. At this point, I am very confused. Because I do not want to hold up any possibility of you sharing your love with another lady that is worthy of it, my answer will be in the next letter that I'll be sending to you within a week.
Best wishes to you in Germany,

Your friend, always,

SA Julia Holton

Julia walked to the quarterdeck and dropped the letter into the out-going mail slot. Confused, she could not get the thought of Mitchell's love for her out of her mind. She didn't want him to be in love with her, even though she liked him a lot. She was not ready to admit she might be in loved with him. Often she looked at his picture on her mirror, and the one on her desk at work. Why did she do that? Was it because she cared about him as a human being, did she care about him because he was her pen-pal, or did she do so because she was sublimely in loved with him? And if she was in love with him, was it something she was willing to admit to him? She knew she could not be his because there was no way she deserved his love. She wanted things to stay the same between them, but the soldier wanted her as his lady. Julia had a lot of thinking to do. She would take the whole week to sort things out.

CHAPTER 26 -- REJECTION

When Mitchell received the letter from Julia he felt a bit relieved. Though he did not receive an affirmative answer regarding her acceptance of his love, he kept his hopes high while he waited for her second letter to come. Many days after receiving the initial letter she sent to Germany, his anxiety ran wild with anticipation of what she'd have to tell him. Would she say yes to his love for her, or would she humbly decline his feelings. When he was stateside it seemed as though her letters were always quick to come. But he noticed across the ocean the letters seem to take many more days to arrive. To keep his mind off of the long and monotonous days of waiting for her answer, he busied himself with his unit. If he was unoccupied and he found himself thinking of Julia, he would visit with his buddies.

It took fourteen days for her next letter to arrive, but to him it seems like an eternity. When the mail was passed out in his unit, all eyes were on the pink envelope Julia mailed him. Anxious to read the letter in private, he stuffed the envelope in his pocket and waited for his next break. When break time came, he found an empty table. He sat down then pulled the letter from his pocket. Julia's letter was a full two pages and inside of the letter he found a photograph of her. He looked at the photo and smiled. Though it was of her in her uniform, secretly he hoped she would have sent him a photo of her in civilian clothing. But it was alright. He was happy to have the picture. He turned the photograph over and read the note she had written on the back; *To Mitchell Lauers, with great fondness, Julia Holton.* Though it was just a common statement, he was happy. His heart beat wildly and a large smile came upon his face. He looked around, hoping no one was nearby. There were soldiers scurrying about with their own agendas at hand; none of them paid the lone soldier, sitting at the table, any mind. With excitement he unfolded the letter; it read:

January 3, 1967

SA Julia Holton
Operations Admin
Patuxent River, Maryland 20670

Dear PFC Mitchell Lauers,
As I write this letter to you, I am praying it finds you in the best of health and high in spirits. I hope you had a wonderful New Year's Day and spent time with your comrades. I didn't get a chance to visit my family but I had a nice quiet New Year's Day here at the base. I went to church and the service was beautiful. I said many prayers for you and your fellow soldiers, and thought about you all of New Year's Day.
I have also thought about your last letter to me. I must admit it did catch me off guard. I am still trying to get over the fact that you want me in your life. I have had a lot to think about and I promised you that I would give you my answer of my acceptance or rejection of your love in this letter which I am sending to you.

As I've pointed out, I have never thought of you in a romantic sense. It is not because I didn't want to, but more so because I never thought a fine person, such as yourself, would ever give me the time of day about anything. I've always accepted you as a friend and that was good enough for me. Though I've admired you and your determination towards your life's goals, never would I remotely allow myself to think of anything other than being a pen-pal to you. Why would someone as handsome and kind as you want anything to do with the likes of me? I can't figure it out. But I do love you, I just don't think that I am the one that is worthy of your love. This bothers me, so therefore, I do not think it is fair of me to accept the love you have in your heart for me. You deserve so much more than you could ever receive from me. Trust me; you do not need me in your life. Of all the beautiful ladies in this world, why me? Though I only know you from the Greyhound Bus ride and the many letters you and I have shared with one another, I can honestly say I do care so much for you. But I have had many problems which have plagued me; problems which I cannot even begin to tell you. Things too hurtful to explain. A couple of those difficulties I believe I have brought upon myself due to being too trusting to unworthy people; and during those critical moments I failed to use common sense. Bad choices, that's what they were; plain and simple. I cannot let you into my life which could possibly encompass you into my problems. I will not allow myself and my chaos to become entwine within your life.

Thank you for considering me as a girl that you are interested in, but in all fairness to you I can only remain a friend. I will continue to write to you as long as you would like me to. But I won't let our lives to be woven into a tapestry of love.

If you are not interested in remaining friends, then I sincerely understand.

Best wishes to you always,

Seaman Apprentice Julia Holton

PFC Mitchell Lauers could feel a lump in his throat. His chest was tight and though the building was cool, perspiration beads dotted his forehead. No lady had ever turned him down. He did not know how to handle this rejection. He wanted to call the wave, he needed to talk to her and explain how much he loved her; but he didn't have a telephone number for her. And though he knew calling state-side would cost him a fortune, he would have used his whole month's salary just to plead his undying love to her. If he knew the number to her naval base he would have immediately dialed it. He found himself sad the little wave did not want to be a part of his life. His divorce was final from Brenda, and he thought it was perfect timing God placed the wave onto the Greyhound Bus with him. He felt God wanted him to have the lady; and he wanted her. Mitchell was determined to let Julia know they were meant for one another. And though she was only eighteen years old and he was twenty-three, he knew she was the one for him. He loved her and now in her letter she even admitted to loving him. She mentioned something about problems she was going through. *Well join the rest of the world*, he thought; for Mitchell hadn't known a soul who didn't have a few complications within their lives. He felt his life would not be complete unless he was sharing it with her. He wanted to re-read the letter, but reading it the first time pained him. He was sure the stress of the letter was showing upon his face. Mitchell looked around to make sure none of the other soldiers were nearby; there was no one in his vicinity. Discreetly he wiped the welling of tears from his eyes. Why would she not want him to be her man? What could have gone so terribly wrong in her young life for her not to even give it a try with him? He was a good man. Not the type of man to run around on his woman; not the type of man to dog his woman and put her down. Not the type of man who would withhold love, kindness and understanding from her. Mitchell wanted her badly. Though he did not know what her real reason was for rejecting the relationship with him, he felt a strong determination to continue to win her complete heart; not just part of it.

~ ~ ~

Mitchell waited for another letter to come. Surely Julia Holton would write again and tell him she had been wrong; that she loved him deeply and to please ignore the previous correspondence sent to him. He kept thinking the letter was all wrong; just a mistake on her part. Mitchell worried for three and a half weeks waiting for a letter that never came. He hadn't written to her because he was sure she would have a change of heart and write, asking his forgiveness for trying to deny him her love. Impatience got the best of him. It was not as though he was in the states where the letters came quickly. He began to wonder if he lost the love which he had only met once. Why hadn't she written to him? She said she had no special man in her life. Was she afraid now that he put his true feelings for her on paper? He didn't know, but he did know he needed to hear from her, and soon. Unable to stand the long wait anymore, he decided he would write to her. But he would not write her a letter of his own. He would return the letter she'd wrote to him with notations in red regarding the comments she made to him.

He did not know what was going on with Julia and he found himself worried about her. He wanted so much to exclusively love Julia, and for her to exclusively love him. And he wanted to be in her life, through the loves and the troubles of her live. He needed to be with her even moreso now that he knew there were problems which pained her. He could help her through them, if only she would let him into her life. Mitchell was sure she didn't even know it, but by him loving her so deeply, he was already involved. He was concerned and he wanted her to know he would do anything to comfort her. With the lack of another letter from Julia, his mind played tricks on him. Had she become some sailor's sweetheart, had she taken ill and was in the infirmary, or did she simply want nothing more to do with him. He wanted to know; he was desperate to know. With her letter placed on his desk and a red ink pen in his hand he carefully went over her written words. Some of her writings he left, and what was not relevant to his way of thinking he wrote beneath her wording, writing his true thoughts and feelings. After rearranging her original letter with his own feelings he dropped it into the outgoing mail. Her letter drained him. He found himself worrying that the letter he returned to his love might cause him to lose her permanently. It was a chance he would take.

That evening some of the other soldiers from his Screaming Eagle Jump Division, invited him to go out on the town with them. He did so and for the third time in his life he drank hard alcohol. As his head swam from the booze, he thought of Julia. He was so lonesome for her; he thought she was giving him the runaround. When he had not received the correspondence he wanted to come, he felt like she had turned a cold shoulder towards him; maybe even playing hard to get. What was it with the lady that he loved so much? He drank heavily to soothe his hurt. The more he thought about her, the more he drank with his trooper friends. The more the attractive waitresses sat and talked and drank with the soldiers, the more he drank. The more the other soldiers pulled out their wives and girlfriends photos, the more he drank. In fact, for Mitchell to be a nondrinker, he drank so much that he became ill. On the way back to the compound, he threw up on the floor of the cab. All of the troopers got out of the cab and ran, but they were chased down by the cabbie and the military police; and Mitchell was ordered to pay for the cleaning of the cab's interior.

CHAPTER 27 -- RED INK

Yeoman Cross arrived from the mail room with all smiles on his face as he stopped at Julia's desk. "Wow, I'm surprise. You got a letter from the soldier. It's been a while since he sent you a piece of mail, ain't it? Is everything alright?" He looked at the envelope, then in a surprised voice said, "Humm, no flowery envelope this time; what's going on Holton?"

"Cross, just give my letter to me. Besides, it is none of your business anyway?" She hated it was his duty to pick up the mail from the downstairs mailroom. But because he and YN2 Hurley were the only two sailors with top-secret clearance, the responsibility at the time was his. Everything was a production with him, and it seemed as though he loved acting like an idiot when it came to Julia's mail from the soldier.

Still toying with Julia, he flapped the envelope in the air, then put it to his nose. "Umm, no cologne this time. You must have done something wrong. What'd you do to make him mad, Holton, huh?" He glanced at Julia, then with an arched eyebrow he added, "Had to be something?" He tossed the letter onto her desk; gave her a stare of pity as he shook his head. He added, "Look like the love affair is over, poor Holton."

Julia was happy when he finally left her desk. She realized Yeoman Cross could be a real jerk when it came to delivering her mail. Why couldn't he just put it on her desk and go about his business, like he was supposed to do. She knew he got a kick out of seeing her squirm regarding the soldier's correspondence. Yet each time, she'd play right into his hand instead of ignoring the sailor. She thought, one of these days he just might catch her in the wrong mood and she would let him have it. But deep inside, she knew that wouldn't happen. She picked the letter up from her desk, and took note of the plainness of the letter. Whatever Mitchell had written on the letter inside, she figured it could not be good. She knew not to lift it to her nose. Yeoman Cross was correct; it was in a plain white envelope with the traditional airmail red, white and blue border. She knew it was more than likely his letter telling her it was over. If he couldn't have her as his lady, he no longer wanted her as a pen-pal. Julia's day at the office was going very well and she didn't want to spoil it by reading Mitchell's letter. She put the letter inside her purse.

Julia sat in deep thought at her desk. Even though it was still early in the afternoon, she decided she would not to go to chow after work. Lately she didn't have an appetite for food. Already she'd whittled down to ninety-two pounds; eating was next to impossible when something heavy was on her mind. Now she weighed even less than she did when she arrived at Pax River. Her being in the military and Mitchell's letters were the two things that made her happy. But now she may have placed part of her happiness in jeopardy.

When her two o'clock break rolled around, she got up from her desk and slung the long strap of her navy purse over her shoulder. "I'm going on my break now, be back in fifteen minutes." As she got up to leave the office, Yeoman Cross blurted across the office, "Hey Holton, you gonna read that Dear John letter that the soldier sent you?" She gave him a distained look, and walked out of the door. *"God, he gets on my nerves,"* she mumbled beneath her breath.

She thought of Mitchell's letter ever since Yeoman Cross placed it on her desk. It worried her that the letter was not frilly like the previous one. Now there was a possibility she might have upset him to the point of no longer writing her after this one letter she had in her purse. She knew she would have a very tough time without his letters. He always gave her so much hope and happiness whenever she read and re-read his letters. Now with Mitchell possibly no longer wanting to write to her, a nauseated feeling shrouded her. Julia refreshed herself, then sat in her usual spot on the bench in the empty ladies lounge. Unable to take the suspense of the letter any longer she pulled the envelope out of her pocketbook. With no eyes upon her she sniffed the envelope. There was no scent of Wild Country. She could feel her heart sadden. She ruined a wonderful friendship. A friendship which had blossomed into a love, against the wishes of Julia. She really did love Mitchell and it saddened her that she would lose his communications. It pained her to think he may very well find another lady to send his beautiful letters to. *Oh God, please help me. I don't know what to do. I can't afford to lose him as a friend.* And no sooner than she said the silent prayer to herself, God answered, *Read the letter, Julia.* She ripped the envelope opened and braced herself for the let-down. She looked at the letter; she was shocked to see the same letter she mailed off to him over five weeks ago. She noticed Mitchell's writing, in red ink was added onto her letter. He wrote between the lines of her words. This startled her, and before she began reading, she knew it was over. She forced herself to read the complete letter. After reading his red-inked words, she read the letter again. It read as follow:

~~January 3, 1967~~ February 16, 1967
~~SA Julia Holton~~ PFC Mitchell Lauers
~~B-42-22-45W~~ 17 Long Range Recon Patrol
~~Operations Admin~~ Gibbs Concern
~~Patuxent River, Maryland 2067~~ APO AE 09008

~~Dear Mitchell Lauers,~~ Dear Julia Holton,

As I write this letter to you, I am praying it finds you in the best of health and high in spirits. I hope you had a wonderful New Year's Day too. Mine was not as great as it could have been because I did not have you here with me. I didn't go to church on New Year's Day, but I did pray for you. Julia, I pray for you at every moment I think of you. I pray that you are safe and I pray that you will fall in love with me as I have fallen in love with you. Yes love, I did think of you all of New Year's Day, even read some of your old letters that you sent to me (not this one, it made me sad. That is why I am returning it to you).

As I have pointed out to you, I think about you constantly. I must admit your letter did catch me off guard. I am still trying to get over the contents of it.

When I think of you, I feel like there is peace in paradise in my soul. I have always thought of you in a romantic sense. I have accepted you as a friend only in hopes that your love would come. I do love you; and I know that I am worthy of your love. You deserve so much happiness and I know I can give it to you; to us. I have tried not to overburden you by revealing my affection for you early on. Please understand that I am a patient man. I am willing to give you the time and space you may need to make sense of all of this.

Many nights I think about you and though I only know you from the Greyhound Bus ride and the many letters you and I have shared with one another, I can honestly say that I do care and love you deeply; I gladly give my love to you. You deserve the best, and I can give that to you. I will always measure up to your standards and if I disappoint you, it will never be because I intentionally sat out to do so.

Julia, I worry about whatever the problems are that plague you. Whether they are problems which may have been inflicted upon you, or difficulties you feel you may have brought upon yourself, I care! I want so much to be by your side to help you through anything that may trouble your pretty little head. Julia, my love, I would die for you; that is just how strong my love is for you. If you would only let me into your life, I will always be there for you. Love, I truly believe that with you and I together we can move mountains and handle any complications that may block our path of happiness. Together, our love for one another will keep us strong.

Please bath in my love and in return shower all of your loving affection onto me. I love you intensely. I do want you, not only as someone to write to, but as my woman as well. And if you will accept my love, I would like to have you as my wife. I know this letter might make it sound as though I am desperate, and that's okay. Because I am desperate, I am desperate enough to let you know that I will fight to keep you in my life. I know this might be too much for you to comprehend, but please say that you will be my woman, Julia Holton; not just for a little while, but forever. I love you more than you will ever know.

I boldly sign this, Always your man,

Mitchell Lauers

Julia wanted to read the letter again, but already she lost track of time and it was 1417 hours, two minutes past her break time. As she rushed back up to the third deck her brain was flooded. Mitchell still loved her; she could not believe her good fortune. Yes she loved him, why was she trying to deny it? But how could that be? How do you fall in love with someone you only met one time, and simply wrote to one another? Is that even possible? *Apparently it is possible*, she thought. Was she dreaming when she read his letter? Couldn't have been; she read it twice and even the second reading blew her mind. Why wasn't Mitchell angry at her? Why did he still want her? She did not know, but she did know that the man was someone special. She was anxious to get home and write to him. She wanted him to know that she did love him, that she wasn't playing immature games with him. She was just afraid. Terrible things had happened to her; how could she tell him that she was no longer pure. The thought of divulging that part of her life to Mitchell frightened her. Would he still want her to be his, or would he just want to take advantage of her. His letters had extracted her love; a love she didn't even realized was within her. She wanted him now more than ever, and with the both of them being thousands of miles away from one another, she found it unbearable. Why hadn't the two of them figured out their feelings before he left for Germany? They could have been visiting one another while stationed within hundreds of miles, not thousands of miles and a big ocean between them.

Julia walked into the office. She didn't even know she was smiling until Yeoman Cross announced, "Must have been some good news in that plain envelope. You're smiling from ear to ear. What did he say, Holton? I guess he didn't dump you after all? Huh?"

"Cross, don't you have some correspondences for Commander O'Shea to type?" she said loud enough for Yeoman Hurley, and Yeoman Kampschroder to hear. She continued to smile as she sat herself down in front of her electric typewriter. She was happy, and didn't care who at work knew it.

When Lieutenant Kadowski entered the office, he said to Julia, "So, what did that soldier have to tell you in the letter, Holton? Is it still on with you two lovebirds?" The other yeomen all start laughing again; and Julia laughed with them out of embarrassment. She wasn't about to tell the sailors and the officer what Mitchell had written. She smiled the rest of the day at work as she tried to remember all of the beautiful things Mitchell had penned.

~ ~ ~

When Jim pulled up to the air terminal loop Julia got onto his bus with such enthusiasm the bus driver did a double-take. "My, my, my. Somebody's in a good mood," he said in a pleasant voice.

"Yes I am, Jim. It's Friday, the end of a pretty good work day; and I'm in a terrific mood. Hurry up and get me home." She didn't pay any mind to the other sailors and the few waves on his bus.

"Hurry up and get you home? Gal, how come?" he asked as he steered the bus onto the main road.

"Can't tell you," she said as the bus rocked sideways, shaking and grunting as it made its way up the small hill onto the straightaway.

Jim drove, stopping at the Navy Exchange for some of his passengers to get off, and the mess hall where most all of the sailors and waves disembarked. There would be no mess hall for Julia today. Why would she need food now after learning the beautiful contents of Mitchell's letter? Besides, Virginia had been working an odd shift for the past couple of days so she would not be meeting the photographer at the mess hall for dinner. That was just as well, her stomach was filled with Mitchell's love; there was certainly no room for food.

Jim finally reached the WAVES Barrack. Excited, Julia rushed across the quarterdeck to get to her room. When she entered her quarters she took Mitchell's photo from the mirror, kicked her shoes off and sat down to read his letter once again. Every now and then after reading a certain point in Mitchell's letter, she would glance at his picture, then gently place her lips on it. The letter soothed her. She laid down upon her bunk and napped with Mitchell's picture and letter lying next to her on her pillow.

CHAPTER 28 -- ACCEPTANCE

When Julia got up Saturday morning, she was well rested. She felt as though she could stay up a straight forty-eight hours before she needed to lie down again. It was a wonderful sleep and she knew it was because of her new found love, Mitchell Lauers. She was happy, and for the first time in a long time she wanted to have breakfast. There was a whole beautiful day awaiting her. It was still early in the morning, 0630 hours, and she wondered if she should use the quietness of the Saturday morning in the barrack to write Mitchell. She didn't have any fancy paper; she still had a few of the pink envelopes one of the waves gave to her and some perfume. She sprayed two sheet of the paper with the floral scent of the perfume and allowed it to dry.

Julia started writing the letter to Mitchell as soon as her thoughts were together. She wrote:

February 25, 1967

SA Julia Holton
Operations Admin
Patuxent River, Maryland 20670

My Wonderful Love,

I do love you. I thought I had lost your love through my determination of denying my affection for you. But I can see you are a diligent man and your persistence is extremely strong. Never did I want to admit my love for you; I only wanted to continue to write to you with no strings. You, however, want us to do more than write to one another; you want us to be in love and this makes me nervous. You are going to have to help me through this process; it is something very new to me. Right now, I am so confused about this complete change in our friendship. But if this is the direction in which you want our friendly relationship to go, than I freely give my love to you. Mitchell, I have always had you in my mind; now you are in my heart. It was easy for me to keep love out of the equation and I was hoping you could do the same. Now that we are willing to give our hearts to one another, I have one question for you. My darling Mitchell, why are we in love? We've only met once and we don't really know anything about one another. Is our love for one another all in our heads; or is it very real within our hearts? I don't have the answer to that, my sweetheart; all I know is what I feel at this moment. And what I feel at this time is love for you. It is easy for us to experience these emotions while we write to one another. But who is to say that once we meet again in real life, the love we've shared in our written words will remain? I guess we will have to wait to find out.

Thank you for loving me. Please know that I love you passionately.

I boldly sign this letter, Always your woman,

Julia Holton

She wanted to sign it *Always your Lady*, because she did not feel mature, like a woman would be. But she remembered Mitchell writing *please say you will be my woman* in his previous correspondence. Julia was excited as she proof-read the letter. She wished she could think of more to tell Mitchell but she felt it was a completed correspondence. The last thing she wanted to do was give him reason to have his doubts about loving her. She had never had anyone tell her that they loved her. Julia looked at her alarm clock, it was 0718. She placed the letter into an envelope, addressed and stamped it then placed it in her purse. She gathered her items for the shower, placing them into her little shower tote, put her robe and flip-flops on, then left her room; locking the door behind her.

The shower stall was empty. Though the lights were on in the shower area, she preferred to shower in the dark. She turned the lights off. There were two fragrances in her shower tote; Rapture and White Ginger. She sensually rubbed her body and lather up with the scented liquid soaps. She had never used them before; but today was special. She declared her love for Mitchell and though he was nowhere near her body, she wanted it to smell as though he was. Smelling the flowery fragrances reminded her of the letter she had just written to him; like love, pure acceptance of love. Her heart and mind was opened to the concept that Mitchell could actually be in love with her. And it was a warm feeling, an adoring sensation of happiness; just like the soft, supple water that flowed smoothly onto her face, and down the front of her breast. The shower sprinkled her in all of the sensualities she was sure Mitchell and she would experience once they were reunited. As the water trickled gently upon her body, she thought of Mitchell. She touched herself softly and wished she could feel Mitchell inside of her; but she knew it would be a long while before that would become a reality. She wanted him so much that she imagined him naked in the small stall with her; kissing her delicate lips, as he pressed her body against the ceramic tile of the stall. She felt his mouth on her breast, hungry for her love. Through her vibrant imagination, the gentleness of his hands tantalized her and his kisses consumed her body with trickling tingles. The euphoric ecstasy embraced every inch of her soul as she allowed her mind to thrust in passion. The mental sexual joy gave her permission to experience fulfillment. And when, in her dreamy state she became complete, she felt a sense of rapture and the sensual shower had come to an end. Completely drained from the stimulating shower, she was relieved to realize the man she committed herself to had such a mental effect on her. When she was done showering and fantasizing, she was exhausted, but still she knew she must get herself together. She wanted to mentally feel Mitchell towel-dry her off, but she could not afford to get herself locked into another vivid fantasy so she dried herself off, put her clean under garments on, then covered herself with her robe. She returned to reality when she stepped out into the corridor.

PART SIX

CHAPTER 29 -- OLDER WAVE

Many months passed and gradually the memories of the rape left Julia's mind. She found solace in studying for her next pay grade. She did not want to be an E-2, seaman apprentice, any longer than necessary. The sooner she could advance in her field as yeoman, the sooner she could receive more pay in her monthly paycheck. Her plans for her future were big; and in order to make those plans happen she knew she needed to study hard. It was her dream to do the best she could; she was well on the road to becoming the person she wanted to be. Virginia was instrumental in encouraging Julia to keep her studies up so she could advance. And though Julia liked her other friends of the barrack, there was a special place in her heart for the friendship she had nourished with Virginia.

~ ~ ~

There were many waves that often hung around in the lounge area. And since there was sometimes nothing to do, it was not uncommon for a group of them to use a corner of the lounge area to sit around and shoot the breeze with one another.

Virginia was a quiet wave; and though she pretty much stayed to herself, she was wise to keep abreast as to what was going on around her. Many times she would overhear conversations from the other ladies. Always, she kept her voice out of the conversations and formed her own opinions. She knew who was promoted, who was considered a outstanding wave, who had been given special assignments, who was sleeping with whom, and who was pregnant and wanted out of the navy. Many conversations she overheard when no one was even aware of her presence.

One conversation in particular came from Adrianne Hess. Adrianne was the oldest wave in the barrack; she came from Queens, New York. Her voice was loud and raspy; and when she talked she wanted everyone to hear what was coming out of her mouth. The wave had an innate desire to be heard. But the other waves deemed her as desperate and kooky.

One evening as Virginia was walking down the corridor, she heard Adrianne Hess' loud obnoxious voice. She was in the middle of a conversation with Geraldine Burts, "What do you mean, you've never sucked a dick?" When Geraldine told Adrianne it sounded so gross and she would never do such a thing, Adrianne looked at her and said, "Don't knock it till you've tried it." Adrianne turned and walked down the hall; she and Virginia's eyes locked as they approached one another. She stood directly in front of Virginia and stared her down, then said, "What are you looking at? I suppose you've never sucked one either? You goodie-two-shoes make me sick." Virginia stepped aside, to go around the angry woman. But Adrianne's large girth blocked her movement.

In her quiet demeanor, Virginia warned the older wave, "You have five seconds to stop blocking my path."

"Or you'll what?" Immediately she placed her thick finger in the center of Virginia's forehead then gave it a quick shove. Before Adrianne could say another word, Virginia punched her in her face. The punch caught her off guard and the big wave staggered out of Virginia's path. As the astonished wave reached her hand to soothe her face, she angrily said, "You young waves think you're so much. You don't know shit about how to please a man. You'll find out; it ain't all about straight sex. Men want different stuff and the older you get the more you will come to realize what I am saying is right." She stormed off to her room. Her door echoed as she slammed it shut to emphasize how angry she was at the young, stupid waves who thought they knew everything. They didn't know anything as far as she was concerned. She didn't like being thirty-two years old and the oldest of all the waves in the barrack. And though other waves tried to befriend the woman, they found her brunt opinions a little too hard to take. Virginia was unlike any of the other young waves. She would not try to pacify the woman, even if Adrianne was older. In fact, she didn't have an interest in trying to impress any of them. Her only concern was to be the best photographer for the naval air base's newspaper she could be. She loved working for Patuxent River NAS Daily News. She refused to let anything or anyone sap up her energy with total nonsense. The only interest she had as far as friendship went was with Julia. There was something she liked about the wave and she wanted to help her in any way she could because she considered her as a sister she never had.

~ ~ ~

Saturday morning, March 25, 1967, Virginia and Julia caught the Greyhound and headed for Washington, D.C. to see the cherry blossoms, a few monuments, and part of the Smithsonian. Julia had never gone anywhere on the outside of the base with Virginia. She wanted to look her best so she purchased a new burnt orange skirt and matching jacket. She wore a navy colored, straw, Panama hat and a silk scarf to accent the suit. Julia was excited to be on the Greyhound Bus with her friend.

The two well-dressed ladies enjoyed the bus ride to D.C. And though Virginia was hoping to have a nice quiet ride to Washington, D.C., Julia talked the complete hour-and-a-half of the ride. She talked about the air traffic control tower, how AC1 Diane James took time to show her around the tower. She explained to Virginia why she liked her commanding officer,

Commander O'Shea. Constantly, Julia rattled on telling the sophisticated wave her love of the navy, and how she was going to make a career out of the military. Occasionally Virginia would smile to convey to her friend, she really was interested in what she was saying even if she was not participating in the conversation. Virginia was happy to see Julia in her normal upbeat disposition.

When the bus was twenty-five minutes from D.C., Julia finally got Virginia to join in the one-sided conversation. Julia asked, "Virginia, how well do you know Adrianne Hess? You know; the hospital corpsman who lives next door to me?"

Virginia, hoping she could cut the subject short about Adrianne said, "I don't know much about her." Which was true. She did not want to get into the explicit sexual conversation she heard Adrianne Hess speak of. The classy brunette was hoping that would end the conversation, but it did not.

"Do you know a while back I saw her coming out of my room? I was coming from the shower and she was closing the door to my room."

"What? Are you sure?"

"Yes Virginia. Sure, I'm sure. I didn't say anything; besides, I didn't see her carrying anything from my room."

Even Virginia knew Julia should have confronted the wave. She shook her head in disbelief. Virginia worried about her; she felt Julia was way too timid when it came to standing up for herself. She witness it many times how she would let the other waves take advantage of her. "That's odd."

"What do you mean, 'That's odd'?"

"Julia, have you always been so trusting? Why would you think she didn't take anything from your room, just because you didn't see her carry anything out? Do you know Adrianne is one of the biggest thieves in the barrack?"

"Uhh, well I, umm."

"No, let me take that back. Adrianne Hess is not one of the biggest thieves in the barrack; she is the only thief in the barrack. So like I said, just because you didn't see her with anything in her hands, doesn't mean she didn't steal something from your room." She shook her head; Julia knew her friend was trying to educate her but she felt she was being a bit harsh on her for not challenging the hospital corpsman. Virginia continued, "The next time you go to the head to take a shower or use the toilet, make sure you lock your door and have your key with you."

Meekly, Julia said, "Okay."

But what Julia didn't want to tell Virginia was the fact that Adrianne did take something out of her room. There was four dollars missing from her top drawer; and from the bottom drawer all of the unopened letters from D.A. Johnson were missing. She had received five to seven more letters from the odd man. She couldn't quite remember the count, but it did not matter, because now they were gone. That same evening the letters went missing Julia checked to see if the lady stole Mitchell's letters from the top shelf of her closet. His letters were still there.

When the bus pulled into the Washington, D.C. terminal the ladies were filled with excitement. Virginia had been to D.C. many times. A couple of those visits she had gone with a first-class photographer's mate who was romantically interested in her. She was infatuated with the sailor. But when she found out he was married and his wife had just left base-housing to return to their hometown, Virginia dropped the relationship.

Virginia was very familiar with the town. She took Julia to Café Intrigue where the food was phenomenal and the people were interesting. In the café Julia was surprised to see so many people of different nationalities. It reminded her of being on the base. After they had their lunch, Virginia suggested they start with the monuments and then go check out the cherry blossoms. The two ladies made their way to President Kennedy's gravesite and then visited the Tomb of the Unknown Soldier. When they made it to the cherry blossoms, Julia found herself overwhelmed by the beauty. The nice, subtle fragrance of some of the cherry blossoms were intoxicating to her. The array of pink bloom of the many trees she and Virginia viewed were a delightful sight to the young ladies. And though Julia did not want to leave the beautiful blossoms, Virginia reminded her that they had to visit a small section of the Smithsonian.

Julia was enthralled when she went into one of the buildings of the Smithsonian. There was so much to see, and though her friend told her they would never see all of the museum in one day, Julia was happy to take in what few sights they could. At one point they stopped at the case which displayed the Hope Diamond. Virginia made a joke and told Julia, if Seaman Hope Jones had come with them, she could have shown her military i.d. and retrieved her diamond. Of course they laughed at such a notion.

As they were taking pictures, a young man asked them if they would like for him to take a picture of them together. The ladies were happy to have the opportunity so they posed happily together with big smiles as the man snapped their photo with each of their cameras.

That evening when they were back on the bus, heading for Pax River, they were filled with beautiful memories of their excursion in Washington, D.C. Julia was happy; she knew Virginia had treated her to something special. And if she never made it back to the thriving city, she knew she had had a most eventful moment in her life, there in Washington, D.C., during that particular time.

On the bus ride home, Julia was too tired from the excitement to talk. She slept the entire bus ride back to Lexington Park.

CHAPTER 30 -- SUBMARINE

One evening Natalie and Lucy, came into Julia's room. "Aren't you ready yet," Natalie asked. Lucy was a little short colored wave who came from Jacksonville, Florida. She loved to tell jokes and liked getting together with Jasmine and Natalie most every other Friday night to go to the Dance Spot. Julia had been to the club a few times with the waves. As Julia was doing a last minute touch up on her lipstick, Natalie went over to the mirror where she stood. Natalie saw Mitchell's photograph; she picked it up. "Lucy, look at this." She rushed over to Lucy to show it to her.

Lucy snatched the picture from Natalie's hand, then said, "Julia, who is this?"

"It's some guy I met on the bus a while back." Julia felt no need to tell her fellow shipmates the circumstances regarding her attachment to the handsome soldier. She figured Lucy was going to say something smart, and she was right.

"So when did you start dating white boys?" she snickered and Natalie laughed.

"Give me my picture," Julia said as she snatched at the air to retrieve it. Lucy toyed with moving it out of her reach each time she grabbed for it.

"Girl, don't you know once he go black, he ain't goin' back?" Lucy kidded with Julia. She playful examined the photograph.

"Umm, he ain't even a bad lookin' guy. You ain't really interested in this white boy, are you?" She handed the picture back to Julia.

Julia took the picture before Lucy could toy around with it again. "I don't know if he is white; to tell you the truth, I never noticed his color. Just seemed like a nice guy; that's all."

"So what are you doing with his picture, Julia?" Natalie asked the wave.

"He sent it to me."

"But this guy is an army guy. What's wrong with you?"

"Come on. Let's go?" Julia took one more look in the mirror, patted her hair in place then shooed her friends out of her room. They took the bus to the guardhouse of the base, walk off of the base and grabbed a cab to the Dance Spot.

~ ~ ~

Jasmine was already at the Dance Spot shooting pool. She was a tall thin, chocolate brown wave, with long black soft hair. The wave was the only one amongst the colored waves who actually step foot on a college campus. And though she informed the waves she had once been looked at by the navy as officer material, she never told any of the ladies why she was just an enlisted person, same as they. All of them had their own reasons why they were in the military. Some were noble reasons, some were simply survival alternatives, some for their patriotic duty and some were for the sense of adventure, just like the pamphlets offered. None of the ladies ever questioned one another as to what was their catalyst for joining the military.

When Jasmine saw her friends come into the club she waved at them to come over to the pool table where she was shooting pool with Bradley. Natalie went towards her while Julia and Lucy stood at the bar.

"I got a big table in the corner," she yelled over Sam and Dave's, *Hold On, I'm Comin'*. "Dot is sitting at it." Natalie looked at the tall brown man that Jasmine was shooting pool with. She knew he worked at the Supply Hanger and had seen him in the mess hall a few times. She noticed every time she came to the Dance Spot with her friends he was always there. But he usually hung around with other patrons; this time he was shooting pool with Jasmine.

"Okay, we'll meet you at the table," Natalie told her friend. She rounded up Julia and Lucy then headed for the table in the back.

"Hi Dot," Natalie spoke to the woman. "Thanks for saving these seats for us."

"No problem ladies; sit on down." She looked at Julia, then asked, "Who's the new girl?"

Lucy spoke up, "She's been stationed here for about six months or so. Dot, this is Julia; Julia met Dot."

"Nice to meet you, Dot." Julia waved her hand and Dot gave her a nod.

"How come I ain't seen you here before, Julia?"

"I've been here a few times with Natalie. I probably just blended in with the crowd. You probably didn't know I was a wave from the base."

"Could be. Anyway, it's really a pleasure to know you. So you're in the navy?"

"Yeah, I am." she answered as she twisted the strap on her purse.

"Lucky you," Dot said to Julia. The attractive brown lady was a civilian who looked as though she was twenty-one years old. But she was thirty-seven with six children to raise; and she lived in Lexington Park.

When Jasmine came back to the table Bradley was with her. They sat at the table and Jasmine announced, "Hey everybody, I beat the shit out of Bradley for two games of pool." That was Jasmine. She always wanted to be the best at whatever she did. She knew a lot and she loved letting people know she knew she was smart and capable of handling herself. "Bradley, I think you know everybody at the table. I'm not for sure if you know this one," she touched Julia on the shoulder. The wave looked Bradley's way and said hello to the gentleman. He nodded, then draped his arm over Jasmine's shoulder. When the waitress came by and took everyone's order, Julia, ordered a coke. "Ahh hell naw," Jasmine said. She looked at the waitress then said, "Give her a Colt 45," and the waitress wrote it on her small note pad then trotted off to the bar.

Everyone was having a good time dancing and talking. Jasmine was always the one the other waves looked up to. She was five years older than most of them. The wave was more outgoing and always knew how to approach man or woman. As the drinks were flowing and everyone was having a good time, Jasmine talked about ordering some food. Then she winked at Julia and said, "Julia, you want a submarine?" And all of the waves laughed, except Julia. When Dot asked what was so funny, Jasmine told her, "The night Julia arrived on the base we asked her if she wanted a submarine."

"So, I still don't get what's so funny about that?" Dot questioned.

"It's hilarious because she thought we were talking about a real submarine; you know the underwater kind? She thought we wanted to take her on a submarine ride. Ain't that something?"

Bradley took a drink of his Cutty Sark on ice. He rubbed on Jasmine's thigh, looked at Julia and smiled. "Leave the kid alone," he told her. "She was new to the place. Hell, I might have thought you were talking about a submarine ride, myself. After all we are in the navy." He looked at Julia, then said, "The poor girl just didn't know a sandwich on a long roll is called a submarine sandwich." He lifted his drink in the air and added, "Here's to innocence."

Jasmine's sarcasm kicked in, "Innocence, or dumbness. She probably thinks that Colt 45 she's been sipping on is a gun." She gave a loud laughter and everyone but Julia laughed. She was feeling like the brunt of their jokes, and she did not like that. She'd endured jokes at her expense all of her life. She was not going to laugh with them at what Jasmine said about her.

Dot, who was a mother and an insightful mother at that, was smart enough to know the group's laughter hurt Julia's feelings.

To get everyone off of the subject of Julia's inexperience of things, Dot said, "Hell, y'all can laugh at Julia all you want. At least she was smart enough to get herself into the navy. Shit, I'm thirty-seven years old and got a house full of children." Everyone at the table looked at Dot in disbelief. They knew she was a civilian who live in Lexington Park. They just figured she was slightly a few years older than they; not almost a whole decade. Dot knew she caught them all off guard so she said, "Yeah, I'm an old-ass woman. Don't let all this makeup and my young-lookin' body fool you." She leaned over and touched Julia's hand. "Honey, fuck what these fools say to you. They don't mean anything by it, I'm sure." She looked daringly around at the waves and, with the exception of Jasmine, the waves felt badly about their insensitivity. Dot looked at Julia, then said, "Hey Julia, I wish I did have sense enough like you did to get myself into the navy. I bet you one thing, I wouldn't be stuck here in Lexington Park."

Natalie said, "My goodness, it was just a joke." Lucy even mentioned she was sorry about laughing. However, Jasmine, with a disgusted attitude, told Julia she shouldn't be so thin-skinned.

Not wanting to get into the waves' disagreement, Bradley finished his drink, stood up and said, "Hey look, I got to get out of here; duty at 0430. I'll catch y'all later."

When he left, Dot, desperately wanting to lighten the air, asked, "Anyone here like chit'lings."

"Yeah, I love them," Lucy said.

"So do I," Jasmine admitted.

Dot offered, "Have you ever ate them fried, I fry mine. My kids can't stand them so I got a lot left over. If you guys want some you are more than welcomed to come to my house and eat till your heart's content. I got greens, cornbread and sweet potato pie too. Hey, I might not have no man to cook fo' but I cook me a mean dinner every now and then. Y'all interested?"

They were all interested, except Julia. She wanted to get back to the barrack. Julia was funny like that. Whenever she felt people were attacking her, she would stick her head in her shell and clam up. Her evening was ruined and she was ready to end it.

"How 'bout you Julia, would you like a nice home-cooked meal."

Trying not to ruin it for her friends, she said, "I think that beer has given me a headache. I'm going to call it a night."

Disappointed, Dot said, "Okay Julia. Come on ladies, let's go get us some real food. This liquor is making me hungry." As they all got their purses and jackets together, Julia began walking towards the pay phone. "Where are you going, Julia?" Dot asked the wave.

"I'm going to call a cab."

"No you're not," the older woman said, "We're not leaving you here to wait on a cab. You're coming with us; I'll take you to the barrack."

"But you can't get onto the base," Julia told her. She knew the guard house would not let the woman through if she wasn't in the military.

Jasmine was tired of Julia's whinny ways. The wave had totally killed the little alcohol buzz she had going on. Careful not to make her look like a fool again, the older wave said, "Julia, she can get on base when we show the security guard our passes. It's not going to be a problem." No one laughed.

"Oh," was all Julia could say.

~ ~ ~

When she got to her room she turned the light on, threw her purse onto the bed, then kicked her shoes off. She plopped her butt onto her bed. What started out to be a fun evening with the waves, ended up being a very trying night; Julia was anxious. To settle her nerves from the incident at the Dance Spot she began cleaning out her drawers. She started with the top drawer, pulling out the clothing, neatly refolding them on her bed then replacing them into the drawers. When she got to the bottom drawer she pulled out all of the clothing and placed them on her bed to refold. In between her dungarees and chambray shirts an envelope fell out. She saw her signature, the date and a message she had written, I DO NOT KNOW THIS PERSON. When she turned it over she spotted the return address, D.A. Johnson. She scratched her head; she thought Adrianne Hess had stolen all of the unopened letters from the bottom drawer. Apparently the thieving wave missed this one. She noticed after the theft of the letters, she never received another one from the man; she wondered why he stopped writing. She hadn't given it much thought because it was as Virginia mentioned the whole thing was just plain creepy.

She ripped open the envelope. When she unfolded the letter she recognized the terrible handwriting, but a little card fell out and when she picked it up and flipped it over, she was not prepared for what she saw. It was a picture of her sister, Josephine. She did a double take. *"Wait a minute,"* she spoke into the air, *"What is Josephine's picture doing in this letter."* Quickly she unfolded the letter and began reading it. It read:

D. A Johnson
#896590
Attica, New York 14011

February 21, 1967

Hi Jewels,

I been wondering how come you haven't been writing to me. I thought we were going to be able to have something special going on. You know what I mean. I had to admit that you had me fooled girl. I know you was just coming with your friend when she visited Cool Man. It was nice of you to sit and talk to me, even though you did not know me. But I been writing you all this time and *not once have you written me back. I take it you ain't interested. I see that Cool Man's girlfriend still come to visit with him. How come you don't come with her anymore?*

Any way, aint no since in me keeping your picture that you gave me during your first and last visit. Sure, you are one fine lady, but I don't think you are the one for me. No love lost. Anyway, I'm working on a plan to get out of this place. And when I do I might just come and look you up.

D. A. Johnson

She looked at the date again; the letter was almost two months old. She never opened up the other letters after receiving the first one. And now she didn't have any of them. She was sure the hospital corpsman stole them. But she hadn't seen Adrianne Hess for over a week. She wondered what the other letters said, and now she had to wait until the wave returned to the base. She put the tangled clothes back into the bottom drawer, dropped the letter on top of them, and slammed the drawer shut. She would make a long distance phone call to Josephine first thing in the morning.

CHAPTER 31 -- IMPERSONATING

It didn't surprise Julia that Josephine answered the telephone. She stayed on the phone most of the time before Julia left for the navy. She sound rushed when she said *Hello*. It was just as well because Julia did not want to be on the line with her sister for any length of time. She was a little upset with the girl and though her sister was a year younger, Julia always felt the girl was much smarter than she. Now she was beginning to have doubts about it. What was Josephine thinking to have a strange person writing to her? She wondered why her sister would give the man her name and address instead of her own.

"Hi Josephine, how is everything at home." She decided she would ease into the reason she was calling.

"Oh my goodness, mama it's Julia," she heard her sister hollering for their mother. Julia tensed up. Before Julia could tell her sister she called specifically to speak to her, the sister yelled once more to get her mother's attention. The next voice she heard on the telephone was that of her mother's, Eleanor.

"Baby, when are gonna come home again? You know it ain't the same without you around."

"Hi mama. I don't know when I'll be home. You know I'm almost two hundred miles away from Philadelphia."

"Yeah, I know. Why you have to be stationed so far away from home anyways? Couldn't you have requested a duty station in Philadelphia?"

"Mama, I have to go where the navy sends me. You know that."

"I just wished you were here. Things would be so much betta, Julia."

Julia knew what her mother was doing; trying to put her on a guilt trip for no longer being a part of the Holton hell. She was not going to buy into it. Thanks to her mother and her father she wanted no parts of the life they chose for themselves. Her mood was jacked-up from the incident at the Dance Spot. The letter from D. A. Johnson made her demeanor sour even more. She did not want to listen to her mother's begging for her to visit as soon as she could. She abruptly said, "Mama, I'm not going to be home anytime soon. I'm sorry. Mama, can you get Josephine to the phone for me, please?"

Her mother did not say anything else to her, but the next voice on the telephone was her sister's. "What did you say to mama? She don't seem too happy," the girl questioned her sister.

"Look Josephine, I didn't say anything that would upset her. She did most of the talking; she wanted to know when I'll be home again. I couldn't give her an answer because I've already had my two-week vacation. I just called to ask you something."

"Ask me what?" she snapped.

"Do you know a person named Cool Man?"

"Yeah, that's Deborah's boyfriend. Why?"

"Do you know some guy name D.A. Johnson?"

"Yeah, that's Cool Man's cellmate? Nice looking guy."

"Huh? Cellmate? What do you mean, cellmate?"

"Just what I said, his cellmate? I went to Attica State Prison with Deborah when she went to visit her boyfriend, Denny. His name is Denny, but they call him Cool Man. Anyway I met his cellmate, Donald Johnson. I was so proud of you, you know, with you being in the navy and all. I pretended I was you and gave him your address."

"You did what?"

"I gave him your address."

"Have you ever visited him since you did that?"

"Are you for real? Of course not; how could I? I'm in the navy, remember? I'm supposed to be you," she said, as if it made logical sense.

"Oh, so now I get stuck with him writing to me, huh?"

"Give me a break, Julia. You know how odd you are when it comes to boys. I figure I was doing you a favor."

"Josephine, what is this person in jail for."

"He's not in jail, stupid. He's in prison. Deborah's boyfriend is in prison for armed robbery. His cellmate, David, is in prison for selling guns. That's what he told me; but it he said the cops planted the weapons at his place. So he's really in prison for nothing."

Trying to keep her composure, Julia asked, "And you thought it would okay to give him my name and address, instead of your own? How did he get your picture?"

"I gave it to him when I visited. Hey, he's in prison, it's not like he can get out anytime soon."

"Well, I got news for you Josephine, in one of the letters he sent to me he says he's working on getting out. And it's an old letter I found in the bottom of my drawer. So he might already be out. I'm not sure if he is, or is not. Anyway, he sent your picture back because *Julia*, that's me, remember…*not you*, did not write to him; and he seems mad."

Josephine asked, "How can he be getting out; and why didn't you at least write him, Julia?"

"Are you insane, Josephine? Why would I write him?" Julia asked.

"'Cause he wrote to you, girl. That's why."

"Josephine, I don't know him. I didn't even know he was a felon until you just now told me. This is really awful Josephine. Just plain awful."

"How come you're calling me, Julia? He's your problem now, not mine."

Aggravated that Josephine was making no sense in such a serious matter, Julia explained, "You should have given him your information, not mine. Now you've got a criminal mad at me because you used my information, trying to pretend like you're so important being in the military."

"What do you mean like *I'm so important being in the military?*" the sister barked back.

"Just what I said. If you wanted him to think you were in the military, you could've just lied and told him you were in the military, and given him *your* name and address, not mine. You're not me. What you did is called impersonating a member of the armed force. It was a very nasty thing to do, Josephine."

"Well honestly Julia, what can I do about it? I didn't expect for the guy to really write me; umm, I mean write to you. Ain't nothing I can do about it now."

Julia shook her head, she said, "Josephine, please don't ever use my name or give it out as an address. You can't go around doing that to me."

"You know what Julia; go to hell. You should have been glad I was thinking about you. You should be thanking me; not trying to make out like you are so much better that I am. What, you think you're so hot just because you got yourself in the navy? Well, you're not. You're nothing, and always will be nothing, just like mama's been sayin'." And with that, Josephine slammed the phone in Julia's ear.

Julia could still hear the nastiness in Josephine's voice after she hung up the phone. She sat in the telephone booth almost in tears. It was a good thing there wasn't a wave waiting to use the phone. They certainly would have heard the aggravation in her voice with the conversation she was having with Josephine. She made her way out of the phone booth then went back to her room. Julia wondered why she no longer heard any more from the convict. As she thought back, the letters from the persistent man stopped around the time Hospital Corpsman Hess stole them. A sick feeling was in her gut. Julia heard the scuttlebutt about the aged wave joining the military solely to find a husband. Adrianne Hess was an old wave and whenever she approached the sailors, whether at work or in social settings, she always came across as desperate. Most of the men would use her once or twice, never to be bothered with her again. Many of her follow waves came and went from the WAVES Barrack with marriage proposals and babies on the way. HM3 Hess was still there waiting for some man, any man to come and rescue her. No man ever showed up. Julia wondered what was going on with Adrianne Hess and the letters the wave took from her possession. She couldn't think anymore; the thoughts in her mind were on overload. Julia put her pajamas on and went to bed. Her brain was exhausted; she fell right to sleep.

CHAPTER 32-- INVESTIGATION

Petty Officer Eunice Brendon was on duty watch for the evening. At the beginning of her watch she was ordered to detain certain waves whose names appeared on a roster. She was informed to ask them if items were missing from their room. There had been another theft in the barrack. This time, over three hundred dollars had been stolen from First Class Karen Infantino's room. If the detainees had items missing and had reported it to the duty officer, it would be in the log. If they had missing property, and simply did not report it to the quarterdeck watch officer, she was to send them into the makeshift interrogation area which was inside of the lounge. There, they would find a master-at-arms sitting behind a folding table to take their statements.

When Julia came in from work, Petty Officer Brendon stopped her at the quarterdeck. "Wait right there, Julia," she ordered. The guard on duty knew the wave; not personally, but just in general. There was another wave standing at Brendon's desk and Julia noticed the both of them were going through the watch log together. Julia wondered why she had to be detained on the quarterdeck.

"There it is," the standing wave pointed at something in the book to Petty Officer Brendon. I knew it was around the first of March. I reported my bracelet and twenty dollars stolen on this day. She emphasized her assurance of the date by giving hard taps with her index finger onto the log book. "See? PN Yack was the duty officer for that night." Petty Officer Brandon added her name and the items stolen along with date and time onto a list marked THEFT REPORTED AND LOGGED.

"Okay, then I'll make sure the master-at-arms get this information. That will be all; that is unless you're contacted for more information." She dismissed the wave with a nod and then motioned for Julia to come forward.

Julia felt a nervous rumble inside of her stomach. She wondered what this interrogation was all about. She took a quiet deep breath, then stepped forward with a smile. "Yes?" she questioned.

"Hello Julia; how are you this evening?"

Julia wanted her to by-pass the niceties and get on with why she was stopped on the quarterdeck. "I'm doing real good; is something wrong?"

"Yes, as a matter of fact, there is. There has been a rash of thefts in the barrack that's been going on for quite a while. Base security has sent a master-at-arms to our barrack to investigate. You are one of many I have to ask if anything has been stolen from their room. Now if you have and reported it to the duty officer on guard duty that day, she would have recorded it in the barrack log." She tapped onto the open book. Julia looked on wide-eyed. She was paying attention to every detail the watch officer was presenting to her. "Have you had anything come up missing from your room?"

Julia looked at the watch officer in puzzlement. She was always worried when confronted; and because she was too nervous, her brain came up with nothing. She just wanted off of the quarterdeck; her feet were hurting and her day at work had been long. The whole thing about theft had her concerned. She replied, "No I haven't missed anything from my room; nothing that comes to mind."

"Umm, that's funny. I could have sworn one of the waves said you did have a missing item from your room. Think she said four dollars."

"Four dollars?" It came to her mind when she heard the duty officer mention *four dollars*. She remembered the four dollars Adrianne Hess lifted from her drawer. But it was only four dollars; who's going to remember four dollars being stolen. "Who told you that?"

"I just heard it in passing while I was checking another wave in. Can't say who mentioned it; just that your name came up as missing the money."

Julia hated being involved with things she felt would jeopardize her life in the navy. She wanted no blemishes on her record; being connected as a victim of theft did not set too well with her. Besides, she had forgotten about the little bit of money. And though she wondered who mentioned the missing bills, she readily admitted the loss of it. "Oh yeah, that's right. I did have something stolen from my room; you're right. It was four dollars; hardly worth mentioning."

"Then get on in there and tell the master-at-arms."

She did as the duty officer suggested and entered the room. The thick neck military police officer nodded at her to have a seat. She sat down in the chair across from the big man. His hair was reddish brown and his eyes were set far apart with bushy eyebrows. As she sat in front of him, she noticed the serious look on his face: his lips were pressed together with no hint of a smile. He spotted her rate on her sleeve, then addressed her in a strict baritone voice.

"Hello Seaman Apprentice; I'm Master-at-Arms First Class Philip Donaldson." She nodded, greeted him then extended her hand to shake his. In a moment of awkwardness he extended his massive hand and shook the seaman apprentice's small hand. "Your full name please; spell your last name."

"Seaman Apprentice Julia Holton; H O L T O N."

He wrote her name down, then gave her a stern look. "And SA Holton, you want to report that you did have something stolen?"

"Yes. Yes I did." She saw the man look at a roster, spot her name on it and start to write down something, but hesitated. "Seaman Apprentice, please verify your room number."

"It's 116."

The master-at-arms wrote the room number down next to her name. "I see." He looked up at the young wave, and continued. "Please tell me what it is that came up missing."

"Well, the four dollars that was in my top drawer."

"Is that all?"

"Yes, that's all I can think of."

"Do you have a theory on who might have taken the four dollars?"

She did not want to get herself involved with someone else's problems; she had enough trouble of her own. She knew with the uniform code of military justice she was mandated to tell what she knew. A big fear engulfed her. Though she did not want to blow Adrianne Hess in, she was forced to tell the master-at-arms it was her whom she had seen coming out of her room. Julia looked him in the eye and revealed the information he needed for his report. "Sir, Adrianne Hess was coming out of my unlocked door when I returned from the head. I saw her closing my door and going into her room. I didn't say anything to her because I figured she made an honest mistake. It's easy to do. That's all I know."

"I see," Master-at-Arms Donaldson said, though he felt she knew more." He asked, "SA Holton, do you know the ramifications of withholding information."

"Sir, what do you mean, withholding information? I've told you everything I can think of." She was beginning to think the man thought she was responsible for the thefts. She heard of waves losing a lot of money due to the robberies. Nervously, she added. "There's nothing more that I know about HM3 Hess. All I know is her room is next door to mine; and when I returned from my shower four dollars were missing from my drawer. That is all I know about the lady. Because of that incident, I've learned to lock my door whenever I go out of my room."

He looked at her with doubt; then asked, "SA Holton, who is D. A. Johnson?"

"I beg your pardon, sir?" the name hit her like a ton of bricks.

"Who is D. A. Johnson? Do you know this person or not?"

"No sir, I don't."

"Then if you don't know him, why did we find his letters in HM3 Hess' room. And why do some of the letters have your name as the addressee on them?"

Julia was getting very anxious and she could feel the perspiration forming in her armpits. *My goodness,* she thought, *those are the letters Adrianne Hess stole from my bottom drawer.* She didn't think the master-at-arms needed that information as well. She figured all he wanted to know about was the money the woman stole from her. She began to panic, and she didn't even know why. What had she done for her name to be tied in with the thefts of the barrack? Without mentioning the missing letters, she knew it made her appear to the master-at-arms that she was trying to hide something. But she was not; she was simply embarrassed about the convict writing to her. She didn't even know he was in the penitentiary. It was sheer luck Adrianne Hess missed the last letter that contained Josephine's picture in it. She knew if MA1 Donaldson knew the man was an inmate, and she was sure he did, it would look bad for her. Surely the navy would want to know why a convict was in contact with a wave of the United States Navy. She said, "Hospital Corpsman Hess stole those letters from my bottom drawer the same day she took the four dollars. I thought you were only interested in the money she took; something of value. Those letters are of no value to me. I don't even know the person who wrote them." She babbled on; determined to tell all that was flooding her mind. "My sister gave him my address, pretending to be me, so he wrote me, thinking I was my sister, Josephine. That is the only reason I received the letters. I never heard of this person until he sent the letters, thinking I was Josephine. That's the honest truth." She wanted to cry, but she held the tears at bay.

The master-at-arms scratched his forehead as he stared at her. "And that's all you know about this man?" he asked.

"Yes. I've told you everything I know. I didn't know you were interested in the letters. If I knew that, it would have been the first thing I'd have mentioned. Honest."

The man bent down and retrieved a handful of letters from his attaché case. There was about twenty letters in his large hand. He tossed them onto the table then said, "Any of these look familiar?"

With both arms she surrounded the letters and pulled them over towards her. She spotted the six letters the man known to her as D. A. Johnson had sent to her. She pulled them out. Strangely enough the remainder of the letters were addressed to HM3 Adrianne Hess. She had to do a double-take when she saw the ones addressed to the hospital corpsman. "Wait a minute, what's going on?" she said, more to herself than anybody else. "This isn't right. Why are these addressed to Adrianne?"

"I was hoping you would have the answer."

"What do you mean? How would I have the answer as to why this jailbird would be writing to Adrianne?"

"Jailbird? I never told you he was a jailbird. How would you know he's been in locked up if you claim you don't know him?"

At that very moment if her sister, Josephine, had been sitting at that table with her and the master-at-arms, she would have strangled her right in front of the law enforcer. She was so angry and it was starting to show in the crackling of her voice. She looked at the man, and asked, "Do you mind if I go and get the one letter that Adrianne overlooked."

"No, I don't mind. Go right ahead," he dismissed the wave with a nod of his head towards the exit.

She rushed to her room, took off the heels and put on her comfortable boondockers. She grabbed the letter Hospital Corpsman Hess failed to steal and quickly returned to the lounge. She thought it strange that no one else was detained to be interrogated by the master-at-arms. Quickly she lean in towards the quarterdeck duty officer and asked, "Am I the last person for this interrogation?" Petty Officer Brendon nodded to affirm that she was. Julia felt sick. She shook it off and then returned to her seat and gave the letter to the master-at-arms. He examines the envelope and then read the short letter, then looked at the photo of Josephine.

What he said next exacerbated the wave. "How do I know you didn't take your picture out and replace it with a photograph of your sister?"

"I would never do such a thing. This is the truth I have told you." She picked up the six letters that Adrianne stole from her and flipped over the first one she had ever received from him. It was very noticeable because it was the only one crumpled up. "See, this is the first one I received from him. I opened it and read it," she explained. "I knew I didn't know him so I threw it away, my friend retrieved it and made me write this notation on it." She pointed to the writing on the back. It read: **I do not know this person, Julia Holton Oct 7, 1966**. Julia picked out all of other letters he'd mailed to her, flipped them over and pointed to MA1 Donaldson her notations on the back of each of them. **I refuse to open this letter / I don't know this person – Julia Holton**. Each dated the day she received them. But the letters were opened, and she figured Adrianne Hess must have opened and read the contents of each one.

"We know that your letters were stolen by HM3 Hess. Do you know why she would steal these letters from you?"

"No, I don't. You should ask Adrianne Hess what would make her take the letters. Who would want to steal someone else's mail? I just don't understand it. Go ask Adrianne why she would want them; because I can't answer that question."

The thick-neck enforcer pulled out a letter and showed it to SA Holton. "Read it," he ordered.

She quickly read the brief letter. It was a letter the con sent to Adrianne. Basically, he thanked her for letting him know that Jewels, which was a nickname he had given Julia, had been shipped out to another duty station. He also thanked her for writing to him since Julia was no longer available. She placed the letter back into the pile of D. A. Johnson's letters to Adrianne Hess. "I see; she wanted this guy for herself. So, if you knew all of that, then why am I being questioned? Why aren't you interrogating Adrianne about all of the thefts, and why she is getting involved with this convict? I never wrote him. It looks like from all of the letters she has received from him, she's been pretty busy winning him over." In a defensive demeanor she added, "You need to be talking with Adrianne. Not me."

The master-at-arms said, "I wish I could, SA Holton. I wish I could ask HM3 Adrianne Hess. But you see, I can't."

"But I don't understand why you can't." Julia was getting concerned, she did not know what would keep the investigation from being place into the lap of the main suspect. Why were they running her through the wringer?

"The fact of the matter SA Holton, HM3 Adrianne Hess was found murdered in Niagara Falls, New York. We have a feeling she was lured to Niagara Falls by this D. A. Johnson person."

"You mean she was murdered? Dead? How? Why would anyone kill her?" She could feel the tears welling in her eyes and there was no holding them back. They dropped down onto her cheeks and she felt weak and faint. She stared at the master-at-arms, tried to get herself together, but she could not. Her tears were dropping onto her hand. The master-at-arms quickly removed the letters away before the tears fell onto what was now considered evidence. The investigating officer wanted to console her but he was steadfast. He reached into his attaché case and pulled out two tissues for the young lady. He felt bad for the wave but it was not his concern to show sorrow for her. He was order to go to the WAVES Barrack to investigate, not so much the theft, but the murder of one of their own.

With a little touch of compassion he explained. "We think she got herself involved with this D. A. Johnson through the letters he wrote to you. She saw the man as a potential husband so she stole money and sent it to him. And when he managed to break out of prison, he promised her marriage and a honeymoon in Niagara Falls. It's in this letter." The master at arms pointed the envelope to her. "What we thought was an AWOL investigation, has turned out to be a murder investigation when the authorities of Niagara Falls, New York contacted us." He continued on. "I don't know what made you decide not to write this guy, but it's a good thing you made that choice not to. Too bad for HM3 Hess. Writing to the convict ended up costing the lady her life." With Julia still sniffling, MA Donaldson dismissed her. The interrogation was over. She left the lounge area and walked across the quarterdeck with her head bowed. She was sobbing hard as she made it back to her room. Her heart was saddened. Though she did not really know Adrianne Hess, she felt deflated. She was so disheartened that Adrianne stole the letters.

CHAPTER 33 -- EM CLUB

That evening, word roamed around the barrack like ivy on an abandon brick building. Most of the waves found out through different sources about Adrianne Hess' murdered. When the information got to Jasmine, Natalie, Lucy and Carolyn they came to their friend's room to find out what happened. Through the opaque glass, Julia could tell it was her friends, and though she did not want to let them in, she climbed out of her bed and unlocked the door. They visited her and wanted to hear the whole sordid story, but Julia was drained and all she could do was sit on her bed while her friends clamored on with their versions as to why Adrianne met her demise. When she could not take the ladies visit any longer she excused herself and laid on her bed. Natalie, Lucy and Carolyn sat on the other bed which Julia had made to look like a couch; while Jasmine sat in the chair at the desk. The ladies talked softly amongst themselves and when they were sure she was asleep, they quietly left and headed for the mess hall.

An hour passed and Julia awoke from her stress-induced sleep. She saw Virginia sitting at her desk. She was going over the course for her next advance pay grade for photographer's mate, second class. "How long have you been here?" Julia asked as she let out an uncovered yawn.

"About a half an hour; that's all. I didn't want to wake you so I busied myself with studying for the exam." She lifted the thick correspondence book and showed it to Julia. "I brought my course with me just in case you felt like company, but just didn't want to talk. I can understand if you don't." Virginia noticed her friend still looked tired, she added. "I can come back tomorrow."

"No, no. I'm okay." Julia got up and stretched, letting out another yawn, covering her mouth as she did so. "As a matter of fact, I was hoping you would stop by. I'm having one heck of a time and I don't know what to do about this Adrianne Hess thing."

"And why are you having a time with this, Julia? Why? What happened to Adrianne Hess has nothing to do with you. This is something she brought upon herself." Virginia forced herself to breathe. She did not want to come across as being tough with Julia at this tender time. She continued on in the most caring voice she could muster up. "Julia, are you going to beat yourself up forever over this matter? This is not your fault and it's up to you to come to terms with that." Virginia gently touched her friend's shoulder; she added, "You are wallowing in pain because of choices that Adrianne made. She paid for her actions with her life; she should never have stolen those letters." Virginia was always there whenever Julia needed her and this day Julia required her presence even more. Knowing Julia needed to stop wallowing in the blame-game she insisted the lady get out of her uniform and into civilian clothes. "You're getting dressed, and we're going to the EM Club tonight. You don't have to be at work tomorrow; it's Friday night and I'm sure they've got a band playing at the Enlisted Men's Club. So get yourself ready; I'll be back in fifteen minutes." Virginia went topside to her room, dropped off her correspondence book then quickly got herself ready to go to the EM Club with her friend.

~ ~ ~

Virginia knew her friend loved dancing and she figured it was one sure way of getting her mind off of Adrianne's death.

There was always some sailor at the club looking for a wave or military dependent woman to dance with. No sooner than Virginia and Julia walked into the door, Julia's mood changed for the better. Almost immediately they both were grabbed by anxious care-free sailors. After the first dance Virginia left the dance floor and found a table for them. Julia finished the second dance then went to their table to catch her breath. Virginia said, "Here, drink this." It was a purple drink and Julia began laughing. "Why are you laughing?"

"I've never seen a purple drink served in a night club before. What is this, Kool-Aid?" She took a sip of the sweet drink then put the tall glass down.

"It's a Singapore Sling."

Julia took a sip of the drink, then said, "Oh my goodness; it's delicious."

As she was drinking the exotic drink a sailor came to their table. He was rather tall and had freckles which dotted his pale face. His hair was so red, Julia was quite sure he was of Irish decent. Though he was not in uniform both ladies knew he was a sailor they'd seen in the mess hall from time to time. He acknowledged Virginia, but stood next to Julia's chair. He bent down towards her ear and shouted loudly over the band's music so she could hear him. "Hi, my name is Stephen." He extended his hand and Julia glanced over at Virginia. Julia raised her eyebrow and made a quick grimace at her friend.

Virginia, knowing Julia was at a loss of words, shouted; "Julia, don't just leave the man with his hand hanging in the air; go ahead and shake it."

Julia gave Virginia a look that said *but why is he approaching me?* She turned and looked up into Stephen's face. Julia smiled; then said, "Hello Stephen, my name is Julia." She shook the sailor's hand, but before she could retrieve her hand, he lifted it to his lips and kissed it. Virginia smiled; but Julia was shocked.

Stephen looked into her eyes, then asked, "Would you like to dance with my brother."

Julia couldn't understand why he was asking her to dance with his brother. She'd just left the dance floor, but being cordial to the man, she said, "Sure, I'd love to."

Julia looked at Virginia; she gave her friend a quizzical smile. Julia thought the sailor should be asking Virginia to dance with his brother; but for some odd reason he asked her. She looked around for the man's brother. He was nowhere in sight. When she asked Stephen where was his brother, the man told her he was sitting at the bar. Virginia gave her a look of approval and Julia got up from the table, took a long swig of her drink, then followed the sailor through the crowded club towards the bar area. His brother was sitting on the bar stool. Stephen used the strength of his arms and hands to pick his brother up around the man's torso to hold onto him. It was only then Julia noticed in the darkness of the club that Stephen's brother didn't have any legs. Stephen said, "Julia, this is my brother, Theodore." He looked at his brother and said, "Theodore, this is Julia. Isn't she pretty?" As Theodore agreed the wave was indeed nice-looking, he extended his hand to shake hers. After he shook her hand, he lifted it to his lips and kissed the back of it. Stephen bent towards Julia's ear, "He was a paratrooper. He lost his legs doing a night jump with his unit last year in Vietnam. I hope you don't mind dancing with the both of us." So the three of them headed towards the dance floor and danced to Mitch Ryder and the Detroit Wheelers', *Sock It To Me Baby*. Stephen held his legless brother in his arms and the three of them dance around the floor. They were the only three on the dance floor. None of them cared about the eyes that were upon them. When the next song came on, Stephen, still holding onto his brother, leaned over and said, "Theodore wants to dance by himself with you. Do you mind dancing alone with my brother? You can't hold him; he's too heavy." He continued to explain, "I can put him down on the dance floor and all you have to do is hold his hands while the both of you dance in one spot."

"Sure." She looked at Theodore, and said, "Are you ready, Theodore?"

"You bet," he happily said.

"Okay, then let's dance." And when the band played The Capitols', *Cool Jerk* they danced to the beat. A smile was on Theodore's face while Julia danced with him; he was very elated. Knowing Theodore was happy dancing with her, made Julia happy too.

When the dance was over, Theodore extended his hand, shook hers, and then kissed the back of it again. He said, "Thank you Julia; you dance so divinely. Most of the ladies see that I have no legs and it frightens them away. Thank you for being so kind." He placed his other hand on top of hers, then added; "You are really someone special." And though Julia didn't plan on doing so, something in her soul made her bend down and kiss the disabled veteran on his cheek. He gave her a new perspective on life. Because even though he had no lower extremities, he had heart; heart to keep on living in spite of it all.

Stephen returned to the dance floor and picked up his brother. He asked, "Theodore, how did you like dancing with Julia? She's a good dancer, isn't she?"

"I loved dancing with you, Julia. And my brother is right, you're a great dancer." The brothers looked so happy after their dance with Julia. Not only had she brightened up their evening; but her evening as well had been enriched.

Julia walked back to the barstool with the brothers. When Stephen put Theodore back on his seat, he said to his brother, "Now don't you go anywhere," and the two of them laughed at the joke. Julia, unsure if she should laugh or not, just smiled. As Stephen walked Julia back to her table, he acknowledged, "You are a godsend. I am so happy you were here tonight. Rarely can I get him to dance with the ladies. Says, he's not normal and can't take the pitiful stares the women lay on him. But when he saw you on the dance floor, for some reason he felt compelled to have me ask you to dance with him." Stephen chuckled to himself, then added. "I can see why; Julia, you look so happy when you're dancing. And seeing that, made Theodore want to be in your presence."

"Aww, thanks Stephen."

"No, thank you for making my brother feel normal for just that one instance." When they reached Julia's table, the sailor pulled the seat out for her to sit, then took her hand and planted another kissed on the back of it. The sailor nodded at Virginia, then turned and walked away.

"Wow, two kisses on the hand? What chivalry," Virginia acknowledged.

"Actually, four. His brother, Theodore, gave me a kiss on the hand, twice."

"Boy, with Stephen being so tall and good-looking, I can only imagine what his brother looks like."

"He's a real trooper, Virginia. A real trooper." She took a sip of her drink and said a quiet prayer for Theodore, praying the best she could pray for the man and his brother. She was happy Stephen approached her to dance with his veteran brother; and she was even happier Virginia insisted she come to the club tonight.

~ ~ ~

As the days passed Julia found herself re-thinking Adrianne's death. The feeling of blame tried to resurface, throwing Julia's life a little bit out of synch again. The more Virginia tried to counsel Julia, the more Julia tried to rationalize the wave's death. Why did Adrianne have to be murdered because of the convict's correspondence? She felt her sister made a grave mistake using her address to impress the prisoner. A military woman was dead, in part, because of her sister's lack of common sense. If Josephine hadn't used her name and address, there wouldn't have been any letters for Adrianne Hess to steal and communicate with the convict. Then she blamed herself for the death of Adrianne. She threw the first letter into the trash bin, but Virginia told her to keep the letter and to make a notation on the back of it. Consequently, she kept all of his following mail; never opening any of them. Always she would write a notation on the back, sign, date and stored them in her bottom drawer. Had she followed her own mind and thrown them all away, Adrianne Hess would be alive. So in a sense maybe it was Virginia's fault as well. The sadness was overwhelming. Julia shook her head. She could go on and on about who was the blame for the wave's murder. It would still come back to D. A. Johnson, the man who killed Adrianne Hess, as being responsible for her death; and the older wave's critical bad choice of stealing the letters. Virginia had simply given Julia advice for her own safety. How would she, or anyone for that matter, know the desperate Adrianne would steal the letters and contact the man?

~ ~ ~

Still, with all that was going on in Julia's mind, she did not want Mitchell involved with the nucleus of her strange life. There was no way she would bring him into something so bad. Julia would not have him worrying about her problems; not at all. It was enough that she had to deal with them.

The correspondence resumed between Mitchell and Julia. Often Mitchell wanted to talk to Julia on the telephone, and she as well wanted to hear his voice. They had even written to one another about making phone calls. But Julia, always conscience about the cost of long distance phone calls, advised Mitchell she thought it would be economical for them to continue their communication strictly through the written word. They both knew it would be hard for them to engage in a three minute conversation which could easily cost them twenty dollars, maybe more.

Mid April 1967, Julia wrote to Mitchell and mentioned on April 20th she would be nineteen years old. Her friends were taking her out to celebrate at their favorite club, the Dance Spot. The four friends felt she needed to get herself out of the barrack. When she received the next letter from Mitchell she was surprised he informed her his birthday was also in the month of April as well. In fact it had already passed. He had turned twenty-four on April 3rd. Julia thought it was pretty ironic their birthdays were in the same month. Mitchell, of course, was not surprised, especially when Julia told him that his birthday happens to fall upon her one of her brother's birthday.

PART SEVEN

CHAPTER 34 -- BUS DRIVER

Julia found being with her friends was interesting. Sure, it was fun when they all got together to go to the Dance Spot, or the Enlisted Men's Club if there was a pretty good band playing. But often during those times she'd wish Mitchell was with her or somewhere close by. And often Jasmine would complain when Julia was out with them in her *I miss Mitchell* mood. One evening Julia was in that state of mind when she was out with the waves. She was a kill-joy for Jasmine, and the wave let her know it.

"Snap out of it. How are you going to miss somebody you don't even know? Haven't even talked with him, except for that one time on the bus." She shook her head, then asked "Did you kiss him on the bus?"

"No, Jasmine; of course not."

"Did y'all do it in the bathroom on the Greyhound?"

"Ouuu! Don't be ridiculous."

"Ridiculous, Julia, is what you're being. So like I was saying, how are you going to miss somebody you don't even know? You've talked to him for maybe an hour and a half on a fuckin' bus ride. You've never kissed him, you ain't screwed him, and you're asking me not to be ridiculous? Give me a fuckin' break."

Julia could never figure out Jasmine's way of thinking. Often when the other waves in the group invited Julia to go out with them she would go if Jasmine was occupied with some other venture. But if she knew for sure the brash wave was going to be in their company, sometimes she would decline.

~ ~ ~

One day after work Julia got onto Jim's bus. She sat right behind the driver. He was full of conversation about his son. "Yeah, that there Jeremiah, that boy is talkin' about goin' to college to be a doctor. Ain't that somethin'?"

Julia knew Jim was only talking to her to be polite. Many times he tried to hold a conversation with the wave, and many times she gave him the impression she did not want to talk to him. Today was no different; but rather than ignore the old man, Julia tried to show an interest in what Jim was talking about. "Wow, Jim. You've got to be very proud of him. What kind of doctor is he going to be; do you know?" Julia asked him, hoping he would make his answer brief.

"One of them baby doctor's, you know, o-ber-tischi-gan, pee-di-tricks, or was it gyno-coli-gister? Aww shoot, I don't know how to pronounce them big fancy words. Anyway Miss Julia, that's what he's gonna be. A baby doctor. Yep, a baby doctor, plain and simple. Now I know what a baby doctor is, just don't know all them big long words them doctors be using to call it what it is."

"Congratulations, Jim. I know your wife is excited."

"Yeah, she's pretty excited, but she'd be more excited if the boy jist got married and gave her some grandbabies. You know what I mean? That would make her real happy. Is yo' mama like that, gal; always askin' fo' grandbabies?"

"No sir, I can't say that she is."

"Humm, I see." He waited for Julia to expand on her statement, but the wave said nothing more. As Jim continued driving the bus Julia found herself happy he hadn't tried to continue on with the conversation; even happier when the bus rolled its way onto the street of the barrack.

~ ~ ~

Jim was a happy-go-lucky soul. He liked being the bus driver on the naval air station. He'd been employed for over fifteen years as the driver; he loved his job. And he treasured most all of the people he met. He was a friendly old man. Even the crudest sailor or nastiest wave couldn't put a damper on his day; he figured their problems were their problems. He'd always chalk up any of his rider's mean mood as *they must have had a bad day*. Rarely would you hear him say a thing about the person in a derogatory light. And it wasn't beneath him to do all he could to figure out what made a particular passenger tick; even if it meant getting information from one of his riders. He loved to have discussions going on with the sailors and waves who rode his bus. He was an older light-brown man with short grey hair. The eyeglasses he wore made him appear distinguished. The man thought of himself as a purveyor of knowledge and he proudly doled it out to the individuals he took a liking to. Many times he saw Julia, on his bus, and often he tried to be friendly with the young wave, but she barely would chat with him. Once, when Jasmine and Natalie were the only ones riding his bus he asked, "Why is yo' friend, you know, that skinny wave, Miss Julia, so quiet?"

"She just is, Jim. She do have a boyfriend, though. Some army guy she seems to think is gonna marry her," Natalie offered.

Jim gave a chuckle, "No kiddin' an army man, huh? That's a new one; I got to say that is a first. I done seen a lot of you young waves come and go. Many with marriage. But a whole lot with babies and no marriage. You know why?"

Jasmine and Natalie already knew the answer but Jasmine thought she'd humor the old man, so she asked, "Why, Jim?"

"Gal, its 'cause they done went and got themselves put in a trick bag by some good-fo'-nothin' sailor; that's why? Me, I'm a marine; loyal and true. Well anyways, a retired marine."

"You were in the marine?" Natalie asked.

"That's right, gal. You got an old retired jarhead shuttlin' y'all to and fro," he laughed at himself. "Anyways, what I'm gettin' at, is this; I ain't never seen one of y'all waves marryin' no army man. Why, that's real different."

Jasmine spoke, "Well, *Miss Julia* is real different. That's for damn sure. She says he wants to marry her. Me? I'll believe it when I see it. He just don't look like the type to marry somebody like her."

Natalie asked, "Why you say that Jasmine?"

"'Cause he don't. You saw his picture, Natalie. That white soldier only got one thing on his mind, and you can believe it ain't marriage. It's about getting himself a taste of that brown sugar."

Jim said, "Wait a dog-gone minute. You sayin' this here army guy ain't even colored."

"He don't look colored to me, and Julia can't even tell you what he is. She just told us he's a nice guy," Natalie said. "Like that's supposed to tell us what race he is."

Jasmine burst in, "Well shit, she can say he's a nice man all she wants. But I'm telling you, he may be a nice guy to Julia, but to me, he's a nice-and-white guy. Aww, now don't get me wrong. It ain't like I would kick him out of bed." She laughed. She most often had one thing on her mind, sex. She had even admitted she thought people should be more opened about sex. So it was of no surprise to Natalie when Jasmine added, "Hey, that's why I'm happy they didn't make me an officer. I'd have to exhibit that conduct-becoming-of-an-officer shit. Where's the fun in that?"

Jim pulled the bus onto the road of the WAVES Barrack. "Well look, you ladies have yo'self a good evening. I'll see you bright and early, 0630, tomorrow morning." He opened the door and let the waves off and sat a moment to watch them as they headed down the long walkway. He noticed how Jasmine switched as she walked, compared to Natalie's regular marching stride. When he saw them make it to the barrack's door, he pulled off. They were his last run of the evening; he couldn't wait to get home to his wife.

CHAPTER 35 -- LIBERAL WAVE

Jasmine had a controversial way of viewing the world from a woman's point of view. She was way ahead of her time. Her philosophy was that men and women were meant to pleasure, to learn and grown from one another, no matter what the experience may be. She scuffed at the waves who would go out and have sex with the sailors or the civilian men of Lexington Park, and then complain that the guy wasn't interested in her anymore. "Did you want to have sex with him?" she'd ask them. And when they admit they did, her unsympathetic answer would be, "Then what are you bitchin' for? He's only being a man; he's not looking for anything but sex from you. You gave him sex, he gave you sex so why the long face? Build a fuckin' bridge and get over it." But sometimes that was not reason enough for the waves to understand her logic; and Jasmine would have to go a bit farther into her explanation. "Look, if he wants to do it again and so do you, then fine. But don't go crying 'cause he's not calling you anymore. Honey, he's just doing what a man does, and you're doing what a woman does. It's call having sex. It's not called love, it's not called relationship, it's not called engagement and it sure the hell ain't called marriage. If that were the case, then I would have been a bigamist many times over. I don't know why women got to put it in their heads having sex equals having a relationship. One ain't got a fuckin' thing to do with the other. He's getting something out of it, and so are you."

Many months rolled by and still Julia and Mitchell were committing their love to one another onto fancy and scented writing paper. Natalie met a sailor on the base that she decided she was in love with and it was the same with Carolyn. Jasmine found herself going to the Dance Spot as a fifth wheel whenever she travelled with the two waves and their boyfriends.

One day in the lounge she challenged them. "Why do y'all feel the need to saddle yourselves with one of these sailors?"

Carolyn, who was always happy, answered, "Me, I just love myself some Ernest. He's the guy for me; that's why I'm with him." Jasmine shook her head and thought what a waste of her time trying to explain anything to Carolyn. She was just as thick in the head as Julia.

"What about you, Natalie? Why is it you feel the need to strap yourself onto Donald? Is it just because he's got a nice-looking car?"

Natalie was not about to let Jasmine accuse her of being the type of girl who looked for material gain. With arrogance in her voice, she explained, "Jasmine, Donald loves me. He really does and I love him. And if you didn't hop from sailor to civilian and back to sailor again then you would know what it feels like to have someone in love with you." Natalie hadn't meant for the words to come out as harsh and loud as they did, but she knew she was telling her friend the truth. And because she was annoyed with Jasmine, her voiced opinion caught the attention of the other waves and their guest in the lounge area. But Natalie didn't care who heard what she said. So when the other waves in the lounge looked in her direction, she snubbed off their stares. She felt insulted her friend would say such a thing about her. Natalie witnessed Jasmine putting down Julia when it came to her love for Mitchell. She was not going to let her get away with one iota of being nasty to her because she had been fortunate enough to find a good man who loved her. If Jasmine didn't have a true love of her own, then that was alright. Natalie just didn't think she should be knocking everyone else who did.

Jasmine saw Natalie shaking her head as though she was disgusted with her. But it was a fact that Natalie hit a nerve with the liberal wave. Jasmine shot an angry look at the small feisty wave, then said in a scorched tone, "What you trying to do, loud-talk me; is that it?" Natalie said nothing. Then Jasmine added the last piece of her thoughts about the whole matter, "You and Carolyn are as pitiful as that idiot, Julia. She's sitting in her damn room writing fuckin' love letters to some damn soldier she probably ain't ever gonna meet again. And you two dumb asses are sitting around in this damn lounge because you believe your boyfriends got duty tonight." She rolled her eyes. "Forget y'all. I'm catching me a cab and going to the Dance Spot. Maybe I'll even say hello to your boyfriends while they're hanging out with their civilian women." She stormed out of the lounge.

Jasmine was use to going out with any of the sailors who asked her. And if they didn't pursue her, it wasn't beneath her to ask them out. Often she'd tell her friends, "This is the 1960's heading straight for the 70's. Nobody's into that old fashion, *Wait until the man call you*, stuff anymore. At least I ain't. It's too damn many men on this base and out there on the beach to be passing up." But this night was different. Jasmine did not have a date lined up which was no big deal for her. She would simply go to the club by herself and if she got a chance to be with a man then that would be good. If she couldn't find someone, then it was no big deal to her; she could always come home and pleasure herself.

~ ~ ~

Jasmine never felt bad about her beliefs; nor did she care about people's concerns of her way of thinking. She left Augusta, Georgia and never looked back. Yes, she had been to college, but it was not easy for her. The young lady got herself caught up in some fool of a man's web. And because of it, she made a decision to cut her loss.

Jasmine started college two years after she had graduated high school by the constant prodding of her parents. Though she got a late start at college, she didn't have a problem picking up the pace once she attended. But then her young professor, by the name of Professor Nigel Benson, took an interest in her; and it was not for her educational merit. When he came on to her, she did not discourage him. Jasmine experienced a sexual and emotional ride with the professor.

Many times Nigel would give her promises of marriage throughout her first year of college. And she knew with her drive, success was not far from her grasp. Through their pillow talk he promised her that he would make sure she passed his classes, she was staunched about making it through the course on her own. How was she going to go into the medical field if she let Professor Benson fudge her grades? From ninth grade to the twelfth grade Jasmine always maintained a 3.0 – 4.0 average. She came from a long line of educators, her father was a principal of a school and her mother was a home economics teacher. Both sets of grandparents had been elementary school teachers. So it was expected for Jasmine to succeed; if not in the educational field, in some field of humanitarian. When she graduated high school she worked for two years in different hospitals. When she realized she was not going any farther than a patient transporter without the college education, she decided to enroll into community college at the age of nineteen years old.

When she enrolled into the college her plan was to obtain her associates degree and continuing on for her nursing degree. But somewhere between the course with the young professor's flirting eyes and her study time, she got off track.

All through Jasmine's first year of college, Nigel pursued Jasmine relentlessly, and she was happy to have him do so because, not only did they both look beautiful when they were slipping around together, but she knew they would be a power couple once they married. Nigel explained to her that she must keep their love a secret. He would surely be fired if word got out he was in love with a student. She promised she would let none of the other professors nor students know.

Many nights in their stolen rendezvous the young man promised Jasmine all sorts of great things that would happen for her as soon as she completed all of her education. To prove he was sincere, about marrying her, he even let her take him home to meet her parents. But they were not impressed. When his visit with them was over and he left for the evening, her mother and father lit into her.

"Jasmine, this is your professor. Don't you know what he is doing is unethical? He's not to have any compromising involvement with any of his students," her father warned. "He could end up fired from the college if this gets out. You know this is wrong and you shouldn't be doing it; send him on his way." She never liked being told by her parents what she should or shouldn't do with her life. And being determined to prove them wrong, she moved out of her parents' house and in with a friend. The reason she could not move in with Nigel, according to him, was because his handicapped brother, Pierre, was living with him. He felt there was no room in his small apartment, and then there was the visiting nurse. But a week before the end of her first year she discovered she was pregnant, and told him so. She thought he would do the right thing and marry her when she told him she was with child. Where was the love, where was the ring and the marriage? When she finally figured he was avoiding her, she knew he didn't have a commitment to stand in her corner.

Through a friend that worked in the personnel office of the college she managed to discreetly obtain Nigel's home address and his telephone number. Jasmine dialed it. When she heard a woman's voice at the other end of the receiver she did not worry. She knew it was the nurse for his little handicapped brother. In a professional voice, she said, "Hello, I'm calling from the book department of Augusta Community College. Is Professor Nigel Benson available?"

The lady answered, "This is his wife. He's not here; he should be at the college teaching summer school biology. Have you checked his classroom? He's there, I'm sure."

Jasmine contained herself. In her mind, she thought, *Wife, he's got a fuckin' wife? I can't believe this shit.* Her professional voice returned. "Oh no, I haven't; his wall chart of the human anatomy has arrived. I'll have him paged; Thank you." She immediately hung up before the woman could say anything else.

She spoke out loud, "*That son-of-a-bitch. If I had known he was married I never would have had a damn thing to do with him. How dare him string me along. He never had any intention of marrying me; his ass is already married.*" She didn't have the heart to tell her parents. The last thing she wanted to hear was how wrong it was for her to take up with the professor in the first place. She drove her beat-up jalopy over to the college. Never had she thought he was teaching summer courses. Nigel had told her that he was not working for the summer. He said he was taking the summer off to spend more time with his invalid brother. Now she had come to realize it was just to keep her away from him. Had he informed her he was teaching summer classes, he knew she would have signed on for summer courses. She was furious; and now she was pregnant. She wheeled the car into the college parking lot. Her campus parking sticker was expired but still she would take her chance that security would not spot her. She rode around until she found his car; then she parked where she could see him approach his car at the end of his workday.

She listened to the radio and her head was spinning from her thoughts rattling around. As she was listening to The Temptation's *The Way You Do the Things You Do*, she spotted Nigel walking to his car. With him was a cute little brown teenager who looked to be a seventeen year-old. He was laughing and the college student smiled and flipped her long black locks, and then smoothing them out by combing the long strands with her fingers. A tinged of jealously seeped into Jasmine's veins. Before she knew it she jumped out of her car and ran over to Nigel and the pretty teenager. "So, what the fuck is this, Nigel?" she angrily asked. "I thought you and I were going to get married. But we can't get married can we Nigel? BECAUSE YOU'RE ALREADY FUCKIN' MARRIED; YOU BASTARD."

Nigel stood in front of the young college student, as to shield her from the crazy woman. "What are you talking about Jasmine? I never told you I would marry you."

"Well, I'll just be damn. You mean you've just been stringing me along?" She shook her head in disbelief. Then she looked over at the young girl and spurted, "I hope he's not stringing you along too, honey. Just be careful with this professor. He's a fuckin' jerk; a married fuckin' jerk at that. He'll lead you into thinking he's all interested in you, but he's not."

The girl looked at Jasmine. She looked at Nigel with a complex scowl about her face. Then, as it finally sank into her head, she realized Nigel had made a fool of her too. The pretty teenager gave Nigel an incredulous stare, then stormed away from him and went straight towards Jasmine. She said, "Thank you for telling me. I thought it was strange that he took an interest in me. I just thought I was his favorite pupil because I'm an A-average student."

"Yeah, well that's how the son-of-a-bitch snagged me into his web. Made me think I was something special in his class; and I, like a fool fell for it." She placed her hands on the girl's shoulders, looked into her eyes and said, "You just be careful; you can't trust anything he says. He is a good fuck though; that's all I got to say." She glanced him up and down then looked back at the girl; "That's about all he is too; a good fuck, because you'll have no future with him." She left the girl standing bewildered as she headed back towards her car. She pulled out of the parking lot knowing what she must to do. There was no sense in her going through a full term with a baby who would have no father in its life. She would have the pregnancy terminated.

Jasmine searched feverishly to find someone who could help her. When she confided in one of her old high school friend about her dilemma, the girl was quick to direct her to Mama Lulu. The old woman's specialty was helping women out of their condition, even though it was against the law to do so. Since Jasmine was early in the pregnancy Mama Lulu did not have to use the barbaric coat-hanger routine on Jasmine. She mixed a special spice and medication into piping hot water and made her drink it down without stopping. Instantly Jasmine obtained the result she wanted; no more Nigel, no more baby.

~ ~ ~

Jasmine remembered seeing the army, navy, and air force recruiting officers at the community college last winter. Now she wished she had picked up one of those brochures. She thought long and hard on her choices and decided navy as her best option so she went downtown to the recruiting office. When the naval recruiting officer heard she had been to college, he told her there was a possibility the navy might make her an officer if she enlisted. She was happy. She dodged a bullet with the professor and now she could get herself back on the right track. However, once interviewed she discovered she had to have an associates degree before entering Officer Candidate School. With only one year of college, Jasmine was informed she would have to be sent to boot camp for the enlisted personnel instead. *Fuck it,* she thought, *Officer? Enlisted? What the fuck do I care. Just as long as I get the hell as far away from Nigel's ass as I can get.*

Once she graduated boot camp she was assigned to Naval Station Norfolk; a year later she was transferred to Patuxent River Naval Air Station. At both duty stations she was much wiser about men. Nigel taught her a valuable lesson. She loved sex and she loved men. She would make sure she was protected whenever she engaged in sex with them and she planned on having her way with them whenever she wanted.

~ ~ ~

So as the cab drove Jasmine to the Dance Spot she didn't feel shameful of what she said to Natalie or Carolyn. They were the fools; not her. You couldn't catch her not going out on the town because a boyfriend told her he was on duty. She was happy she was not wired the same way as the waves were. She was only four years older than they. She wondered if they would always be so dense when it came to men. Jasmine was going out to drink and find some man to have sex with and nobody could make her feel bad about it. She was going to live her life the way she saw fit; did she care about what people whispered behind her back? No. She learned from a great teacher; a professor. Professor Nigel Benson. And because of him she felt proud of herself. She was Jasmine Mamie Fredrick and Jasmine Mamie Fredrick did whatever she liked, with no apologies.

PART EIGHT

CHAPTER 36 -- RING SIZE

It was a beautiful day when Julia received the letter from Mitchell. He sent her an updated photograph of himself and a long letter. When the letter arrived at her work site, she was happy YN2 Cross was on vacation and YN2 Hurley delivered the mail at her desk with no editorial regarding the letter.

When she slipped away on her break she sat in the ladies' lounge and read his letter. It read:

PFC Mitchell Lauers
17 Long Range Recon Patrol
Gibbs Concern
APO AE 09008

July 30, 1967

My Dear Sweet Julia,

I am hoping this letter is finding you very well and happy. I want you to know how lonesome I am over here on my post. Sometimes I want to call and talk to you, but I know you have a concern over the expense this will cause for us. That is why I write to you as often as I can.

We had a mass jump last week. It is an array of 500 to 1000 paratroopers, trucks and tanks being dropped from three planes. It is a beautiful exhibition put on for the sole purpose to display to our top brass. We had no injuries, which is always a blessing.

I so want to be with you; and once I have completed my two-year stint in this army, I can plan our life together. (Though I do that in my head already). I daydream about us whenever there is a lull in my schedule. God, you don't know how much I need you. I wish I could be next to you this very moment.

I am hoping you are taking care of yourself for me. I cannot be right there to protect you, so please be mindful of everything you do. God has sent you to me and I do not want anything to happen to you.

If you will do me a big favor, sweetheart, I would certainly appreciate it. I need for you go to a jeweler and have your ring finger sized. There are beautiful rings here in Germany and I would like to purchase your engagement ring and our wedding bands before I am shipped from Germany. Can you please do that for me, my love? I don't want there to be any misunderstanding by any man, that you have been taken. You are my woman, and I want everyone to know this. It has been something that I've been thinking about for such a long time. Once I have your ring size I can purchase your engagement ring and ship it *off to you. I only wish I could be there to place it on your finger.*

Please take care of yourself and remember that I love you deeply.

With all my love,

Your man, Mitchell Lauers

Julia was concerned. As much as she loved Mitchell, she was so afraid of receiving an engagement ring from him. She knew she could not put this off, but she was too wearied to do what Mitchell wanted her to do. When she was unsure of anything she'd drag her feet until she could figure out what should be done. Mitchell now wanted to purchase their rings. She was both excited and nervous at the same time. Now Mitchell wanted to take their love to a brand new level. She knew he was serious about the sizing of her finger. She could not risk losing the soldier again because of her failure to comply with his request. But why did he want to move so fast with their relationship? Why did he want to give her a ring? His latest request had her head spinning. She had to get herself home; it was taking forever for the clock to tick away for 1630 hour.

~ ~ ~

Finally, her workday was over and before Julia knew it she was walking down the pavement towards the WAVES Barrack. When she arrived onto the quarterdeck, the blonde, curly haired duty officer, asked, "Are you Seaman Apprentice Holton."

"Yes, I am."

"I have a note for you, SA Holton." Julia stood steadfast on the quarterdeck as the wave on duty reach inside of her desk drawer, retrieved the piece of paper then handed it over.

"Thank you." Julia took the note and left the quarterdeck. Once inside of her room she opened it up. It was from Virginia. It read: *Meet me at the Enlisted Men's Club at 1930 this evening. Very Important. Virginia Payne* She was thrilled to be in her room. She would meet with her friend at 1930 hours.

~ ~ ~

The band was country western and there were a lot of sailors; most of them with their wives or girlfriends dress in country western garb. When Julia looked over towards the dance floor she notice a banner streamed over the bandstand. It read: COUNTRY & WESTERN NITE – HEE-HAW. A few of the waves showed up for the gala and even they were dressed for the occasion. She thought, *I wonder if Virginia knew the club was featuring a country and western band.* Julia saw Virginia sitting at a table slightly pass the band and dance floor. Anxiously, she rushed over to greet the lady who, thankfully, was not dressed in leather boots or a cowboy hat. "What do you want to drink," Julia asked Virginia. "It's my turn to buy."

"The drinks are on me and the food as well; I've already ordered. We're celebrating some good news that I want to share with you."

"Yes, we are celebrating good news," Julia agreed. "Because I just got some great news today."

"You did," Virginia said with enthusiasm. "I've had my good news for a couple of weeks already. But tonight is the first time I'm able to share it with you. But you go first! What happened to make your day so special?"

"Okay, if you insist, then I will tell you. I don't even know how to start," Julia admitted. "Oh goodness, let me get my thoughts together."

The waitress came to the table with the order of food. On her tray she had two cheeseburgers, two orders of french fries, and sodas for the both of them. "Here you ladies go; that'll be three dollars and twelve cents," she said as she took the food and drinks off of her tray and placed it in front of the ladies. Virginia place four dollars on the empty tray, thanked her then grabbed her cheeseburger and took a big bite out of it. Julia, grabbed a handful of french fries and then took a gulp of her soda. Anxious to tell her friend all about Mitchell, she started off with, "You're not going to believe this Virginia, but my day at work was great today." If it was one thing Virginia knew about Julia, it was the fact that the wave hardly ever talked about her day at the Operations Admin office.

So as Julia continued to chatter about her great day, Virginia interrupted. "So is that the reason we're celebrating?"

"No Virginia. I was having a real good day and then I got a letter, which made my day even better." With her hands clasped together, she dreamily said, "Virginia, I'm in love. I think I'm going to get married."

The look on Virginia's face was worrisome; "Getting married? To whom?"

Julia, with a big smile on her face, reached into her purse and pulled out the letter Mitchell sent to her. Before Julia could explain the letter, Virginia said, "Oh no; oh no;" she put her hamburger down and motioned several times with the crisscrossing of her hands warning Julia to tell her no more. "Please don't tell me the weird man from Attica has taken up writing to you again." Then she hated herself for saying it; the death of Adrianne Hess had slipped her mind. Immediately she apologized, "Oh, I'm sorry Julia, I totally forgot about Adrianne Hess. Honest, I did."

Don't worry about it, Virginia; I'm okay. Really I am. No this is not from the person who you're thinking about. It's from this guy I met on the Greyhound Bus."

"What guy? I don't remember you telling me about any guy you met on a bus. When did you meet him, last week when you and your friends took the baby basket to Renee's house?" Julia remembered going with her friends to Renee's place. Renee was assigned to Pax River. Pregnant within a couple of months, she put in a request chit to be discharged. It was Jasmine's idea for she, Natalie, Carolyn, and Julia to put together a gift basket, take the Greyhound Bus to Baltimore and present it to Renee.

"No Virginia, that's not when I met him. I think it was back in September."

"September? That was a while ago. Funny, you never mentioned anything about this guy to me. Who is he?"

"You see his picture every time you walk into my room. You know; the picture on my mirror?"

Many times Virginia noticed the picture on Julia's mirror, but she never asked Julia who the fellow in the army uniform was. Julia never mentioned anything about the guy and Virginia never questioned it. "Oh, that guy. Yeah, I've seen the picture on your mirror. Never thought he was someone you were interested in. You say you met this fellow on the bus, huh?"

"Yeah, I did. He's a pretty nice guy too. His name is Mitchell."

"Well, I got to give you credit, Julia. At least this letter has a guy attached to it you actually met. That's more than I could say about the last letter you gave me to read." Virginia reached for the letter and was very surprised when Julia would not let go of it. "Aren't you going to let me read it?"

"No Virginia, I just pulled it out to show you." Julia fanned herself with the letter, "Besides, this letter was too hot for *me* to read; don't want to take a chance with you reading it. You might not want to give it back." Julia held tightly onto the letter. "I've been smiling all day, Virginia. Mitchell really loves me; told me so, many, many times in his letters. Even one time told me he'd die for me." She put the letter back into her purse, and when she looked up, she noticed Virginia was giving her an unusual stare. Her friend looked concerned; too concerned. After seconds passed Julia picked up her cheeseburger and took a bite. Virginia still said nothing and this made Julia nervous. Finally, Julia asked her friend, "So what do you think?"

"Julia, it's not what I think; it's what you think and how you want your life to go. Just remember, you've got to be careful. How many times have you've been with this man?"

Embarrassingly, the wave admitted, "I told you, I met him on the bus."

"Are you telling me you met this fellow only once and now you think you're in love with him?"

Julia ate a few of the fries, looked at her friend and answered, "Yes, we've been writing ever since then. I just liked him because he was somebody to write to; but the more we wrote, the more we fell in love with one another. He wants me to be his wife." She ate some more fries. She found Virginia's attitude about the man was not as she thought it would be. She wondered why her friend was acting so unsure of Mitchell's love for her. The need for food escaped Julia so the cheeseburger lay idle on her plate as she twirled a french fry around in the pile of ketchup.

"Julia, are you sure you want to be this man's wife?"

For the first time, since telling Virginia about the letter, a look of unsureness draped Julia's face. Still, nonetheless she said to Virginia, "Yes Virginia. Yes, I am sure. Already, I love him. I think I've always loved him even from our earlier letters. I'm just a little scared." Virginia shook her head and quietly mumbled something beneath her breath, but Julia could only hear part of what she said. *"Careful with him"* is what she heard. Julia asked, "What did you say?"

"I said, *If I were you, I'd be careful with him.* That's all I said, Julia. I just don't want you to get jerked over. You don't really know a thing about this person. Have you ever thought about that man in the picture which you've got on your mirror? I mean as a person?"

Julia took a drink of her soda, picked up a french fry and ate it. "I really think he is a decent person. Somebody that I met and liked enough to write to. Why do you ask?"

"What I'm trying to say, Julia, is just that. You've always thought of this man as somebody to write to. Correct? Somebody to tell all of your dreams and hopes to."

"Yeah, I suppose."

"Have you ever, even just for a moment, thought of him as the man you would want to marry?"

"Well I hadn't until he asked me to marry him. I didn't know him so why would I think about something like that. So no; marriage never crossed my mind."

"Oh, I see. And now you're so excited because he wants to marry you?"

Julia was becoming annoyed with all of the questions Virginia was firing her way. She wondered why her friend was being hard on her. Why wasn't she happy that the soldier wanted to marry her? It didn't seem right to Julia. She showed the annoyance in her demeanor and voice, "Look Virginia, Mitchell loves me and I love him. I feel it in my heart he is the one I should marry, and believe me, I've never felt this way about any guy. In fact, I made a promise to myself I would never even get married. So this is just as much of a shock to me as it is to you."

Virginia had witness her friend go through many stages; she knew a lot of things that happened to the wave, even of her causing the death of the D.C. rapist. She leaned into her friend and quietly asked, "And have you ever told him about any of the problems you've gone through, Julia?"

The question hit her in the gut. She knew exactly what the wave was referring to. Sharply she replied, "No, why would I want to do that, Virginia? Why would I tell him of any of those disgusting incidents that's happened to me?"

Virginia's elbow was on the table and her chin rest in her hand. She said in a mild voice, "Julia, I'm just saying you're only nineteen years old. Why would you even think about getting married; you've got your whole life ahead of you." Virginia was exasperated. "What about your dream of making the military a career; you're going to give that up?" The brunette shook her head in a negative manner. "And besides, if you're serious about going along with what this man wants, as far as marrying him, then you need to be honest with him and tell him everything that has happened to you. Not only in D.C., but also the abusive treatment which you have received from your parents."

Bringing up the D.C. incident was bad enough. But when Virginia threw in the fact that she should tell Mitchell of her horrible childhood life, she was not happy.

"And what makes you think he's going to reveal the flaws of his life to me, Virginia? Huh? Do you think he's going to tell me anything about having a mean mother; and a father who beat on his mother and his kids too? Why would I want to tell Mitchell such horrendous details about myself?" She tried to control the anguish in her voice, but she was failing miserably. "Why can't Mitchell and I just start with our love for one another? Why do we have to mix such garbage in with our affections?" she nervously played with the straw in her soda bottle. "I mean what is wrong with us giving our love to one another without bringing our sordid pasts into the equation?"

Virginia felt maybe she had taken it too far for Julia; but she was being realistic. Trying hard to make Julia understand her point of view, she leaned in and spoke over the band's rendition of Johnny Cash's, *Ring of Fire*. "Julia, I know you were taken advantage of in D.C., but don't forget, somebody died. Now I'm not saying the son-of-a-bitch didn't deserve what he got, but these are things Mitchell should know. And maybe, just maybe, if you explain how poorly your parents raised you, he just might understand." She touched Julia's hand, "You did say the man said he would die for you, right?"

"Yes Virginia, yes I did. But I cannot lay that stuff on him. Once I tell him those wretched things, I may very well lose him."

"Then if you lose him, maybe he's not meant to be in your life. You really should start by being honest with him. If the love is strong, then it won't matter with him. I'm not saying tell him everything right up front. Continue to write and just see how things go. If he is still bent on marrying you, then when you finally meet him again, sit face to face with him and lay it all on the line. Don't hold anything back. If he gets up and leave you sitting alone, then you'll know his love is not for you. That's all I'm saying."

Angry at Virginia because she did not see things her way, Julia grabbed her purse which was hanging on the back of the chair. "Look Virginia, I see our opinions differ regarding my love for Mitchell and what I should share with him. You want him to know everything about me don't you? I think you want him to pass me up," she accused.

"Julia, I don't want any such thing. I just want you to stop and think before you jump right into it. Besides, I think if you plan on marrying him, you shouldn't withhold this information; he has a right to know." Virginia tried to be sympathetic; but somehow she knew she was not getting through to her friend.

"But what if he turns me into the authorities; then I'll be charged for the man's death. I didn't mean for him to die." Julia shook her head; it saddened her to relive the abuse she went through. "Virginia, I can't tell Mitchell any of that stuff."

"I understand, Julia. Do what you think is best. I'm just giving you my opinion. It is up to you. You are my friend and you did decide to tell me about the man's death; remember? Don't you know as a member of the armed force, I am required to report that conversation to my commanding officer? Did you know that?" Julia's eyes widen. She hadn't even thought when she confessed her ordeal to Virginia she might be setting herself up for prosecution through the Uniform Code of Military Justice, and possibly thrown in the brig. Virginia reassured Julia, "You are my dearest friend; don't worry, your secret will always be safe with me. I will take it to my grave."

The painful memory engulfed Julia; she could not breathe and wanted to get out of the club. Her head was spinning; she thought she would pass out. Virginia was her friend, but Julia felt the brunette was being too hard on her about sharing the secrets with Mitchell which she had locked away. She trusted Virginia; but still she was infuriated. She accusingly spurted, "Sure Virginia. It's easy for you tell me what I should reveal to Mitchell about my life. It's not your life! And what if I tell Mitchell, and he decides he don't want me anymore; then I lose him for good. He is a beautiful man; I'm just a run-of-the-mill girl. Why, he could have any attractive girl he want, but for some strange reason, he wants me." She took a big gulp from the soda, then dug into her purse. As she was searching for two dollars, she continued on. "Do you really think I'm going to listen to you and take a chance on losing the only man who has ever told me he loves me? I didn't approach him, asking him to be mine; he asked me to be his. That's got to mean he loves me and sees something in me that he wants in his life." She tossed the two dollars on the table, then added, "I'm not telling Mitchell anything about my pathetic life." And with that she left her friend sitting alone at the table. The couples on the dance floor were two-stepping to Patsy Cline's, *I Fall to Pieces* as she stormed out of the night club.

~ ~ ~

When Virginia brought up Julia's past in Washington, D.C. it hurt her soul. She didn't want to remember the awful day. She realized she shouldn't have shown the wave the newspaper article about the death of her rapist. Why didn't she keep all of the nastiness to herself? Why did she feel the need to tell Virginia about it when she would never dream of telling another living soul. Deep down inside she knew why. She trusted Virginia and she knew Virginia would not pass judgment on her. They were best friends since day one. Still, all in all, Julia could not help but wonder why Virginia insisted she tell Mitchell every intricate detail of her life.

The night air was cool to her face as she walked back to the barracks. The breeze whisked around her as if to hurry her back to the tranquility of her room. Virginia's opinion regarding Mitchell bothered her. Then it dawned on her; because she was wrapped up in Virginia's concerns, she did not give the lady an opportunity to share her news of celebration. And now that she'd behaved so childishly, she doubt if Virginia would even bring the subject up again. But it did not matter too much at the present moment. She wasn't even sure she wanted to hear

Virginia's news. Her friend certainly made a point of shattering her day of cheerfulness, with all of her *what ifs, why don't yous, are you sures,* and *you should haves.* She was still upset when she arrived at the long walkway to the barrack and refused to think maybe Virginia had made some good points. As she neared the door of the WAVES Barrack she thought more and more about Mitchell and less about her friend, Virginia. Once she was in her room, she closed the door and locked it. She grabbed the shoebox of Mitchell's letters and tossed it onto her desk. She was in her pajama when she plopped herself onto her bed. She sat, indian style, at the head of the bed with her back against the wall. She pulled out some of his old letters and re-read them. Reading the letters over again confirmed her belief; and her belief was the same as Mitchell's in some of his old letters. They were together on the Greyhound Bus for the sole purpose of being united. Why hadn't she figured that out? It took Mitchell to bring it to her attention; and she was happy he had done so. Now in his latest letter he had asked her for her ring size. Virginia had it all wrong; Mitchell did love her and she knew she loved him. And no, she would not chance losing him by telling him what happened to her.

CHAPTER 37 -- APOLOGY

Julia had a rough night sleeping. She remembered the night before, treating her friend so poorly. Now it bothered her that she'd been so mean to Virginia. She arose early and wrote a letter to Mitchell. The whole time she wrote to Mitchell she could not help thinking of the night before at the Enlisted Men's Club. Why didn't she just sat there and listened to Virginia's point of view. Why did she have to be so defensive? Julia was angry at herself for being so abrasive to her friend; the only true friend she ever had at the barrack. What was she thinking? She realized Virginia would never tell her something that was not in her best interest. The brunette cared about her welfare; she owed the lady an apology.

Was Virginia correct? If she was going to take Mitchell up on his proposal of marriage, than maybe she should start off by telling him of the things that have gone on in her life. She shook her head in sorrow. She would apologize as soon as she saw her friend. Julia was paranoid about whom she shared the information of her past; and Virginia was the only one who knew her story. She fought a hard fight trying to prove her point to Virginia Payne. It was the first major disagreement the friends ever had since their friendship began.

Around 0730 the following morning Julia took her shower and dressed. Once she was dressed she went to the stairwell. She was about to put her foot on the first step to start up the stairs to Virginia's room when she saw the brunette fully dressed in uniform coming down the upper set of stairs and onto the landing. She carried a large navy blue suitcase in one hand, her military purse draped over her shoulder and her cosmetic case in her other hand. Julia was in shock to see her friend dressed in uniform and carrying luggage. She immediately ran up the stairs to meet Virginia on the landing.

"Good morning Virginia. I was going to ask you if you wanted to go to breakfast, but I see you're all dressed to go off." She looked at her friend, then at her luggage. "Where are you going on a Saturday morning?"

Virginia dropped her suitcase and cosmetic case onto the floor of the landing and gave Julia a big hug. She was so happy to see her friend. There was so much the wave wanted to tell Julia but Julia ran off the night before. She wanted to let her friend know she was being transferred. She hugged Julia so hard; it was the hardest Virginia had ever hugged her. Virginia said, "Oh Julia, I wanted to tell you yesterday, but I didn't get a chance. First, let me apolo…"

"Oh no you don't. Don't even say a word. I owe you an apology. You have always been there for me. I don't know what got into me. Virginia, I am so sorry I was extremely rude to you last night. Would you please forgive my meanness towards you?"

"Yes, of course I will." She gave Julia another hug. She added, "Hey, me of all people, should not be trying to tell you how to live your life. Lord knows I've got enough secrets of my own." She smiled, "If you feel you don't want to say anything to Mitchell, it is your business. You're right, how do I know if you share your detailed life with him, he won't feel obligated to turn you in to his commanding officer? Now that's something worth considering. Last night, that never crossed my mind and I am so glad you thought of that possibility." She patted Julia on the shoulder. "Look, I've got to go, the cab will be here shortly."

"But where are you going?"

"I'm being shipped off to Paris, France; I'm on special assignment with my chief and commanding officer. They need photographers and they chose me and a photographer first-class to go on the assignment with them."

"What?!"

"I wanted to tell you yesterday, Julia."

Julia could feel her eyes watering. She turned away so Virginia would not see the tears forming. She tried to stop them but when she blinked they just fell upon her cheeks; at that point, she did not care. Anxious, she asked, "Virginia, why didn't you tell me you were going to be shipped out? What's with the secrecy?"

"The orders just came in two weeks ago. But I was informed by my commander to keep it under wraps. Not even I know what the mission entails."

Julia didn't know what to do or say. She depended on Virginia in almost every aspect. Now, on one of the happiest days of her life, Virginia has informed her she is being shipped out. "I'm thrilled for you Virginia. I really am. It's just that I'm not going to know what to do without you."

"C'mon, you'll be fine." She gave Julia another hug, then said, "Look, I've been given a two-week working-vacation. Commander Harding is sending me to Naval Station Pearl Harbor for a combination indoctrination and vacation time. So I won't have to pay for hotel accommodations nor chow rations." She clasped her hands in happiness. "Isn't that great, a two-week semi-vacation in Hawaii. After that, I'm on my way to Paris. I'll write to you when I get a chance." Virginia's thumb rubbed the tears from Julia's cheeks. "Just remember, I will always think of you and pray for you. I may not ever see you again so I want you to do what you think is best for your life. Think your options through when circumstances arise. And pray, *always pray, Julia* that your decision is the best that you can make. God will be right there to guide you through in making the right choice. And remember Holton, with God, you're stronger than you think you are."

It was 0815 hours and the Lexington Park Taxi was tooting its horn. "There's your cab, Virginia Payne. You go take some beautiful pictures over there in Paris." The ladies hugged once more, then Virginia grabbed up her suitcase and cosmetic case and walked down the stairs with Julia.

"Goodbye Julia, it's been so wonderful knowing you."

Choked by her sadness, Julia said, "Goodbye Virginia Payne; I will always remember you." Sadly, she unlocked her door and went into her room. She laid on her bed and cried.

CHAPTER 38 -- LETTERS

Julia saw Mitchell coming towards her. She'd written to him since he first arrived in Germany. Now he was right there with her. He was so handsome and she was completely enamored by the man. When he reached her he picked her up and twirled her around. Gently her feet touched the ground as he gradually let her down from the spin. "I've been waiting so long to be with you, my sweet Julia." He kissed her passionately and then ran his finger down the side of her cheek. "You are my woman and I love you so much." As he laid Julia down on her bed; the wave worried. What if the duty officer used the pass key to get into her room. She was aware of the rules of the barrack. No men allowed as guest into any of the waves' rooms. That was the purpose of the lounge area. If the duty officer knew the man was there she would be put on report. As Mitchell lay in the bed with Julia, he caressed and fondled her. He began to undress her when she felt something sharp and annoying in her ear. She grabbed her ear to ease the pain and the image of Mitchell evaporated into tiny molecules before her eyes. She jumped up; *"Oh lord, that dream seemed so real,"* she spoke out loud. She wished the dream had continued, but the dream was gone. She got herself ready for work.

~ ~ ~

Work was interesting to say the least. Everyone around the office knew Lieutenant Kadowski was having problems with his wife. She never came to the Operations Admin's office, but you would have thought she lived there. The sailors and the wave knew about Mrs. Kadowski's every quirk. Whenever she called the lieutenant, the three yeomen and Seaman Apprentice Holton could hear the officer yelling at her regarding their personal life. Julia noticed whenever Commander O'Shea was in his office, which was a room off of the main office, the lieutenant was sure to keep his voice down. But if the commander was out, the lieutenant didn't mind letting his subordinates know his wife was a thorn in his side. He never cursed her over the phone but Julia was sure he was not a good husband to the woman. She could only imagine what it was like at the Kadowski residence.

Julia was busy typing a document for the commander when the disgruntled lieutenant grabbed his cover, plopped it on his head, and headed for the egress near her desk. She glanced up from her typewriter at the most awkward moment. The officer's eyes caught her's and she quickly advert her eyes back onto the commander's scribbled writings of the legal pad. The officer knew his outburst to his wife was inappropriate in front of the sailors and the wave but he could not control himself when it came the woman. Feeling a little bad about showing his anger towards his wife's telephone call, he said to Julia as he headed for the door, "Women, you can't live with them, and you can't shoot 'em." He stormed out of the office and Julia finished up the letter hoping the wife of Lieutenant Kadowski was not in harm's way.

"Wow, wonder what's going on with the lieutenant?" Petty Officer Kampschroder asked for all in the office to hear.

"Shit if I know," Petty Officer Hurley announced. "Man, I would never talk to my honey-honey like that. I might end up with a pot upside my head."

"You and me too!" Petty Officer Cross added. "How 'bout you Holton, do you think that soldier-boy of yours, your honey-honey, would let you get away with talking to him like that?" Petty Officer Cross enquired.

Not wanting to get into the conversation about the lieutenant's marital problems, she said, "Married people have problems. It's not all that uncommon."

"Yeah, but don't you think it's a little strange he talks to his wife like that in front of us?" the petty officer asked.

"N.O.M.B," she answered.

"N.O.M.B. What the hell is that supposed to mean?" he asked the wave.

"None Of My Business, Yeoman Cross. That's what it means. My opinion of his conversation with his wife has nothing to do with me typing this document for the commander. So that's why I say it's N.O.M.B." The seaman apprentice was always careful not to get caught up with office politics. She didn't want any problems. Keeping her opinion regarding non-related work matters was one way of ensuring she remained in great standings with her co-workers. Yeoman Cross shook his head at the wave, then left the office.

She was busy starting another one the commander's document when Yeoman Cross returned with the mail. "Here you go Holton, your lover from overseas has sent you another letter." He tossed it onto her desk. He did not tease her about the mail. Mitchell's letters were mostly all she ever received. Her mother stopped writing the wave when she could no longer finagle more money from Julia's paycheck. In fact, Julia informed her mother she was going to discontinue the twenty-dollar monthly allotment; and she did. Eleanor Holton took it hard. It pained her to realize Julia no longer felt it her obligation to send money home. And when the mother saw there was nothing in it for her anymore, the letters from home dwindles until they stopped altogether.

As Yeoman Cross continued to distribute the mail throughout the office, he spotted another letter addressed to Seaman Apprentice Holton. "Holton, here's another piece of mail for you." And Yeoman Cross, being Yeoman Cross, started with the ribbing. "Two-timing your soldier-boyfriend, huh? Who's this PH2 Payne?" He sniffed the envelope, "Humm, no cologne. I hope it's just a friend. I'd hate to see you getting that army guy upset again."

A smile came upon Julia's face. It was her friend, Virginia Payne. She thought she would never hear from the wave again. She picked up the letter, looked at it and smiled; she put it into her purse.

When she got to the barrack she locked the door behind her. She did not want any disturbance from her friends. Once out of her shoes and comfortably positioned on the bed she pulled the letters out. She noticed Virginia's letter. The returned address was FPO, Fleet Post Office. *Oh my, she's still overseas. That must be some assignment,* she thought. She placed the correspondence into the zipper compartment of her purse, then reached for Mitchell's scented letter. She turned Mitchell's letter over and saw the letters, S.W.A.K. She was happy; it always pleased her to see his *Sealed With A Kiss* signoff. She kissed the back of the envelope on top of the S.W.A.K. notation, then carefully opened it. As she sat curled on her bed, she read the letter:

September 10, 1967

PFC Mitchell Lauers
17 Long Range Recon Patrol
Gibbs Concern
APO AE 09008

My Darling Love,

It is with great happiness that I send this letter to you to let you know, my sweetheart that I will be coming home soon, very soon. Yes, my love, in no time I will have you in my arms and I look forward to it. I hope our meeting again will finalize our love for one another; I want to please you deeply. I pray, for the both of us, that we will discover that our wait, and the thousands of miles apart, has all been worthwhile.

I love you so much and I am happy that I will soon be in your company. You make being in this army so worthwhile. Just knowing I have your love make everything bearable. I think of you in all of my spare moments and I can tell by your passionate letters you must surely think of me as well.

But as I said, I will be coming home on leave soon. The reason I am returning to the states is because within seventeen days after my leave starts I will be departing for Vietnam. I don't want you to worry your pretty little head about me because I have volunteered for this duty. God will keep me safe over there. But look, we can discuss this once we are together. You are very special to me. There is so much I want to tell you, and so many plans I have for us as a married couple.

I look forward to seeing you, darling, to holding you, to loving you; and I thank God that you want me in your life. I truly hope that I have no reason to worry, but I do. I have a concern because you never sent your ring size to me. I was hoping to purchase our rings while here. Please don't have any doubts regarding my love for you. You make me so happy and I need you desperately. Please have faith in me and know that I am truly yours, all yours.

I will be leaving Frankfurt within one and a half weeks, so please do not answer this letter. Love, I will be home before you know it. If all goes well I will be at my parents' home on September 30th. I plan on spending a week with them and then come to Patuxent River, Maryland to claim you as my woman. I will have you in my arms on October 8th. I truly love you; always remember that, for you are my heart and soul. Please take care of yourself and think of me often.

Your man,

Mitchell Lauers,

The letter made her tremble. *This cannot be. He cannot possibly be coming to see me*, she silently thought. She was hoping she'd misread the letter, but she knew she read it correctly. Once again she rapidly went over the correspondence. She saw something in the letter regarding Vietnam. *Did he say he wasn't going to Vietnam or that he was going to Vietnam? No,* her mind said to her; *No, that couldn't be. He must have said he wasn't going to Vietnam. Let me read the letter again.* She was sure there was some sort of mistake. When she got to the part about Vietnam she slowed down and read with precision. She did read it correctly the first time. He's going to go to Vietnam. He wrote he had volunteered; but why would a soldier volunteer to go to Vietnam? Her friends in high school showed pictures they'd received from brothers and uncles in the war. The photos depicted many, many casualties. She re-read the letter yet again. *Yep, oh my goodness gracious, he's coming to Pax River. What am I supposed to do now?* She wanted to disappear. What would she do when he came to visit with her? What would they talk about? She didn't have a clue. Sure, it was so nice talking to the guy on paper, and sure she promised him she would be his. And while it was through their letters that the two of them fell for one another, why couldn't it have stayed on paper. She was nineteen and still felt like a kid; not a grown-up ready to be some man's special woman. She was so afraid the man would really want to marry her that her heart beat restlessly. Now, everything Virginia said about her being too young for marriage was suddenly making sense. Why did she tell him she would be his girl, his sweetheart, his lady, his love, his woman or whatever in the world it was he wanted her to be to him? Why did she tell him she would even make a commitment to be his? She wished she did not need the man's letters to get her through. Maybe she would have been better off without Mitchell's letters. She didn't know this person; didn't know him at all. She could only hope she hadn't made another bad choice. She went to her meditation corner and looked upon the statue of Jesus hanging on the cross. Beneath the cross was a small table with her bible opened to Proverbs. She placed Mitchell's letter upon the bible, placed her hand upon Jesus' body and closed her eyes. Slowly she bent her head, then silently prayed: *God, I only wrote to Mitchell because he seemed like a real nice guy. That's all. How did this happen that he would want me to be his own? I was hoping he just wanted me as his girl in our writing of correspondences. And when he tired of writing to me, he could break it off in a letter; plain and simple; or just stop writing. Now he wants to come and visit with me and probably to love me too. I am so afraid, but yet I truly believe Mitchell Lauers to be a good man, honest I do. But even that don't take this fear away from me. Since there is nothing I can do to retract all of those letters I wrote to him, I willingly put my life into Your Hands. If You feel it is best for me to share my life with Mitchell, then please give me some sort of sign. But You really should put some thought into this, God. Don't forget that I'm only nineteen years old and don't really know anything about loving or being with Mitchell right now.*

She kissed the cross, picked up Mitchell's letter and held it against her heart right before placing it in her purse. She began cleaning her room; going to the mess hall was out of the question. The bundle of nerves brought on by Mitchell's letter completely killed her little appetite. She would get her a snack when the geedunk truck arrived. That is if she was still awake.

She thought of how she had once been a trusting soul. The past humiliations flooded through her mind. But through it all she chose to be a person who cared, and didn't want to hurt anyone's feelings. She wanted to believe the best in everyone; that people were good, not evil and would never do anything to hurt her. But since she left her parents' home, she found out the hard way it was not always so. She hoped she hadn't set herself up for another attack. Why did she ever give the soldier her address in the first place? She knew the answer to the question. It was because it was the nice thing to do. He had even given her his address, but she never wrote to him. She tossed it in her drawer and thought no more of it until a week later when she received a letter from Mitchell.

After so many months of writing, maybe he really was serious about wanting her as his sweetheart. And not just through correspondence; but in real, honest-to-goodness, life. She knew she would need the wisdom of God to help her with this one. She would not be alone. If Mitchell Lauers showed up, she would not panic, because in her heart, she knew God was going to be there too, watching over her and calming her nerves. And if things look or felt like they were going to go wrong, she knew He would keep her safe from harm. On the other hand, if Mitchell didn't show up, God would still be right there by her side. It may be His way of letting her know not to worry and to continue on the path of the journey He had set her on. Though she had no clue which direction the path was going, nor where the journey would lead her to, a sense of calm came over her. She realized she would be alright no matter which way the Mitchell drama would unfold.

Relieved from the stress of worry, she realized something. The letter he'd written her was dated September 10, 1967. It had taken the letter nine days to arrive. In eleven days he would be at his parent's home, stay a week with them; at least that's what his letter said, and then come to see her. If he really showed up, that meant she would be seeing him in two weeks. The nerves resurfaced again. What would she do? Leave it in the hands of God; that's what she would do.

CHAPTER 39 -- UNTRANQUIL

When the seaman apprentice walked into the office, she greeted her co-workers with a bubbly and happy *Good morning*. She had a decent night's sleep and she woke up relaxed and calm. God came to her in her dream. He said, "MITCHELL LOVES YOU AND IF YOU TRULY LOVE HIM BACK YOU BOTH WILL LIVE IN A PARADISE OF LOVE. I AM SENDING MITCHELL TO YOU; HIS LOVE FOR YOU IS TRUE. YOU WILL LOVE HIM ON SIGHT AS HE WILL LOVE YOU. TOGETHER YOU WILL SHARE PEACE IN PARADISE. MITCHELL NEEDS YOU IN HIS LIFE, AND YOU, MY CHILD, NEED HIM. YOU ARE YOUNG AND INNOCENT; MITCHELL WILL HELP YOU BECOME THE WOMAN I HAVE MEANT FOR YOU TO BE."
And then God anointed her with a kiss on her head, then drifted towards His Heavenly Home. The dream placed her in the best mood. She took extra time to get herself ready for work. And she looked extra sharp in her uniform. As she sat at her desk putting her day's work in order, she was unaware of Yeoman Kampschroder stares.

Chief Burns was newly assigned to the unit. He had a sense of humor and was forever joking with the sailors and wave. When he saw how impressive the wave looked that morning, he kidded, "Why SA Holton you're a rose amongst us four thorns."

"Thank you, Chief Burns," was all she said as she worked on the three evaluations left over from yesterday's workload.

When lunch time rolled around Julia was happy to get out of the office. She went to the small café on the first floor, ordered a cheeseburger and a bottle of soda. The warmth of the sunshine felt refreshing as she walked out of the Operations Admin building. She headed for the bench to sit and eat her lunch but she could not. The bench was filled with the air traffic controllers. "SA Holton, come on over. We'll make room for you," AC1 Diane James waved the seaman apprentice over. Julia admired Air Traffic Controller Diane James. She originally joined the air force, completed her enlistment, then switched over to the navy. Julia planned on finishing her three-year term in the navy and then joining the air force. At one time Julia was interested in talking to the first class air traffic controller about her adventure in the air force, but now, she wasn't so sure she would have to.

"Thank you, but that's okay." She waved at the table of air traffic controllers and headed for the opposite side of the building. There she sat beneath a tree on the grass. She ate her cheeseburger and drank from the bottle of Pepsi-Cola. Julia pulled Mitchell's letter out to read and savor his words. She was excited to know she would be seeing him within a couple of weeks. Julia was almost through the first paragraph of his letter when she heard, "So Julia, how'sa come you lookin' so sharp today?" She looked up and saw Yeoman Kampschroder. An unlit cigarette hung from his lips like it was about to fall to the ground. He tilt the package of smokes and gently tapped until three filters popped their heads up for her to select one. When he nodded that it was alright for her to grab a smoke, she declined. "What, you don't smoke?"

Aggravated because the man invaded her solitude, she stuffed Mitchell's letter back into her purse. With attitude, she said, "No I don't, Kampschroder. You know I don't smoke. There's no ashtray on my desk running over with cigarette butts." She shook her head in disgust, "You've never seen me smoke, so why are you even here? It's my lunch hour."

"Hey girl, I'm just trying to be friendly. That's all."

The hair on the back of Julia's neck rose. This was a situation she did not want to be in; she knew the man didn't have a reason to be near her. She said, "Are you trying to be funny? Because if you are, then you'd make a piss-poor comedian."

"What the hell are you talkin' 'bout girl? I jist thought I'd come out and keep you company durin' yo' lunch. No sense in getting a wild hair up your ass. Besides, I noticed you got a picture of a white guy on your desk. Figured you'd like a lit'le bit of white meat to go with the rest of your sodie-pop, girlie." His smirk of a grin made her nervous. She shook her fear off and stood up so fast she knocked the rest of her drink over. She knew what came out of his mouth was inappropriate and she felt violated. Just where he got wrong, she was going to set him right. Never had she gone to any of the yeomen's desks looking at their photographs beneath their plexiglass. Mitchell chipped the bone in his ankle during a night jump in Germany. He sent Julia a picture of himself in a leg cast, on crutches and sporting a beautiful smile. The thought of Kampschroder standing at her desk looking at his photo made her skin crawl. She was furious. Kampschroder was a slob of a sailor and it was not uncommon for her co-workers, including the chief, to make comments about his slothenly dress and behavior.

Not wanting any trouble from the yeoman second class, she abruptly said, "First of all, how I look is none of your damn business, second and most important, I am not a girl nor a girlie, I am a wave, which makes me a young lady in the navy. You are to refer to me as Seaman Apprentice Holton, SA Holton, or just plain Holton; take your pick; I don't care. But you are never to refer to me as *Julia, girl,* or *girlie*. And third, stay away from my desk. My pictures and positive affirmations on my desk have nothing to do with you. That is my desk, not yours."

Angry that SA Holton, a mere E-2, found the gumption to stand up to him, an E-5, made his blood boil. Not only was she of far less rate, but she was a girl; and worst yet, a colored girl on top of it. Fuming mad he nastily said, "Don't you go actin' like no uppity nigga with me, girl. I just happened to notice the damn picture on your desk, and he don't look like no fuckin' colored person to me. Got me to thinkin' you might be likin' to be a'layin' down with white men." He spat on the ground, not far from her purse; then gave her a very nasty look. The yeoman, second class, turned his back and walked towards the building. There was a flurry of cigarette smoke trailing his head. Though he scared her terribly, she knew she could not show it.

It was moments like this she wished her friend, Virginia Payne, was there to help her regain her calmness. But she was not; then she remembered the letter. She was so caught up with Mitchell's news of coming home, that she'd forgotten about the mail from Virginia. She picked up her purse, carefully maneuvering it so the long strap did not touch any of the spit the angry yeoman left behind. She retrieved the letter from the inside zipper of her pocketbook as she stood leaning against the oak tree. Normally she would carefully open the envelope with a fingernail file or an unraveled paperclip, but she didn't have either. She opened it as carefully as she could and pulled out the contents. There were three photos wrapped inside of the air mail letter. She looked at them, Virginia in front of the Eifel Tower, Virginia pretending to be holding up the Leaning Tower of Pisa, Virginia at the Great Wall of China. A smile instantly appeared on Julia's face. She unfolded the letter and read:

PH2 Virginia Payne
Box 2690
FPO AE 09627

October 2, 1967

My Dear Friend, Julia,

How are you doing my friend? I certainly hope everything is going spectacular for you in your life.

First off let me apologize for taking so long to write you. Julia I cannot begin to tell you how busy I have been with my chief and commanding officer. I have had the opportunity of traveling Europe exploring many countries. So many that I have a hard time remembering them all. As you can see I have sent you photographs of a few of the places we have traveled to; France, Spain and China. We have also gone to Italy, Morocco and Japan. I am the chief's photographer assistant. Myself and a sailor by the name of PH1 John Divito. We are fortunate to have him with us, because though Commander Harding is fluent in Italian, PH1 Divito is a master of four languages, French, Italian, Chinese, and German. The sailor has saved us through quite a few awkward situations with the language bearer over here. We are photographing the different naval bases throughout Europe. The photographs we are taking are to go into enlistment brochures. The bigwigs figure that our photos of foreign naval bases may entice many new recruits. We have also met some wonderful military personnel along the way. Right now I am on a short liberty and decided I'd better take this time to jot this quick note to you before we are off again . Oh, by the way. I made second class. Boy, what a difference in pay. The advancement test was hard, but I managed to pass and I am happy for that.

I am wondering how your romance with Mitchell is going. Is it still strong as it was the last time we spoke? I am so proud of you Julia for knowing what it is you want. It must be nice to recognize when a man is deeply in love with you and you have the same strong love for him. I can only wish I can find someone that loves me the way your Mitchell loves you when I am ready to get married. What a wonderful feeling for you to realize that you and Mitchell are meant to be together. But Julia, I know you don't want to hear this, however, I still think with you being only nineteen, you have your whole life ahead. Even if you and Mitchell are so madly in love, maybe you can hold off getting married until you at least fulfill your three-year obligation to the U.S. Navy; give it some thought.

When you get a chance, write to me. I can't promise where I'll be. We're constantly moving from country to country, but I am sure that the naval post office will forward your mail to me.

Take care of yourself, Holton. Try to remember all of the fun-things we did together and how much we tried to safeguard one another against some of the pain we've endured. Don't forget, I love you as the sister I never had.

Be safe and Remember God will Guide you...if you let Him.

Your friend, always,

Virginia Payne

Julia was happy she remembered the letter at that very point in time. After the Kampschroder incident, Virginia Payne's words were just what she needed. Virginia wasn't physically there, but she was there in Julia's heart. And her letter saved the wave from the anguish that would have engulfed her upon returning to the office. She wasn't the least bit surprise the poised and confident wave managed to use her photography skills to point, focus and click her way across the ocean into another world of wonderment. God, was she excited for her; and she was pleased they had become good friends.

When Julia got back into the Admin Office, she didn't even look towards Yeoman Kampschroder's way. There was a large smile on Julia's face and all she could see in her head was the man who loved her, Mitchell and the best friend she had ever known, Virginia. She never noticed the angriness on Yeoman Kampschroder's face as he scowled at her entrance into the office. The rest of her day went by like a breeze.

CHAPTER 40 -- ARRIVAL

When Mitchell Lauers was right out of jump school, in Fort Bragg, North Carolina, the officers asked him where did he want to be stationed. When he indicated that he wanted to go to Vietnam, he was sent to Frankfurt, Germany. Once in Germany he signed every waiver that was posted for deployment to Vietnam. Three times Mitchell signed the waiver to go to Asia, and three times it was shot down. Finally, he received his orders. When he was called to come before the colonel, the officer asked Mitchell why he wanted to go to Vietnam. "Sir, I am ready to die for my country," was his reply. The colonel granted Mitchell's request to go to Vietnam.

Before he left for Asia to fight in the war, Mitchell was promoted to E-5 sergeant and granted military leave. He was flown back to the states to spend time with his family and friends. He had a seventeen-day delay before he was to report to Vietnam. There were a few people he wanted to visit and he couldn't wait to see them.

~ ~ ~

Mitchell arrived in Cresaptown, Maryland on a Sunday afternoon. His father was working on the side of the house when he saw the Queen City Cab pull up in front of his home. Unable to see who was in the cab the old man walked towards the front.

When he saw his son Mitchell getting out of the cab, he dropped his rake and walked hurriedly towards the side door to call for his wife. "Matilda, Matilda! Come here, woman. Come here." Matilda came to the screen with a dishtowel in her hand. She looked at Jeremy through the screen. "Matilda, you're not gonna believe who's here," he said in a loud voice.

"Jeremy, I'm standing right in front of you. No need for you to be yelling so loud; the whole neighborhood can hear you." No sooner than the words came out of her mouth she saw her son appear onto the side of the house. "Oh lord, my word. Why look at you, boy. Why didn't you tell us you were coming home?" she screamed with joy. "I don't have anything fixed at all for you, Mitchell. You know I would have your favorite foods cooked for you, son." She opened up the door, walked out with the dishtowel thrown over her shoulder. As the woman walked towards her son, she took her apron and dried her hands off. She reached up and hugged her son. "Oh Mitchell, son, what in the world are you doing here?" She gave him one last squeeze and then released him. She stood back and was marveled by the sight of him. She loved seeing her son in his uniform. He was so handsome and she was so proud of him.

After the excitement of seeing Mitchell had calmed her, the woman was on the telephone. Mitchell went into the living room, tossed his duffel bag down onto the floor then seated himself into the chair across from his father. His father was lost for words; he asked, "Can I get you a beer son?" He lit up one of his Chesterfields and took a long drag from it.

It had been so long since Mitchell had been with his father; he said, "I'll take a beer, dad. You sit, I'll get it; do you want one?"

"Yes I do, son. While you're in the kitchen, grab that shot of whiskey that I got poured. I left it on top of the washer."

"Okay dad."

Mitchell came back with their drinks. He was happy to be home, but he knew he'd have to tell his parents why he was there. While his mother was on the phone telling everyone she could tell her son was home from the army, Mitchell filled his father in on all of his accomplishments in the military. He had learned Morse Code, he was a paratrooper, he had been on many different bases, including the one he had just come from in Germany. But he did not tell him about Vietnam.

Matilda got in touch with her friends and neighbors and soon there were a lot of people in the small house. They were there to see Mitchell. There was food from the neighbors, pastries from friends and some of the family brought more drinks for the soldier's celebration. She could not believe she was actually sitting in the house with her son. All of the friends and neighbors were interested in listening to Mitchell's adventures in the army. They were quite impressed that he was a paratrooper. How courageous he was. A paratrooper? Why, they didn't know a soul in Cresaptown who had the guts to jump out of an airplane; they were fascinated.

When the crowd left for the evening, it was then that Mitchell sat his father and mother down at the kitchen table. The same table the family had shared many dinners, the same table they had all told stories, the same table they had sang songs, and the same table they had played cards. There, at that kitchen table, Mitchell laid it all on the line. He explained why he was home. "Mom and Dad, I just want to let you know I am going to be leaving for Vietnam within two week." Mitchell never believed in sugar-coating what needed to be said. He believed in putting the facts straight forward.

"Oh my God. No, no. Son, are you sure?" Matilda knew her son was going to Vietnam. She just did not want to accept this fact as reality.

Jeremy reached for Matilda's hand and patted it. "Matilda, yes he's sure. C'mon now, let's finish listening to what our son has to say." The father held steadfast onto the tears that wanted to come. He was proud of his son, but deep down he did not want him going to war. Jeremy had the same sick feeling as his wife. There was a war going on, and he was concerned about his son being a part of it.

"Now this is something I have to do," Mitchell emphasized.

"But son," Matilda said in a strong voice, "I know we've taught you well. It's just that we don't want anything to happen to you. Why, I'm gonna be worried sick while you're over there. Honest son, can't you get out of this?"

"No mom. My orders have already been issued. I'll be leaving in seventeen days."

Jeremy took his wife's hand, "Honey, Mitchell is a strong-willed man. If he's being sent to Vietnam, than it shouldn't surprise us he goes willingly. I don't know why they chose him to go, but it looks like they did."

Mitchell said, "Dad, they didn't choose me to go, I volunteered."

"You what?!" his mother blurted out.

"I said that I volunteered, mom. I feel if I go to war, it will keep my brothers safe from ever having to be sent to Vietnam," he explained.

His mother said nothing more. She got up from the table and left the room. Mitchell looked at his father and quietly said, "She'll be alright, dad. I think she just needs a moment to herself." But Jeremy knew his wife was having a rough time with the news; he knew, because he certainly was. Jeremy motioned for his son to go after his mother and comfort the woman. The dutiful son did. When he found his mom she was sitting in the oversized chair in the living room. She was puffing on a cigarette. She tried to give up the bad habit of smoking but the news of her son going to war rattled her nerves. Mitchell sat in the chair near her. She turned her head away from him. He stood up from his chair, went over to his mother and placed his arm around his mother's shoulder. "Mom, please don't worry about me. God is going to protect me; you know this, don't you?"

She turned and looked up at him. Mitchell was happy to see his mother was not crying. She was a strong, strong woman and she gave her all to teach her children not to be weaklings. What would it look like to her son if she sat there sobbing? She would have plenty of nights of which to cry when no one could see her tears. Matilda said to her son, "Yes son, I know He will protect you. I know He will."

~ ~ ~

For six days Mitchell travelled the small town catching up on news of his friends and relatives of Cresaptown. He caught up with his first cousin, George Paguet, and asked his cousin, "Hey George, do you know where Patuxent River, Maryland is?"

George replies, "Yeah man, that's a navy base. My sister, Shirley, her ol' man is stationed on that base. In fact, they live in the base housing."

"No kidding? Man I didn't know that. Anyway, I've got to go there."

"Oh yeah? When do you gotta go?" his cousin asked as he took the last drags from the butt of his non-filtered cigarette.

"I was hoping to go tomorrow morning. There is a lady I want to go visit before I'm shipped off to Nam."

George did not want to tell Mitchell he was short on funds and even shorter on car gas. There was barely enough gas in his tank to get him around town. The base was over one-hundred and seventy miles away. And after all it had been quite a while since he visited with his sister and her navy husband. He didn't want to give his cousin the impression he didn't want to take him. So he came right out and said, "Man, I wish I could take you. Damn, it would be a nice trip and I could take my girlfriend, Charlene with me. Truth is Mitchell, I don't have a damn cent for gas."

Mitchell dug into his back pocket and pulled out his wallet. He immediately snagged a ten dollar bill from his wallet and handed it to George. "Will this fill up your tank?"

George took the money, "Sure will. Me and Charlene will pick you up bright and early, eight o'clock, okay?"

"Yes, it is. I'll be standing outside waiting for you."

~ ~ ~

The ride out of Cresaptown, Maryland put Mitchell in an elated state of mind. He sat in the back seat as George drove and Charlene talked endlessly to both of the men. When George made it so far he got lost. Trying to figure out the correct direction without alarming his passengers he made several backtracks. Mitchell, always alert, asked George, "Isn't this the third time we've been around this beltway?" He was anxious to get to Patuxent River to see Julia, and he thought he could depend on his first cousin to get him there. What he discovered was the fact that George didn't have a sense of direction.

"I don't know, Mitchell. I'm too busy trying to drive this car and get us to the base," he explained; as if driving the car and paying attention to the road signs at the same time were too complicated.

Charlene, in a calm voice added, "Yes George, this is the third time. I think you should stop and asked for directions. I thought you said you knew how to get to the base."

George had called Shirley the night before to let his sister know he would visit with her. When she asked him if he needed directions, he informed her he did not. But now he was lost, and though he would not ask for help, Mitchell's military instinct kicked in. The first thing he did was make George stop at a gas station so they could get directions. They arrived at Patuxent River Naval Air Station a half an hour later.

CHAPTER 41 -- QUARTERDECK

Julia received a telephone call from Mitchell the night before, letting her know he would be there around 1000 hours the next morning. The following morning she was dressed by 0942 hours and ready to meet the man. At 1000 hours Mitchell hadn't arrived. By 1030 hours the wave figured he was not coming. When he didn't show up by 1100 hours, her brain went into relief mode. She figured this was God's sign for her to continue her journey without Mitchell in her life. And though she was somewhat relieved, Julia realized the man had gone to a great length for the elaborate ploy. The joke was on her. Maybe he simply said he loved her because he figured that was what she wanted to hear. Had she been in love with thin air; a love which had never been there? Right now he must be somewhere having a good laugh. He even said his cousin, driving him to see her, had a sister living in base housing, right there on her base. *Yeah*, she thought, *sure his cousin lives on this base.* How coincidental would that be? Just like his birthday was in the same month as hers. But what if everything he said was true? What if something happened? Anything could have delayed his visit. Julia tossed the prank scenario aside and concern for the soldier came into her mind. What if his cousin crashed the car while trying to get to Patuxent River? She prayed it was not the case. She could easily take it as a trick that Mitchell had played on her, rather than people getting hurt, or killed trying to make their way to the base to visit with her.

It was 1128 hours when she heard, **"SA Holton, SA Holton, you have a guest on the quarterdeck. SA Holton, you have a guest on the quarterdeck."** The message blared over the public announcement system for all to hear. She felt a tight knot in her stomach and somehow could not get her legs to work. So it wasn't a hoax the soldier played on her; so there was no car accident. She was excited and fearful; what would they talk about? She knew the army man came a long way to visit with her. She could not let her nerves hold her back from meeting the man who claimed her heart through their letters.

Julia took a deep breath and walked out her door. She secured her room, then headed for the quarterdeck. When she swung the door to the quarterdeck opened and saw Mitchell standing there, her heart pounded and she felt weak. He was not in his uniform. But uniform or not, he looked so striking. Julia took a few steps onto the quarterdeck, then stopped in her tracks from nerves which overwhelmed her. She loved him as soon as she saw him. When his eyes met hers in a loving glisten, she dropped her head with embarrassment. Was this a dream, or was he really there on the quarterdeck? She couldn't tell. Mitchell sensed his new love was nervous; without saying a word, he walked towards her. She thought she would faint when he took her by the hand and lead her onto the barrack's enclosed porch. Alone on the porch, he faced her, put his finger under her chin and lift her face upwards. Mitchell said, "Oh my darling Julia. I've loved you from the moment I met you. I've been waiting so long to feel you in my arms." He bent down and kissed her. She was mesmerized when she felt his tongue slip between her lips. The kiss seemed to go on forever; she had fallen in love, in the flesh, with the soldier. It was no longer a correspondence of love; it was real live love. When Mitchell gently pulled away he leaned back to look into her eyes. She still hadn't spoken a word to him; she was too afraid her voice would ruin the moment. Mitchell's eyes were filled with happiness as he stared into Julia's brown eyes. He said, "Oh, Miss Holton, you make me feel so good. Do you think you could love me forever?"

Julia wanted to yell, not just to Mitchell, but to the world, YES MY WONDERFUL LOVE, YES I CAN LOVE YOU FOREVER. But she stared into his eyes, and simply said, "Yes Mitchell, I love you deeply." A wider smile came across his face and then before she knew it, Mitchell picked her up and whirled her around, then gently placed her down. "Oh, my goodness Mitchell, can this really be happening. Are you sure it's me you want?" Her head was bent down and once again she was looking towards the floor.

Mitchell, wanting so much to take in the beauty of Julia's brown face, asked, "Miss Holton, why do you look down? I've come such a long distance from overseas to see your pretty face; please don't look at the floor."

Julia didn't know what to say. Bravely, she lifted her face and looked into Mitchell's eyes. A weak smile came across her face. She felt as though she was having an out-of-body experience. As she looked at him, she said, "Mitchell, I'm so nervous. I've never been in love before. I love you so much and I really don't know what I've done in this world to deserve your love. This whole meeting again, this being in love with you, it…well…umm, well it just don't make any sense."

Mitchell worked so very hard to win the little wave's love. He was not about to let a technicality like her not understanding the evolution of their love ruin it. He was happy they were finally together and he hoped she felt the same way. With love in his eyes, he said, "Can't you simply except the fact that our love is meant to be? I certainly can. I don't question God's reason for putting us together; you shouldn't either." He kissed her on the forehead, then tapped her little nose with his finger. He looked longingly into her eyes, then said, "Don't worry your pretty little head about it." Then he said, "Are you hungry, Julia. I saw a diner outside of the base where we can get a bite to eat."

~ ~ ~

The two of them got on the navy bus and took a ride to the gatehouse. They walked to the nearby diner and ordered their food. Julia held her head down almost the whole time the two of them sat and ate. She ate a few forkfuls of her macaroni and cheese and took a couple of bites from the open-faced roast beef, but that was it. And though Mitchell did all he could to put the young lady at ease, he knew she was having a hard time. For God's sake, Julia told him that she'd never been in love before. Maybe this was too much on her. But all he knew was the fact that he did not want to lose her. As they sat in the restaurant, Mitchell told Julia he had once been married. He let her know after fourteen months of marriage he filed for divorce. He informed Julia they didn't have children and his ex-wife left him early in the marriage. He explained to the wave he did not want the information to frighten her away; that is why he never mentioned the marriage and divorce in any of his letters to her.

And even though it was the perfect opportunity for Julia to tell him about the rapes and the death of her second rapist, she could not bring herself to do so. Still thinking he would hold the hideous acts against her, she was too afraid to divulge the pains of her past to Mitchell. She toyed with her food while the soldier kept the conversation going. Finally, there was no more conversing on Mitchell's part. He looked passionately at the wave. And though she saw the love that showed in his eyes, still she could not bring herself to tell him of the awful incidents. She said nothing.

~ ~ ~

Mitchell wanted to be alone with Julia. He was a gentleman, but he was a gentleman in love. And though he wanted to make love to her, he did not want to be imposing upon his lady. He touched her hand and played with her small fingers. He toyed with the finger on her left hand, she felt uneasy. Mitchell asked, "Do you know the size of your ring finger?" Julia did not answer and when he looked at her, he noticed a nervousness about her face. With a serious gaze into her eyes, he said, "Julia, I need you so much." He kissed her fingertips, then confessed, "I want to make sweet love to you."

Not knowing what to say, Julia held her head down and looked at the plate of food which she long ago abandoned. She spoke into the plate, "I need you too, Mitchell," she admitted. "Would you like to be alone with me? I really would like for you to hold me in your arms?" She self-consciously looked at Mitchell and there was a radiance of attraction in his eyes.

He picked up her hand and kissed her ring finger. "God, I love you. You mean the world to me. Yes, my love, I want to hold you in my arms as well." He looked Julia in her eyes and she could see his love for her. She wondered if he knew the depth of her love for him. Mitchell could sense the anxiety in Julia; but being as delicate as he could possibly be, he carefully worded his desires. He softly said to her, "My lord, I want you so badly. I wish I could hold you, could touch you. I wish I could have you." He felt he was making Julia increasingly nervous. But when their eyes met again, Mitchell knew. At that very moment he could tell, she wanted him too. He glanced out of the window of the restaurant and noticed Hotel Lexington within walking distance from the diner. Julia's eyes followed his. Mitchell asked, "Should I get us a room, my love?"

Without hesitation, Julia answered, "Yes."

CHAPTER 42 -- PERMISSION

While Mitchell had some days left he wanted he and Julia to go to Philadelphia so he could ask Julia's parents for her hand in marriage. However, the thought of spending a weekend in Philadelphia with Mitchell did not appeal to her. They were definitely in love. And though Mitchell felt the need to ask Julia's parents for her hand in marriage, she did not think it was necessary. Even though she loved her mother and father, with all of their faults and flaws, she saw no reason for Mitchell to ask their permission. She hated to admit she was embarrassed by their lack of civility towards one another. But since he wanted to make this gesture, she hoped they would be on their best behavior when she and Mitchell arrived at their home.

It was two days later the two of them met at Julia's parents' apartment. She arrived a day ahead of him. The following day Julia's mother took her to the Philadelphia airport to pick Mitchell up. Julia was so proud to see him in his military uniform. The last time she saw him in uniform was when they initially met on the Greyhound Bus.

Once Mitchell was in the car, Julia worried. As Eleanor drove home the mother made small talk with Mitchell, asking him how was his flight and how long he had been in the army. Julia prayed no curse words would slip from the woman's mouth. When the car pulled up to the curb of their home, Julia was relieved her mom refrained from using bad language. As the car doors open all of her little brothers and her two sisters were there at the car to greet him. Mitchell was enthralled by all of the attention Julia's siblings gave to him. Not since his own childhood, had he been surrounded by so many children. He marveled at them and was pleased to know the lady he was going to marry was the oldest from a family as big as his. As Julia's sister, Josephine, walked with him up the walkway to the house, she gently placed her arm into his. Walking arm in arm with the soldier, the eighteen year-old whispered to the man, "I'm going to steal you away from my sister." Mitchell continued walking with the teenager, choosing to ignore what she said; he did not want any trouble. The man was there on Julia's behalf; nothing more, nothing less. He knew his reason for being there. It was for the sole purpose of asking Mr. and Mrs. Holton for their daughter's hand in marriage.

~ ~ ~

Jake Holton was a good man to everyone, including his children, when he was sober. His wife, Eleanor warned him, "Jake, remember Julia called and said she's bringing somebody special home with her. I want you to act like you got some damn sense." She was weary they would have another one of their fights while the soldier was visiting. It had been a tough life for her; after nineteen years she managed to still put up with the dominate man. Through every black eye he gave her, every stabbing she inflicted upon him, and every harsh syllable of filthy language they'd spew at one another, they were still together. Eleanor Holton did not want anything embarrassing to happen, but if something jumped off, she knew she would not bite her tongue.

~ ~ ~

Mitchell remained in his uniform, and all of Julia's siblings seemed to like him. This made Julia so proud she gave in to his request. Mitchell insisted all of the kids eat before he and Julia.

Before Jake and Eleanor could fix their plates, Mitchell said to them, "Mr. and Mrs. Holton, if you have a moment, I would like to speak with you." As the children all found their spots to sit down and have their meal, Mitchell politely addressed Jake and Eleanor Holton. The four of them were in the living room when the soldier started the conversation with Julia's parents. Mitchell said, "I can't tell you how wonderful it is for you to open your home to me; I'm a total stranger to you all."

"Aww Mitchell, you ain't no stranger. You're a friend to our daughta, Julia," Eleanor said.

"Yeah Mitchell; man, it ain't no big thang," Julia's father added as he chewed on his stubby cigar.

Julia said nothing; she just sat and listened. He continued on, "Well actually, Mrs. Holton, I'm more than just a friend to Julia."

Eleanor, surprised by the soldier's statement, thought the very worst. "I just be damn. What the hell is that supposed to mean, *you're more than just a friend to our daughta?*" Then her attack turned towards her daughter, "Julia, did you go and get yo'self knocked-up by this here man?"

"Mom! God no! Why would you say something like that?"

Julia's father came to his daughter's defense. "Eleanor, don't go talkin' foolishly. It's bad enough I done knocked you up when you was eighteen. Rememba? And then you go and force me to marry you? Julia has her act together." The father turned his attention back to Mitchell, and said, "Mitchell go 'head, man. What was you sayin'?"

Julia just shook her head. Somehow she was not surprised by her mother's allegation. She could not wait until this procedure, a procedure which Mitchell insisted on putting them through, was over with.

"Mr. and Mrs. Holton, I am in love with Julia. And she, thank God, is in love with me. I would like to have your blessings as I ask for your daughter's hand in marriage."

Julia's mother got up from the sofa. Anxiously, she walked over towards the stereo console with her fist clenched. "Oh lawd, oh lawd. You mean you actually want to marry this skinny chile of mine? How come? She looks like a string bean, got that little frail-lookin' face and the girl can't even cook." Eleanor shook her head in disbelief. She wondered what underhanded motive the soldier had in regards to the skinny girl."

"Mrs. Holton, I can always buy a cook book for Julia. If she wants to learn how to cook, she will learn. I'm not really worried about such a minor detail. All I know is that we love one another and she has agreed to take me as her husband; of course with your blessing."

Jake Holton reached over and shook Mitchell's hand. He replied, "What Eleanor is tryin' to say is welcome to the family, future son-in-law." Mitchell stood up from the sofa and so did his bride-to-be. Mitchell held tightly onto Julia's hand. He squeezed the palm of her hand to give her assurance that he felt it went well. Mitchell wanted to kiss her right then and there, but he decided he would wait until they were alone. Jake Holton got up and stood by the couple. He put his hand on Mitchell's shoulder then said, "Mitchell my man, come go with me." Julia gave Mitchell a questionable look. She did not want him to go off with her father. With a nod of confidence he let his lady know he would be alright. This was something he had to do to win the confidence of his future father-in-law.

~ ~ ~

"Mitchell I'm gonna take you to one of my ol' hangouts. If you gonna marry that daughta of mine then you should have some fun before you go makin' that big jump." Jake pulled away from the curb. He drove about an eight of a mile straight ahead to Collin's Tavern. It was a short ways; in fact, you could see it from the apartment. Mitchell wondered why they didn't just walk the short distance.

When they got out of the car, Jake said, "Hey man, it's a lot of pretty ladies hangin' out in this place. You might get lucky!" He nudged Mitchell in his side and chuckled.

Mitchell did not want to be in a bad light with Julia's father, but he also didn't want to be with any other lady either. He found his woman and he had no intention of getting caught up in somebody's trick bag. Not Julia's sister, and certainly not Julia's father. Boldly, and in all clarity the soldier said, "No thank you, Mr. Holton. Julia is the only woman I want and the only woman I will ever need."

The older man gave the sharp-looking soldier a hard look. He looked the man up and down; then said, "Shit, you cain't tell me a good-looker like yo' ass is gonna be stuck with just one woman for the rest of yo' life. Aww, hell naw." He gave a devilish look at Mitchell, then added, "Let me tell you somethin', Redbone, guys like you ain't no one-woman man. I know what I'm talkin' 'bout." But when he saw Mitchell shake his head, indicating he just was not interested, Jake knew he was not getting through to him. "Aww the hell wif it. I see she done got yo' nose wide open. Yeah, I see those big-ass mac trucks parked in both of them nostrils." He laughed, then added, "I cain't help you man, you done went and got yo'self caught up in some love. Well Mitchell, I hope thangs work out for you. I sure do." He gave the army man a pat on the shoulder and they walked into Collins' Tavern. Once they were inside the bar Jake introduced Mitchell to the bartender, and his few friends in the place. It made Jake feel like a big-shot being in the presence of the young military man.

One of Jake's friends came over to see who the man in the uniform was. He asked, "Jake, who the fuck is this?"

Jake, trying to show a little bit of class for himself, and a lot of respect for the army guy, warned his friend, "Man, watch yo' mouth. Show some respect for this man. Can't you see he's in uniform, you fuckin' moron?" Then he put his hand up in the air as he apologized for the profanity that escaped his mouth. "Sorry 'bout that, Mitchell." He looked at his friend, then said, "Man, this is my daughta's ol' man, Mitchell. Sergeant Mitchell to yo' ass. Mitchell, this is Big Head." He slapped Mitchell's chest, then added, "That ain't his real name but that's what we call him, 'cause he got a big-ass head." Mitchell shook the man's hand.

Big Head looked at Mitchell's uniform. He said to him, "Man, it's a bad time to be in the fuckin' military, Sergeant Mitchell. I hope you don't get sent off to that damn Viet-ta'ma-mese war."

Mitchell smiled, "Actually, I'll be leaving shortly for Vietnam."

"Man, you gotta go over there and fight. Damn, they just grabbin' everybody they can get they hands on to send 'em over there. Sorry son t'see they done ordered you to go ov'r there." Big Head told the soldier.

"Sir, they didn't order me to go to Vietnam. I volunteered."

Jake Holton downed a shot of whiskey. Surprised by the sergeant's statement, he blurted, "You what? You volunteered? What are you…fuckin' crazy? Nobody volunteers for some shit like that?"

A few of the patrons noticed the sergeant. How could they not notice him? He looked white, in an all-black tavern, he was in an army uniform, and he had just informed Big Head he'd volunteered to go to Vietnam. An old black man, named Beasley, got up from his chair. With the aid of his cane, he made his way to the bar, laid a five-dollar bill on it then whispered something in the bartender's ear. He went to the sergeant and said, "Son, my name's Beasley. I heard you say you volunteered to go to Vietnam. Let me tell you son; that is the most commendable thing you have done, putting your life on the line for our country. I was in the Korean War. Yes sir; I got wounded over there, too." He pulled up his right pants leg, then tapped the brown specimen with the wooden cane. A hollowed sound was heard loud and clear by all in the establishment. "Landmine, took it off son. But I tell you what, not one day have I ever regretted going to war for my country." The old warrior put out his hand and the sergeant shook it. He continued, "I put five dollars on that bar; I want you to go order whatever you want to drink."

Mitchell didn't have the heart to tell the man he wasn't much of a drinker. Instead, he said, "Look Mr. Beasley, I'll have a beer and that is all I want. I thank you for your generosity. Sir, please use the rest of the money on yourself. You deserve it," then he shook the man's hand again.

~ ~ ~

Jake's chest was swollen from the pride of being around Mitchell with his friends at the tavern admiring the soldier. After about an hour and a half they returned to the house. Mitchell felt the busyness of the day catching up with him. Though it was only five o'clock, he asked Mrs. Holton if she'd mind if he took a nap. Julia took him to the bedroom which she had once shared with her sisters while growing up. Once he was situated on the single bed, she returned to the downstairs where most of her family was. After the young lady figured Mitchell was asleep, she went up to the bedroom and laid down on the bottom bed of the bunk in the same room. She was just as tired as Mitchell, and a nap would do her good. Julia slept for an hour while Mitchell slept in the bed across the room. It was Mitchell who awoke first. He sat up in his bed and looked at his lady lying asleep in the bottom bed of the bunk. She looked so peaceful, and though he wanted her, he knew it was not the right time, nor place. He was surprise when she awoke within ten minutes of his awakening. When she opened her eyes and smiled at him, he said, "I didn't know you over there sleeping all of this time. Come sit on the bed with me." She got up from the bottom bunk bed and walked over to where Mitchell was now sitting on his bed. She sat next to him. He draped his arm around her, and then quietly said to her, "Before we leave Philadelphia, I am taking you to have your ring finger sized. I have found some beautiful diamond and wedding band sets." He pulled out four small flyers of wedding ring sets. "Which one do you like?"

"I would like you to pick out the ring set, Mitchell," Julia begged.

"No Julia, this is something the bride-to-be must do. So please choose the one you like best, love."

Julia looked at pictures of the four different sets. She hand Mitchell the flyer of her favorite ring. When she glanced at her future husband, she saw a smile on his face. He folded it and placed it into his wallet behind a photograph of her.

"Now, that wasn't so hard, was it?"

When Julia said nothing in response to his question, he asked, "What's on your pretty little mind, sweetheart? Is it the ring that I want to get for you? I've noticed you always shy away from my request for your ring size."

Hesitantly, she explained, "Bad things have happened to me, and I don't know if I'm even comfortable telling you. I've been told that I should, in fact I promised myself that I would; but now, I'm not so sure."

Mitchell put his arm around her shoulder again and pulled her as close as he could. "Are you getting cold feet about marrying me, Miss Holton? I certainly hope not because I cannot bear the thought of you not being in my life."

Julia replied, "No I'm not getting cold feet. I want to marry you, Mitchell, but my past is horrible."

Mitchell said, "Sweetheart, your past is over with. I am concerned about your future; our future." He gently leaned away from her and looked into her eyes. He thought about the old black man at the tavern, then added. "Julia, I cannot marry you before I go to Nam; I want you to know that. I have no knowledge of how I will return. I am hoping to come back in one piece to start our life together. And if it is in God's Will for me to return safe and sound, I promise I will always be around to take care of you." She looked at him, then touched his face. He added, "What I am trying to say is, we've got a lot of living to do. Even right now. Let's take advantage of the time we have together now; not waste it on things that happened in your past or even my past." He finished by affirming, "If you don't feel the need to share whatever it is that is hurting you, I'm alright with it. If you ever want to tell me what it is that have you in so much pain, I will always be here for you. I will do my best to understand and accept whatever it is that's troubling you. And never will I judge you, regarding it." He kissed her on the forehead; "I am a man. I am your man. And as your man, my loyalty and love is to you; not a damn other soul; and certainly not to your past. My loyalty is to you, Julia; the here and now you; the present you. There's nothing in your past I need to know if you are uncomfortable telling me. I love you, Julia; and nothing that happened in your past, can ever make me stop loving you."

Julia's heart was racing. She was nervous because Mitchell was so convincing. But as genuine as he sounded, she did not want to chance losing his love. Instead she bargained with him. "If we get married, and after five years I don't want to be married anymore, will it be alright with you?"

He looked at her, smiled and then shook his head as if to indicate that she still didn't understand the depths of his love. He said to Julia, "Sweetheart, I love you enough to let you go. That's just how much I love you. Even though it will hurt my heart, I promise, you can leave. I want you to be happy; and I will do everything in my power to make sure you are. But if you are not, I will present no roadblock in letting you be on your way." Mitchell kissed her on her lips. "Whether we are married for five years, or forty-five years, I will always love you." I will love you until the day I die, Miss Holton." He got up from the bed, then gently pulled her up into his arms. Mitchell kissed Julia softly, then said, "Don't worry your pretty little head. We will be alright."

PART NINE

CHAPTER 43 -- VIETNAM

Sergeant Lauers served with 101st Airborne Division which was stationed out of Fort Campbell, Kentucky. The deployment from Fort Campbell to Vietnam contained thirteen-thousand soldiers. It took one-hundred and five C-141 aircrafts to get the personnel to Vietnam. There were one-hundred and twenty-five soldiers in each of those planes with the exception of the one that Sergeant Lauers was in. Sergeant Lauers rode in a C-141 with a maximum of twelve army personnel. His flight, besides the dozen army men also included all of the tanks, jeeps, and an assortment of other military equipment needed in Vietnam. Sergeant Lauers was assigned to the caravan with so few military men because his MOS was critical. He was one of the top in his field of Morse Code. Therefore, he was chosen out of many soldiers to be the colonel's communications man. Everywhere the colonel went, Sergeant Lauers and his radio were right by his side.

~ ~ ~

Vietnam was nothing like the sergeant imagined it to be. Once the C-141 landed in Vietnam many troops were packed on open trucks and then driven to the airport hangers. There they bunked down in the hanger, until moved to their post. Once outside of Wade, the men pitched a tent and bunker. Water was flown in to the troops and showers were taken in makeshift showers.

Outside of the compound there was a small village. From the community, women were selected to work inside of the army compound. The ladies were picked up at the perimeter by Sergeant Lauers. The Vietnamese women worked hard for six-cents a day to fill up sandbags which were used for bunkers within the compound. Sergeant Mitchell was placed in charge of thirty-one Vietnamese women. It pained him to know top headquarters were paying the women so little money. The lady who cleaned his bunker and clothing, he paid her twelve cents a day. Later, top management found out about it and the sergeant was ordered to cease the overpayment because the other Vietnamese women were squabbling about it.

Specialist Mayran was a friend of Sergeant Lauers. He was the compound's switchboard operator. Specialist Mayran was happy working in the underground bunker. It was protected by ammunition boxes which were filled with sand. On top of the sand boxes was a corrugated steel to cover the bunker. Every now and then the specialist would have a visitor from the compound to step into his world below. Once a fellow soldier came down to visit with him, he asked the specialist for a smoke. "Man, give me one of them cigarettes," the soldier begged.

Mayran told him, "Sorry man. I can't give you any of my cigarettes. Don't you know these things are valuable?" Actually he would have given the soldier a cigarette, if it was a cigarette. But it was not. Each month, Mayran's girlfriend would send him a box of marijuana and a carton of cigarettes. Patiently he would unroll the whole carton and re-roll them with the dope. So no one could ever bum a cigarette from the soldier.

One night while on duty, Sergeant Lauers heard advancement upon the bunker he was guarding. He called top headquarters to see if it was alright to shoot. Orders came back, "Sergeant Lauers, do not shoot. Wait until they get close enough for you to beat them with a stick." The sergeant could not believe what headquarters was telling him. What were the bigwigs thinking?

But he was only a sergeant and they were top brass in charge of calling the shots. As a soldier he was going to follow those orders even if he felt it was a great risk to the protection of the bunker he was guarding. He waited, and waited as he could hear the advancement growing closer. His orders of waiting until the Vietcong were close enough to use a stick on them ran through his mind. And even though he felt he was taking a great risk following the top executive's orders, he did just that; waited. When the advancement of the troops came closer, the sergeant was prepared to shoot once they came within range enough to hit them with a stick. The sergeant was prepared; the sound of the advancement came closer; the sergeant had his finger on the side of the trigger of his M-16. He was prepared to slip his finger onto the trigger and pull it when he heard one of the men say, "Damn these grenades are heavy." A cold chill went through the sergeant. He was close to shooting one of their own. He panicked when he realized if he'd taken it on his own to open fire, he would have killed their soldiers. It came to his mind how close to friendly-fire he had come. He even recognized the man's voice. It was a friend of his whom he'd gone on maneuvers with once before. His concern of taking the life of the Vietcong was replaced with anger. Why hadn't the lieutenant in charge of this maneuver informed top headquarters his unit would be outside of the perimeter? Immediately he got on his radio and call top headquarters. That evening the lieutenant in charge of the maneuver was busted down to a sergeant right in front of his men.

~ ~ ~

Many times Mitchell thought of Julia. He missed her and when times got very tough for him he would think of the moments they shared in one another's arms. When it was time for mail call the sergeant would get a letter from her; but then some days when he was out in the field, he would not receive his mail. When he returned to the bunker, he would get five or six letters she'd sent. In one oversized package Mitchell was pleasantly surprised to find a sexy photograph of his Julia that he requested her to send. The sergeant's mail made other soldiers shake their heads; they wished they had received such a vast amount of mail. As Sergeant Lauers collected all of his mail in front of his comrades, a slight smile came across his lips.

~ ~ ~

One evening a grenade hit the aviation fuel tank, sending fuel into the bunker of Sergeant Lauers. He was burned severely. The sergeant suffered burns on his feet, hands, an ankle and the right side of his face. Immediately he was medevac to a Japanese hospital.

CHAPTER 44 -- BURNED

There was a knock on Julia's door at three o'clock in the morning that woke her from a deep sleep. It was her friend, SA Lucy Platts. Lucy was on quarterdeck duty. When Julia answered the door, Lucy said, "Julia, you have a call on the quarterdeck. It's Mitchell." Julia slipped on her robe and slippers and followed Lucy to the quarterdeck. She answered the telephone. "Hello," she said.
"Hello Sweetheart. How are you doing?"
"Mitchell, where are you?" Julia was surprise to hear his voice.
"I don't want you to worry, but I've been burned in an accident. They had to medevac me out of Vietnam to a hospital in Japan. I'm alright, Julia. I'll be back in the states in about a month, so I'll call you when I get to a state-side hospital. I love you, Julia. I can't wait to see you, love."
"I love you too, Mitchell. I'll see you soon. Bye Mitchell.
"Bye, Julia."
Though Julia was concerned of the extent of Mitchell's injuries, she was relieved he was out of the war zone.

~ ~ ~

A month later, when Mitchell arrived at Walter Reed Hospital, he called Julia. The following weekend Julia went to the hospital to see him. Mitchell was proud she came. She sat with him by his bedside; she noticed the broken men who returned from the war. Men with a missing arm or leg. Men with both legs missing. Men with many sorts of battle scars, both visible and invisible. It was a devastation to see the veterans in such a state of pain and injury. Mitchell told Julia one of the men with no legs had been wheeling himself around the medical bay and was always in a happy mood. But then one day when he saw the soldier, the man looked like he was down on his luck. Mitchell asked him what was wrong, and the soldier said, "The doctors say I have infection in both my arms. Now they want to take my arms." It was so much pain in the large hospital room, and seeing the injured soldiers made Julia tear up. She wanted to get out of the bay of injuries. She asked Mitchell if he would like to sit out in the large, empty corridor, and he said he wanted to. She helped Mitchell up and with his crutches he walked with her to the empty hallway. Being away from the other wounded soldiers gave Mitchell the opportunity to kiss his lady the way he wanted to. He found himself happy she suggested sitting in the empty corridor. As they sat on the bench Mitchell held Julia in his arms and kissed her. He leaned away from her and took a good look at her. His eyes and quiet demeanor told her how much he needed her. It seemed like forever since he'd last seen her. He was so happy to be out of the war and once again in his woman's arms. They continued to sit on the bench and embrace one another. As Julia snuggled in his arms and gave him all the kisses she had saved for him, at that very moment the war for Mitchell was just a faint memory. He was now back with his woman, holding her, caressing her and accepting the love she offered him. And even though the rawness of the burns were excruciating, with the love of his Julia, he knew he could endure the pain.

~ ~ ~

Mitchell was healing well and the doctors agreed he was okay enough to be discharged from Walter Reed Hospital. Mitchell's complete unit of 101st Airborne was still over in Vietnam. But his burns, though they were healing, were too severe for the commanding force to send him back into the warzone. The army assigned him to 82nd Airborne of Fort Bragg, North Carolina.

~ ~ ~

The Friday of Mitchell's first free weekend, he made his way to the naval air station to see his Julia. A diamond ring was in his pocket. It was 1750 hours when the Lexington Park cabbie picked the sergeant up from the Greyhound Bus Depot and dropped him off at the WAVES Barrack. Julia was on the enclosed porch of the WAVES Barrack awaiting Mitchell's visit. He was dressed in his soldier uniform. Julia had just come home from spending a long day at Operations Admin; the wave was still in her uniform. Julia ran up the long walkway to greet him. As she approached him, he dropped his satchel to the ground. She ran into his opened arms and he kissed her. She could taste the butterscotch candy in his mouth, as the flavor flowed into hers. He was happy to see her; and when their kiss ended, Mitchell stepped back to look at his lady. He smiled, then lifted her chin and gently kissed her again. After the second sweet kiss, he said to her, "I have missed you desperately, my love."

"I missed you too Mitchell. I love you so much," she told the soldier.

It was at that point Mitchell kissed her again, then asked, "Miss Julia Holton, will you marry me?"

Without hesitation, the wave smiled, and said to the soldier, "Yes, Mitchell. Yes, I will marry you."

Right then and there Mitchell took the ring out of his pocket. He nervously held her small hand as he placed the diamond ring upon her finger. Then he kissed her upon her forehead. He hugged her tenderly, then said, "Oh God, I love you. I am so happy you love me too. I promise I will take care of you. I will protect and cherish you always, Miss Julia Holton." Julia could feel the butterflies floating inside her heart, her head, her stomach. She was so much in love with the man; she was unaware of the waves and the guest as they walked pass them on the pavement.

The two of them walked to the enclosed porch, though Julia could not tell you how she got there. She felt like she was floating on a cloud. As they sit on the rattan davenport, Mitchell said, "I'm so hungry sweetheart. I've got to get some food in me, and I know you need nourishment too. Did you make the hotel reservation so I'll have a place to stay for the four days I'll be here?"

"Yes, I did," she told him.

~ ~ ~

After the couple had dinner, they took the cab to the best hotel in Lexington Park. When the clerk saw the couple, all of a sudden, the room which Julia reserved for Mitchell's stay suddenly become unavailable.

"What do you mean, you have no more rooms?" Mitchell asked in an authoritative voice.

The big, burly white man looked as though he was upset at the presence of the young people in uniform. With his big hands clasped on top of the counter, he took a look at Julia, then glanced back at Mitchell. He leaned forward and repeated, "Sir, I said we have no more rooms. Sorry we cannot accommodate you and your lady friend."

This angered Mitchell. He wanted to grab the man by his collar and force him to give up the room which was reserved for him. But he learned a long time ago to control his temper. Mitchell looked the man in his eyes, and said, "I will have this place shut down. I've just came back from Vietnam and you are going to deny me a room; a room which was placed on reserve for me?" He stood so close to the man it made Julia nervous to see the two big men face off.

"Come on Mitchell, there's other hotels we can go to."

With his eyes still on the man behind the counter, Mitchell bellowed, "No, there's no way we are going to another hotel. The cab dropped us off here, and we're staying here."

Julia, stood back, and then she nervously walked away to a far corner of the lobby. She hadn't ever seen Mitchell angry; she feared he would get into a fight with the man. And she had a right to fear such a possibility. Mitchell hated prejudice. When he was fifteen years old he beat up a white classmate for telling him, he did not have the same privileges as the white kids. And though Julia never liked trouble she knew she must let the man handle the situation. Mitchell believed in standing up for what was fair and right; and trouble, though he never went looking for it, he also was never afraid of it. Within three minutes of Julia hearing muffled conversation, she noticed Mitchell walking towards her in a huff. "Come on honey," he said. He had a roughness to his voice which she had never heard before.

Stressed and nervous from the entire episode, Julia asked, "Do you want me to use that payphone to call for a cab?"

"No Julia, no need to. My room number is 418."

CHAPTER 45 -- OFFICE

The weekend was beautiful for Julia. She spent time with the soldier and throughout the weekend, the two of them would take a cab back to the base for Julia to shower and change into civilian clothing. She and Mitchell went on a picnic with Carolyn and her boyfriend, Ernest; and Mitchell got a chance to meet Natalie, and Lucy. Jasmine, as usual, was nowhere around on the weekend.

Mitchell had two more days to be with the wave and Julia thought it would be perfect to take the soldier to work with her. So Monday morning, Mitchell took the cab to the WAVES Barrack and met up with Julia. She was pleased to see he was back in his uniform; she greeted him with a kiss.

When Jim's bus pulled over to pick up Julia, the old bus driver was surprise to see a man in an army uniform standing next to her. He nodded at them while they boarded his bus. As Julia and Mitchell sat together, she could feel all eyes on them. Every now and then she could see Jim looking in his rear view mirror trying to get another look at Mitchell. When Jim pulled up to the air traffic control building Julia and Mitchell were the last two people on his bus. Before Julia and Mitchell got off, Julia said to the driver, "Jim, this is Mitchell, the man I'm going to marry."

Jim's eyes widen and his big smile revealed a perfect set of teeth. He smiled at the soldier and shook his head. Once he got over the shock of Julia's introduction, Jim said, "Well I'll be damned. You really do look white. But I've been around; even got half-breeds in my own fam'ly. You might be foolin' them other people, but you don't fool me none."

Mitchell, so use to people confusing him with the Caucasian race, simply said, "I'm not trying to fool anyone, sir. I am, what I am. And what I am is colored. But I understand why people are confused. I'm colored; always have been, always will be."

Jim reached out and shook Mitchell's hand. "Hey soldier, I don't mean no disrespect. It's just that everybody's been sayin'..." Jim thought about Miss Jasmine's accusation that the soldier was only after Miss Julia's brown sugar, so he had to stop the words before they came out of his mouth. "Aww heck, never mind. It ain't important. I want you to know Mr. Mitchell, it is nice to finally meet you. I've heard so much about you; and not from Miss Julia either. She hardly says a peep when she's on the bus. I tell you, If I was younger, I'd give you a run fo' yo' money," he announced, to let the soldier know he had been something in his younger years. Then he added, "You is a wise young man, sir. You got yo'self a good gal there; yes sir, a mighty good gal."

~ ~ ~

Julia introduced Mitchell to all of her co-workers in the office. When Commander O'Shea walked into the office he saw the sergeant sitting in a chair next to the wave's desk. Commander O'Shea was pleased to have the opportunity to meet the army man who had stolen the heart of his lady sailor. Julia had a smile on her face when she saw the commander. Immediately, Commander O'Shea walked towards Mitchell and extended his hand. Mitchell stood up and shook it. As they were still shaking hands, the commander greeted the sergeant, "Sergeant Mitchell Lauers, I presume?"

"Yes sir, I am."

"It's nice to meet you young man. I'm SA Holton's commanding officer, Commander O'Shea. The scuttlebutt around the office is that you've just returned from Vietnam. Got wounded over there; is that true son?"

"Yes sir it is."

"So, are you the army man that's got my sailors all in a buzz over SA Holton's love life?" The commander gave a loud, hardy laugh after making the comment. That caught Julia off guard. She'd never heard Commander O'Shea laugh and it seemed a bit out of character for the grey-haired man. She always knew him to be serious; never did he so much as smile, not even a little bit.

Mitchell's face was beaming. He replied, "God sir, I certainly hope so. I've waited a long time to be with Seaman Apprentice Holton." Julia tried to act serious, but she could not lose the nervous smile.

"Good for you, son. Good for you." Commander O'Shea nodded at the soldier then continued on towards his office. Mitchell took his seat and continued to remain by his lady's side while she worked on reports. Seaman Apprentice Holton smiled the entire morning as she sat at her typewriter pounding out the Lieutenant's documents.

When lunchtime came, Julia and Mitchell walked out of the building to be amongst the beautiful day. There was a small grassy knoll and the two lovers sat upon it eating sandwiches which Mitchell purchased from the café. As Commander O'Shea was driving out of the parking lot he spotted them. He stopped adjacent to where they were and spoke loudly from the car to the lovers. "What are you two still doing here? SA Holton, don't let me see you here when I return from lunch. In fact, don't let me see you for the rest of the day."

~ ~ ~

Julia was elated that Commander O'Shea had release her from work for the remainder of the day. She and Mitchell caught Jim's bus and headed straight for the guardhouse. They walked to the Lexington Park diner and ordered some submarine sandwiches and sodas for them to eat later on in the evening. After they purchased their food, Julia called for a cab to take them to the fancy hotel. Once inside, they wrapped themselves in the rapture of their love.

It was later in the evening when they opened the submarine sandwiches and sodas. As they were having their meal, Mitchell said, "Julia, I am not for sure if I can get any more time off. We won't be able to get married until I'm discharged in two months." He saw a disheartening look on Julia's face. Concerned, he questioned, "Sweetheart, what is it?"

~ ~ ~

For a few weeks she had heard her friends poke holes in her relationship with Mitchell. *What does he want with you? Julia, do you really think you're his type? Don't look like y'all got anything in common. Ever think he might be using you? And anyway, have you even seen his divorce papers?* Then there was Jasmine, who summed it up, *He's not going to marry you Julia. He's probably still married, with kids.* As if her military friends weren't bad enough her mother sent a hot letter disapproving the union. The mother noted Mitchell was not only too old, but also far too experience for her. According to her mother, a young girl like Julia was easy pickings for him to marry and take advantage of. Even with everyone's concerns, she had enough sense to put all of their apprehensions aside and placed her faith in the man who was in love with her. But now Mitchell has told her they can't get married for two more months. Had the naysayers been correct?

Somehow, she knew she must stop overthinking what people were saying about Mitchell's love for her. She trusted and believed everything her future husband told her. God sent this man all the way around the world, and then God sent him back to her. All in one piece. All in the spirit of still loving her;

even more so now. Would God do that if He knew the soldier was just taking her for a ride?

And then she started having concerns about being in love. Why did the man she love have to come along so early in her life? And wasn't she the one who said she was never getting married? Sure, but that was before she fell in love with Mitchell; it was too late to turn it around now. She blamed their falling in love on Mitchell because he was the one who changed the paradigm of their correspondence. She begged him to keep it the way it was; two friends writing to one another. But noooooo, that was not what he wanted. She even wrote him and pointed out she was not the one for him; but he wasn't hearing any of it. What does he do? Returned her letter with all of that red ink in between the lines of her writing.

Then she got to thinking, maybe her falling in love was not Mitchell's fault. She figured she should put the blame right where it should be; on herself. If she studied hard enough she would have passed the health portion of boot camp, then she most certainly would not have met Ruthie York and made a promise to go to Cresaptown to meet the recruit's brother and family.

~ ~ ~

"Julia? Julia? JULIA! Love, is there something wrong, sweetheart?" he again asked her. "What's is it?" He wondered why Julia seemed so distant. With this visit, they shared a beautiful time together. He did not want her to be in this melancholy mood, so close to the time when he would have to leave her. "Love, please tell me that everything is alright. You seem to be so deep in thought." She said nothing, "Sweetheart, if our love is going to last, we cannot shut down on one another when something is bothering us. What is it, love?"

In a low voice she asked, "Are we getting married?"

"Why of course we're getting married, honey. Are you afraid that we are not?"

"Yes, I am. And I'm afraid if we don't get married next weekend, I don't think I can go through with it. Mitchell, I think I'm getting scared again," she admitted.

This sadden Mitchell, and he was not sure how to take her comment. He'd gone through a lot to win her love. He had loved her from afar, while in Germany. He saved all of her love letters she wrote to him while he served in Vietnam. And now she tells him she feel frightened about getting married. He knew it was just nerves; but he also knew she could overcome them.

He took her left hand and kissed the ring he'd placed upon her finger days ago. "Julia, do you know I love you?"

"Yes, Mitchell. I know you love me; and I love you, but I am so afraid," she admitted.

"Don't be afraid, my love. All we need to know is the fact that our love for one another is real." He looked sincerely into her eyes, then explained. "I just want you to know, love, if we get married when I get out of the army, we will be able to have a beautiful wedding and we'll be able to go on a honeymoon. But if we get married next weekend, as you want to do, the only thing we will have is the preacher to perform the ceremony and that will be it. There will be no big wedding with lots of people, no three-tier cake, no honeymoon. Is that what you want, Julia?

"Yes, Mitchell. I prefer it simple. I don't need all of those fancy things. Why, it sounds like such an expense and I don't think we need to start our lives together with spending money on a big wedding. I have never known anyone who got married in a fancy wedding. I always thought average people just went to the justice of the peace, or to a preacher to get married."

Mitchell could not believe what Julia was saying to him. Was she really telling him she only wanted to get married without all of the fancy trimmings of a wedding? All he could think of at the moment was the wedding expense he'd gone through with the marriage of his first wife.

Julia's voice quivered as she continued on, "The way you're explaining things, it sounds awfully expensive." She shook her head in a negative way. "That would be money we can spend on something else. What if we start our family right away? That's money we can use on things for the baby."

Mitchell's heart fluttered. He loved Julia and he thought about her all the time; but he never thought of them having a baby. His eyes lit up and there was a look of astonishment on his face. He stared at his wife-to-be because it was all he could do. The joyous words could not come. When his breath came to him the anxious words finally came out. He said, "A baby? You and I have a baby? Oh Julia, I would love to marry you and for us to have a little baby." The soldier was ecstatic, why hadn't he thought of that possibility. Here he was, thinking she would want a big wedding, and all she really wanted was to marry him in a simple ceremony. He felt elated knowing he would be marrying a young lady who was not selfish. A lady who was concern about their life together as a family. And most importantly, a lady who was in love with him and wanted to have his baby. He could not believe his good fortune. He kissed her long and passionately; he knew his love for her would be forever. After their passionate kiss, Mitchell smooth her hair, then said, "Julia, you are so right. Why spend the money on a big wedding, when we can plan on starting our family immediately." He wanted to make sure it was truly a dream of hers. With a gleam in his eyes, he asked, "Sweetheart, do you really want to start our family right away? Are you sure that's what you want to do?"

"Yes Mitchell. Yes I'm sure," she confirmed.

So often Mitchell wished he had a wife and children, someone who loved him and he could love them right back. He thought how fortunate he was to have found Julia; a mate whom God sent just for him. Soon he would be on his way to becoming a husband to Julia, and if the good lord saw fit, a father to their babies.

If Julia wanted a simple wedding by this weekend, then so did he. Mitchell would obtain their marriage license and notify the preacher so they could marry. And since the state of Maryland requires no blood test, the soldier was positive things would go smoothly for them. And so it was set, they would be married in Cresaptown, Maryland in the little church that Mitchell's family attended. While they sat in the hotel room and he finalized the quick arrangements with her, he could not help notice she was smiling. It made him happy. This would be their last evening they would spend together before their marriage.

Mitchell gave Julia the fare for the Greyhound Bus trip to Cresaptown but she would not take it. And though she refused the money, Mitchell stuffed it into her military purse and gave her a look of contempt when she tried to remove it and return it to him. "You are my woman, Julia. I am your man, soon to be your husband. It is my responsibility to always take care of you." Julia left the money in her purse. By 2300 hours Mitchell put Julia in a cab and paid the driver to take her home. As the Lexington Park cabbie drove away, Mitchell chest swelled with pride; he could not wait for Saturday to come; the day Julia would become his wife.

CHAPTER 46 -- SURROGATE

"SA Holton, Commander O'Shea wants to see you in his office," Yeoman Hurley said to the wave. She marked her spot on the memo's rough draft and turned off the typewriter.

Julia had never been inside of the commander's office. When she opened the big metal door and closed it behind her, she was surprised to see that the commander's office did not look like an office at all. It looked more like a strategic command post. There were large metal panels wrapped around the walls with dials, knobs, meters and lights. Commander O'Shea was sitting to the left of the entrance door. He was the only person in the strategic room.

"Ahh, SA Holton, I call you in here because Lieutenant Kadowski has given me your request chit to get married this Saturday." Julia could feel a lump in her throat. She was hoping she had not made a mistake on filling out the request chit because Mitchell was making all the arrangements for their wedding day. The commander continued, "I just want to let you know that I have approved your request for the marriage. But I also want to show you something, SA Holton." He pointed to the extra leather swivel chair which sat next to his. "Please have a seat." The commander dug into his pocket and pulled out his wallet. He retrieved an old black and white photograph from the wallet. It was a picture of a beautiful, young woman, dressed in a white floor-length wedding dress. She had a long veil draping her hair, shoulders and flowing down onto the floor. He held it for Julia to look at. "This is my wife. We've been married for forty-five years, and I still see her just as she is in this picture." Then he picked up the request chit and looked it over. He asked, "Do you love this soldier?"

"Yes sir, I do love him," she nervously answered.

"Outstanding, that's the way it should be. You should be so much in love with him that you can't stand to be apart from him. Tell me, Holton, does the soldier love you?" He had a quizzical look as his eyebrows furrowed.

"Oh yes, commander, he does love me. I feel it in my heart that he truly loves me and wants me to marry him." Julia felt it was the truth; that Mitchell was madly in love with her; though she couldn't figure out why.

"Outstanding," he said with a big flashy smile. "I am so happy to hear it. That is the best way to start your marriage; with love and care for one another. It's a beautiful foundation for a marriage. I can see on your request chit that you and your soldier, Sergeant Lauers, are getting married in Cresaptown, Maryland but your family resides in Philadelphia, Pennsylvania."

"Yes sir, that's true."

"Will your family be attending the wedding?"

"No sir, they won't be able to make it. With their finances, sir, it's just impossible." She added, "They couldn't afford to come to see me when I graduated from boot camp, sir."

"Umm-umm, I see. It's okay, though. I know if there was any way they could be there at your ceremony, they would be." The commander gave her an affirmative nod. "I'm sure of that," he added. "Even though your father and mother will not be able to attend, just remember, they will be there in your heart. Now I can only speak for myself, but if I were your father, I would be extremely proud of you. You're smart, you've got a great personality and you're a very good yeoman." He gave Julia a long look, then added, "SA Holton, I think you and the soldier will make a wonderful couple. It's not too many men who would volunteer to go to war for their country. He is an excellent soldier; and he's about to marry a charmingly, responsible navy wave."

Julia squirmed in her seat. She wasn't use to people giving her compliments. "Thank you, Commander."

He rubbed his chin, then gave the seaman apprentice some sage advice. "SA Holton, I want to instill this in you, always look towards your husband for love and guidance and he should do the same with you. Once you are married, you two are a team; and a team must work together in order to succeed. I want to let you know, Holton, that marriage is a beautiful thing for the couple who love, cherish and honor one another. Now with that said, I must inform you, there's going to be a lot of people, temptation, and bumps in the road which may come your way. It's up to the soldier and yourself, working in tandem, to sidestep problems. As husband and wife, you have to be diligent in dealing with both the good and the bad to keep your marriage intact. And if, by chance, a shroud of ugliness wants to tear your love apart, it's up to the both of you to reinforce the strength of your love; less the ugliness will win, and your marriage will be ruined." The commander smiled, then added, I pray that the two of you get an opportunity to be married as long as my bride and I." He looked at the photograph once again, then tucked it back into his wallet.

"Yes sir, I'll remember that, sir. Thank you for the fatherly advice. It means a lot to me, sir." And Julia meant that too. For so long she wanted a father and a mother who acted like loving parents, to explain things to her, to nurture her and guide her into adulthood. Julia had come to realize for that one instant, Commander O'Shea stepped willingly into the role to fulfill her needs. He and the picture of his lovely bride; they had been her surrogate parents.

The commander gave a nod, then said, "That's all, SA Holton. Congratulations on your upcoming marriage to Sergeant Lauers." He handed her the signed request chit, then said, "You're dismissed, Holton." And with that, the seaman apprentice left his strategic office.

~ ~ ~

It was a beautiful, sunny day in Cresaptown on the day of Mitchell and Julia's wedding. The birds sang lovely melodies, and the sweet smelling hyacinths graced the air. The small neighborhood church had been decorated with white roses on the end of each pew. On the podium was a beautiful bouquet of two dozen white roses. Mitchell wore a dark-blue suit and Julia wore a beige pleated skirt with matching top. As they walked down the aisle together of the near empty church, Julia saw Mitchell's fourteen year-old sister and a teenaged boy sitting with her in the front row. Reverend Moses stood in front with his bible in his hand.

After the reverend preformed the brief ceremony, the newly husband and wife kissed and they both were happy to know they had committed themselves to one another. No longer would the two of them have to be concerned about their relationship continuing on in its traditional correspondence. No longer would they have to figure out if it was a love relationship only through their written word. Now they knew it was a true and very real love. A real live relationship; they were married now in real life. And though it still felt like a dream to Julia, she knew, with the wedding bands they had placed upon each other's fingers, she belonged to him and he belonged to her.

They had fallen in love simply by writing to one another in the course of a year and a half. What they discovered was a love so strong, it could not be contained strictly by their written words. Their love was real, as real as heaven above; and God had given Mr. and Mrs. Mitchell Lauers their Peace In Paradise right there on His Beautiful Earth. God loved them, as He knew they surely loved Him; and He would keep them safe.

The End

Edwards Brothers Malloy
Oxnard, CA USA
September 22, 2014